A Killer's Moon

A Jo Pullinger Novel

Thomas Fincham

Contact

Visit the author's website:

www.finchambooks.com

Email:

contact@finchambooks.com

Jo Pullinger Series

Contents

PROLOGUE

Though the eastern part of the state was still getting hammered by snow, the west was enjoying mild temperatures. Misty rain fell from the sky. The motorcycle had a large windscreen, and Peter was wearing his helmet. Even so, it became difficult to see.

Thankfully, the road was desolate. At this time of night, the only living things he saw were bats flitting overhead. And the red taillights of the car glowing a half mile ahead of him. He focused on it. He'd be okay if he just kept his two wheels between the lines.

His mind was free to wander. What was the young woman in the car thinking about? What was she doing? Listening to music? A podcast? Maybe an audiobook. Some kind of guide on how to invest millions of dollars of inheritance.

Peter knew it was a young woman in the car. He knew exactly what she looked like and how tall she was. Some of what he knew came from things his friend had told him. Other things he knew because he had been following her for hours. Ever since she left the assisted living facility.

He decided she was probably listening to music. Maybe it was outdated information, but Peter had heard she liked early 2000s pop music. The stuff she listened to as a kid. He was sure that hadn't changed. That sort of thing never changed. It stuck with a person for life.

Peter wondered what she would do if she could never listen to her music again. He didn't think that was a probable outcome of the night's events, but he didn't really know what would happen for sure.

Everything was up in the air.

What should I do with her when I have her? It's not like I can throw her on the back of the bike like saddlebags. I'll have to take her car. Put her in the trunk. I can get a new one somewhere along the way. Hers will be too hot once they figure out she's missing.

But he was getting ahead of himself. Before worrying about any of that, he had to find a good time and place to grab her. The assisted living facility wasn't it. Broad daylight. Too many people around. There was even a cop parked at the coffee shop across the street.

No way he could have done it there.

So where?

She would have to stop for gas at some point. Since it was late at night, she'd probably be the only customer at any gas station she stopped at. But there would still be a clerk. A potential witness.

Dead ends down every avenue of thought.

There was good news, though. She was going all the way to Seattle. That was hundreds of miles away. Since she hadn't stopped at a hotel yet, Peter figured she was going to drive through the night. That gave him plenty of time.

While he was busy thinking, the young woman increased the distance between them. He could barely see her taillights anymore. Peter hit the gas. The rain splattered harder against his helmet. The wind shot up his sleeves, filling his riding leathers with cold air.

Once the gap was back down to about a half mile, Peter slowed. He was sure she had already noticed his presence. He was the only other motorist on the road. Just so long as she didn't get suspicious...

The car's right blinker came on. The woman was entering a rest area. Slowing to a crawl as she drove up a curving ramp.

Perfect, Peter thought with a grin. *I doubt there's anyone else here. And I have to pee, anyway.*

He drove in after her.

ONE

Despite the size implied by its name, Pacific City, Oregon, was tiny. It was home to a little over a thousand people. Agent Jo Pullinger felt like every single one of them was at this bar, surging around her.

She didn't even remember the name of the place. She barely remembered the name of the town. It was just where she had ended up. All she knew was they had good beer.

She took a sip of her glass and turned a page in her book. It was a tattered paperback she had picked up at the local thrift shop. Good thing it was a book she had read before. With all the noise around her, she could hardly focus.

Someone bumped against the back of her seat. Pushing her forward. She looked back with the slow calm of a woman who knew she could take down anyone in the place. She caught the wide eyes of a young guy in a bright polo shirt.

"Sorry, sorry," he slurred, raising a glass. "Sorry, didn't mean to... anyway..."

He stumbled into the crowd, vanishing.

Jo looked at the time. She was going to wait until she finished her one beer and felt completely sober before leaving. But now she was considering an early departure. The late-night crowd had settled in for the long haul. And they were an obnoxious bunch.

She picked up her beer and started chugging it. The foam proved to be overpowering, and she set her glass down, coughing.

The bartender, a rotund man with salt and pepper hair, approached her. "Getting ready for a second one there, miss?"

Jo shook her head. "Just thinking I should hit the road soon. Do you know how much alcohol's in this?"

"You picked one of our stronger beers," the bartender replied. "It might hit you hard. But I don't claim to know your tolerance. You look tough."

"I am," Jo said with a smile.

The bartender laughed and moved to his next patron.

Jo read the next paragraph in her book. She realized she had no idea what it said, so she read it again. She was on her third readthrough when she decided it was hopeless. Sighing, she dog-eared her page and set the book down.

She pulled out her wallet. Found enough cash to cover the beer and a tip. Left the cash on the counter.

"Don't tell me you're leaving right *now*," a man said behind her. "After I finally worked up the gumption to come over here."

Jo turned her head much faster this time. Not only was this man in possession of a rich, suave voice, he didn't even sound drunk. His face matched his voice perfectly. He was ruggedly handsome. His face bristled with stubble. There seemed to be a permanent sardonic expression on his face. It was locked in and surrounded by wrinkles.

"I was thinking about it," said Jo.

"Maybe I can help you think about something else," he shot back without hesitation. Then he chuckled. "Maybe that sounded too suggestive. I have no idea how these are supposed to work."

She raised an eyebrow. "These?"

"You know... approaches. Men going up to women in bars, trying to win their favor."

"Well, you're at least doing a good job of being direct," she said.

For the first time, she noticed what the man was wearing. A faded Motörhead t-shirt. A trucker hat with the silhouette of a naked lady on it. The words *Big Dom's Truck Stop* were emblazoned just above the rim.

"That's something." The man grabbed the back of the stool next to Jo. "Mind if I sit here? If not, I think there are two or three other empty seats in this place. Although, I see half-empty glasses sitting in front of them. I guess those people are just in the bathroom."

"Then I guess you can sit down," said Jo. "But I have to warn you. I could blow this joint any minute. I make no promises. And no, you cannot buy me a drink. I'm switching to water."

TWO

The man in the trucker hat sat down. It seemed this was as far as his planning went. He didn't say anything else, just tapped on the bar and anxiously watched the bartender.

"He was just over here," said Jo. "I don't think he'll be back in our neck of the woods for a few more minutes."

"I was just going to order a rum and coke," said the man.

Jo took another sip of her almost-finished beer. "That's a good drink. But I had you pegged for a margarita man."

"Why is that? Is it the tan?" he asked. "The name's Ted, by the way. Ted Campbell. If you need a load of frozen food hauled across the country, I'm your guy."

"What if I need to have a memorable conversation at a bar?" asked Jo.

"Then you could do a lot worse." Ted shrugged.

Jo looked him over again. Her line of work had taught her to pick up on subtle cues. How to tell what someone was after. What kind of person they were. Right now, she didn't see anything worth worrying about.

"I'm Jo," she replied, offering her hand.

He shook with her. His eyes went wide. "Wow. You're strong. Grabbing onto a steering wheel for a thousand miles in a row can develop some good grip strength, but not like *that*. Can I ask what you do?"

Jo decided she was done with her beer. So far, she was having a fun time with Ted, but she didn't want to let her mind get any foggier. Just in case he had something nefarious in mind. You could never be too careful.

"You can," she told him. "And I guess I'll answer. Vaguely. I'm in law enforcement."

The bartender arrived. Jo asked for water. Ted ordered his rum and coke. It was delivered to him. As he took his first sip, he stared at her. She maintained eye contact.

"Yeah, you're a tough one," Ted said with a grunt. He set his drink down. "How about we play a quick game? I ask three questions. You answer them honestly. Don't worry, they won't be too invasive. After I get my three answers, I'll try and guess exactly what your job title is."

Jo shrugged. "Sure. Why not?"

"All right, first question. Do you work here in Pacific City?"

"Nope," said Jo. She decided to be generous. "Actually, I've never been here before tonight."

"Okay... What city *do* you work in?" asked Ted.

"Seattle."

"All right. Big city. We're getting somewhere now. If you don't mind me saying, you look very fit. Do you work out on a regular basis?"

Jo used the straw to stir the ice in her water glass. "I try to run at least a few miles most mornings. I have a calisthenics routine I run through four times a week. When I feel ambitious, sometimes I hit an extra workout at lunch."

Ted had a huge grin on his face. "Yeah, that's what I thought. FBI agent."

Jo's eyes went wide. She couldn't help but laugh.

"I guess that means I'm right. Phew." Ted ran a hand over his forehead. "You know, I was only about fifty percent sure. I was right, wasn't I?"

Jo gestured to her jacket pocket. She reached into it and gave Ted a quick peek at her FBI badge.

"Never seen one in person," Ted gasped. "Very shiny. Feel free to tell me to take a walk off the pier, but can I touch it?"

"Take a walk off the pier," Jo barked. "Not literally. The water's probably ice cold. Now I'm going to guess you, Mr. Ted Campbell. You're a truck driver."

"Wow, how could you have known?" he said sarcastically. "Oh wait, maybe it was the hat. Or the numerous references I've made."

"By the way..." Jo pointed at his hat. "Where exactly is Big Dom's Truck Stop?"

"Just outside Peoria, Illinois," Ted replied. "Great place. I always take a shower there. Good hot food, too. Now I'd love to shoot a question right back at you, but you probably can't tell me much. I'll do it anyway. Have you had any good cases lately?"

Jo pulled her water glass closer, gazing into the cold depths. "That depends on your definition of 'good.'"

THREE

"There isn't much I can tell you," Jo went on. "It's just too recent. But it was somewhere in Oregon. A weird little town whose name I'll keep to myself."

The town was a place called Lapse. Until she was stranded there, Jo had never heard of it.

"I was driving with two of my fellow agents…"

Lewis McKinley and Edward Swann. Good men, both of them.

"We were on our way to a different field office. A blizzard hit, and we decided to stop in this town. It turned out something weird was going on there."

People were going missing at a disproportionate rate. All young people. Something sinister was happening in Lapse. Jo and her fellow agents bore the brunt of it.

She didn't give any of these details to Ted. But the thoughts and memories flashed in her mind. It had all happened just a couple of days ago. She was still on her way back to Seattle after the events in Lapse. Taking her time.

"Things went south there," Jo added. "But I'm still here. And now I almost want to start drinking again, so I can try to forget."

"You know I'm happy to buy you another drink," Ted told her. "But no pressure. Sounds like you've been having a rough time at the office. But what brings you to Pacific City?"

"Funny story," said Jo. "My drive to this unnamed town in Oregon was supposed to be a leisurely cruise. A sort of vacation. After what happened, my boss said I could take my time getting back to Seattle. So I've just been driving around. Slowly making my way west. Now that I hit the coast, I guess it's time to start moving north."

"And that's why you stopped at one beer." Ted indicated her water glass. "You're planning on hitting the road tonight."

"I have to pick some people up from the airport. My brother, along with his wife and daughter. So I need to make up some miles."

Ted suddenly became lost for words again. He went back to nervously scanning the bar. He wasn't looking for the bartender this time. His glass was still mostly full. Jo thought he was trying to think of something to say.

Or trying to pluck up the bravery to say what was already on his mind.

"I don't know your schedule," he finally said. "But maybe spending the night in Pacific City might not throw it off too badly."

"It might not," Jo admitted. "But you never know what might happen out on the road. I like to leave some wiggle room in case something crazy decides to pop up. That tends to happen to me."

"Maybe *I'm* that crazy thing." Ted poked himself in the chest. "What do you say? Stay another night? I'll buy you another free water or something. We can talk a bit. Maybe, I dunno, go for a walk on the beach."

"The cold, windy beach," Jo said.

"All right, maybe not the best plan," Ted replied with a laugh. "But my hotel has a hot tub. And your hotel... well, you don't even have one, I guess. So I win."

Jo took a long drink of water as she came up with a plan for letting Ted down easy.

Why do I care about letting him down easy?

She glanced at him and realized why. She kind of liked him. Maybe staying another night and spending it with him would be harmless fun. But it felt like an irresponsible thing to do. The type of thing a kid would do. Not a grown woman with an FBI badge in her pocket.

Still, the temptation was there. And the longer she sat at this bar, the stronger it got.

"I can't," Jo said softly. "But maybe your truck-driving adventures will bring you to Seattle someday soon."

Ted perked up. "Yeah. I hit Seattle now and then. Nice city."

"It can be," Jo said. She grabbed a cocktail napkin. Ted was ready; he handed her a pen. Jo wrote the number for her personal cell. She slid the napkin to him.

Ted carefully folded the napkin and put it in his wallet. "The first thing I usually do when I get to a city is find a place to grab a burger. But next time I'm in Seattle, calling this number will be my first move."

"Then I'll just leave and anticipate hearing from you," Jo said. To avoid a long and awkward goodbye process, she simply got up and left. At the door, she turned back to give Ted a wave. He returned it with gusto.

FOUR

Jo had trouble finding her car in the lot. She still wasn't used to the rental. She wandered the crowded rows for a few minutes, scanning the vehicles. Finally, she had the idea to mash the unlock button. Normally she would have defaulted to that, but she was distracted.

Thinking about Ted.

She caught a blinking light from the corner of her eye. A moment later, she was sliding in behind the wheel. She rolled out of the crammed parking lot, away from the hubbub of the bar.

There was an abrupt change as she entered the streets of Pacific City. They were lined with tiny bungalows and scrubby pine trees. A heavy mist hung in the air. A fine drizzle speckled her windshield.

It wasn't a good night for driving fast. Thankfully, she wasn't in a hurry. She wandered eastward, keeping her eyes open for main road signs.

She passed a mansion on her left. It was situated on a hill, its windows peering down at her. It turned out to be a medical facility. There were no lights on. Other than the bar, the city was sleeping.

Jo turned north and followed the speed limit. She turned the radio on, scanning through local stations. Mostly it was static. Nothing much was going on at this hour of the night.

She settled on a country station. It reminded her of Lapse, where country music was the only thing the radio had. Bad memories, for sure, but she had come away with a slightly higher appreciation of the genre. It had a certain mood that was fun to fall into.

A Reba McEntire song was playing when Jo saw the sign for the rest area. Suddenly, she realized her bladder was full. The beer and water were catching up. She glanced in the rearview mirror and saw nothing. She didn't bother turning her blinker on as she drifted into the rest area.

She couldn't see much through the rain. But the rest stop looked like a typical place. A long, narrow parking lot. A small brick building with trash cans and drinking fountains outside. Jo parked a few spaces down from the building and got out. She pulled up the collar of her jacket.

There was only one light, glowing above the drinking fountains. It was full of dead bugs and struggling for life. Barely giving off any light. The whole place had a creepy atmosphere.

Jo noticed another car in the lot, and was glad for it. However, the person that car belonged to could be anyone. Maybe they were perfectly normal. Or maybe they were like a character from a horror movie. Stalking the highways of America by night. Lying in wait for victims.

On second thought, maybe being alone would be preferable.

Jo almost grabbed her handgun from the glovebox. But she thought better of it. This was just a rest area. Nothing bad would happen.

FIVE

Jo approached the building and heard a hand dryer blowing inside the men's room. *That must be the person with the car,* she thought.

She went into the women's room. There was a young lady at the sink. Washing her hands. She made eye contact with Jo in the mirror. The woman had dark hair and pretty green eyes. She looked tired but otherwise fine. As soon as she noticed Jo was looking at her, she went back to scrubbing her hands.

Her presence seemed to complicate Jo's theory about who owned the other car. But she realized it could still be explained. They were driving together. The young woman and whoever was in the men's room.

Just a nice couple on a late-night drive. The same as Jo. It didn't matter why they were out here or where they were going. They just needed to use the bathroom.

Jo went into the end stall and shut the door. She was relieved to see that the toilet was clean. She took a seat and pulled out her phone. There were no notifications. She put it away again, sighing.

What were you hoping for, Jo? A desperate call from Ted? A goodnight text? Are you really that lonely?

The woman at the sink finished washing her hands. The dryer came on. The sound of blasting air filled the bathroom. It mostly masked the sound of the young lady's departure, but Jo heard the door swing shut with a bang.

Rain fell on the metal roof with a sound like sizzling bacon. It was a soft sound, and Jo heard voices through it. The man and the woman were outside, talking.

Jo couldn't make out the words, but the cadence made it seem like a conversation between two strangers. People who just happened to bump into each other. The man asked a question. The woman answered it politely.

Maybe they didn't come together. Then why is there only one car?

Jo flushed the toilet and left the stall. She washed her hands quickly. Anxious to get outside in case there was trouble. Logically, there was no sign that this was the case. She knew she must have just missed the other vehicle.

But she had a bad feeling. Sometimes, your gut provided better information than your eyes and ears.

Other than the air dryer, there was also a paper towel dispenser. Jo used the latter. She didn't want the dryer's noise. She wanted to keep listening to what was going on outside.

Now that she was closer to the door, she could make out words.

"I'd better get going," the woman said. "Lots of driving to do. Good luck."

A moment later, there was a scuffle. The woman screamed, but the sound was quickly muffled. Jo imagined a hand being pressed over her mouth.

Jo let the wet paper towel fall to the floor. She yanked the door open and ran outside.

SIX

Jo rushed around the corner of the building. The hum of the vending machines filled her ears. A silent battle was being waged in front of them. A struggle between two people.

In the weak light over the drinking fountains, Jo saw all she needed to see. There was a man wearing a hooded sweatshirt. Wrestling with the young woman. Trying to subdue her.

"Hey!" Jo shouted. She reached for her hip, then remembered leaving her gun in the glovebox.

The man glanced at her. She couldn't make out his face. He reached up with one hand. Inside his hood, he grabbed the edge of a ski mask and pulled it down, covering his features.

Other than that, he did nothing. Only a second passed, but it felt like a full minute. The man watching Jo. Jo watching him. Neither of them quite knew what to do.

There was enough time to think. To run through what had happened here and make sense of it. The other car must belong to the young woman. This kidnapper had parked somewhere else, out of sight.

He had followed his prey to the restrooms. He went into the men's side, waiting for her to come out. He used the toilet and dried his hands.

It was the dryer. The loud rush of air. That was why he had no idea there was a third person at the rest area. It had drowned out the sound of Jo's arrival.

In lieu of her handgun, Jo produced her Bureau credentials. She held them at an angle, so the light would bounce off her shield.

"FBI!" she cried.

That made the man react. He took a big, leaping step backward. At the same time, he shoved his victim forward. She tripped and landed on her hands and knees. The man took a step toward her, reaching as though to help her out.

"Don't move!" Jo ordered. She put her hand near her hip. "I'm an armed federal agent, and I'm perfectly capable of blowing you away."

Maybe she was coming on too strong. Or maybe this guy was smart. He stared at Jo as he slowly walked backward.

"You don't have a gun on you," he said. "It must still be in your car, right? That means I can get away. Have fun."

With that, he turned and ran out into the parking lot. A dead sprint.

SEVEN

Jo was torn. She watched the kidnapper go. The rain was falling heavier now. He disappeared quickly behind a curtain of mist. She couldn't even see her own car anymore, parked nearby. Another reason he hadn't known she was there.

There was a decision to make. Should she follow the man? Or stay to help his victim?

Maybe both were possible.

Jo knelt beside the woman, taking her arm. "Are you all right?"

"Fine," she groaned. "Last time I skinned my knees, I was eight years old and trying to learn how to skateboard. I forgot how much it hurts."

"No time for pain," Jo told her. "Get up."

She helped the woman to her feet.

"You need to catch that guy," she told Jo.

"I will. But I need to make sure you're safe too. Come with me."

They hurried through the drizzle. Jo hit the unlock button on her key fob. The lights flashed through the fog. They got into the car, buckling their seatbelts.

"This is weird," the woman said.

"It is," Jo said with a grunt. She put the car in reverse and backed out. Turning toward the direction the man had run. "I try and take a vacation, and this is what happens. Why is it always me?"

"I'm the one who almost got kidnapped," her passenger complained.

"Been there, done that," Jo said with a sigh.

"Really?"

Jo smiled. "No, I guess not. But I'm sure it'll happen eventually. All right, so that guy was running pretty fast. Eleven or twelve miles an hour, I'd say. Nowhere near what a car can do. We should catch him in just a few seconds."

She drove along the curve of the parking lot. Letting the engine surge up to thirty miles per hour. She felt the anti-lock brakes engage. She slowed down, allowing her vehicle to regain traction.

She reached blindly, pressing a button near the steering wheel. The radio switched from country to static.

"Damn, where are the high beams in this thing?" Jo growled. She glanced at the young woman. "It's a rental. I'm still figuring it out."

She took her eyes off the road, searching the instruments. She found the right button and pressed it. The high beams came on, bathing the parking lot in light.

They saw the kidnapper, running down the very edge of the asphalt. He looked over his shoulder, squinting.

"There he is," Jo said with a grin.

The man dove to the side, into the trees.

"There he goes," the passenger moaned.

Jo drove up to the spot where the man had entered the trees. She stopped, waiting. Trying to decide if she should pursue him on foot. It would mean leaving the woman alone. Vulnerable.

There was a roaring sound from the trees. An engine coming to life. A motorcycle came ripping out between the tree trunks. It hit the pavement, skidded, righted itself, and surged toward the main road.

"There he goes!" the young woman said again. This time with a lot more enthusiasm.

"I see him." Jo hit the gas, trying to match his speed. "Don't worry. I won't let him get away."

EIGHT

The motorcycle's driver never looked back. He kept his eyes on the road. This was his one attempt at safe driving. He maintained a reckless speed, often slipping and nearly losing control on the wet pavement.

"He's not even wearing a helmet," Jo observed. "This guy is nuts. I can keep up with him, no problem, but catching him is going to be tricky. Getting into a fatal car crash isn't on my list for tonight."

Jo sighed. But in truth, she was having a good time. It was a refreshing change of pace from her most recent case. A relatively low-stakes chase through the night. A single perpetrator, who apparently didn't have a gun. Unless he just wasn't crazy enough to shoot an FBI agent.

For her passenger, it was a different story. She was crying, hugging her knees to her chest.

"Do you have your seatbelt on?" Jo asked.

The woman nodded.

"What's your name?"

"Kari Cross," the passenger said.

"Well, my name is Jo Pullinger. You're safe now. Even if I don't catch this guy, I'll make sure you get to wherever you're going."

"I thought you said you wouldn't let him get away," Kari reminded her.

Jo shrugged. "He's going ten over the speed limit. On a rainy night. On a motorcycle. On a curvy road. He's got a lot to lose by letting me catch him, and he's going to do whatever he can to make sure that doesn't happen."

Kari wiped tears from her eyes. She turned her head to look through the rear window.

"My car," she said.

"We'll go back and get it later," Jo told her.

She gritted her teeth as she followed the kidnapper around a radical bend in the road. She had to slow down to make the turn safely. The motorcycle didn't slow down at all. It sped up, if anything. Somehow, he pulled the turn off and rocketed into the distance.

As soon as her car straightened out, Jo gradually pushed the pedal to the floor to try and catch up.

"Do you have any idea who this guy is?" she demanded.

"Not at all," Kari replied. "He's just some guy."

"Did you get a good look at his face?"

Kari scrunched up her face. Concentrating hard. "Not really. It was dark. He's a young guy. Maybe twenty or something? He told me his car broke down on the main road. He wanted a ride to the nearest town."

"You turned him down," said Jo. "That's hard to do. It takes courage."

"I made him mad." Kari started crying again.

"All you did was throw a wrench in his plan," Jo told her. "He obviously doesn't have a car. He has a motorcycle. And it's working just fine. He wanted to take *your* car."

"With me in it?" Kari asked.

"Most likely. I assume you're his primary target."

Lightning flashed across the sky. The harsh glow framed the kidnapper ahead of them. The tail of his leather jacket flapping in the wind. The way he was hunched forward. Desperately trying to get away. He still didn't look back.

The lightning continued for several seconds. Turning night to day. Shining through the mist and giving them brief visibility. The motorcyclist saw a potential way out.

It was a dirt frontage road, running parallel to the paved one they were on but separated from it by a ten-foot-wide shallow ditch.

The kidnapper made his move. He dropped his speed to slightly below suicide-level. He bumped his way across the gap. Down one side of the ditch. Up the other. He was nearly shaken off his seat but held on tight. He made it to the other side.

He finally looked back. Watching the car. He obviously doubted Jo would be able to follow him. He was counting on her changing her mind.

Which was why she had to keep going.

"Crap," Jo groaned. "Have I told you this is a rental? I don't even want to know what kind of fees this will incur."

She turned the wheel to the left. Drifting toward the ditch.

NINE

The ditch was deeper than it looked. As the nose of the car tipped down into it, Jo had the sensation of falling into the Grand Canyon. She tensed up. Gritting her teeth. The car ground and bounced its way down the slope.

"Say a prayer for the undercarriage," she said.

The front wheels maneuvered onto the flat bottom of the trench. The ground down there was mucky, soaked with rain. A good place to lose all her speed. To combat this, she hit the gas hard. The wheels spun for a second. Kicking up mud. They finally managed to catch on to something.

Jo and Kari climbed up and out onto the other side. The car struggled again as the rear wheels hit the same muddy patch. But Jo persevered through a few more surges on the gas pedal.

The kidnapper was still moving forward. Along the frontage road. He had dropped his speed significantly to make it over the gap. He was still moving at that reduced speed. Gawking at the car that was following him.

He didn't see the telephone pole until the last second.

He tried to steer out of the way and almost succeeded. His left handlebar clipped the pole. His front wheel went sideways, and his bike locked up. He flew over the handles and splattered into the wet dirt.

Jo reacted, increasing her speed to intercept him. The kidnapper jumped up in terror, continuing his getaway on foot. His only choice now was to go where her car couldn't follow.

He ran into the bushes. Disappearing into the wild, overgrown foliage.

"He's just not going to make it easy, is he?" Jo stopped the car, leaving the keys in the ignition as she popped her door open. "Do you have a phone on you?"

Kari nodded. "Right here in my pocket."

"Good. Lock the doors and call the police. You should be okay until they get here. If anything happens..." Jo opened her wallet, grabbing one of her contact cards from the small stash she kept inside. She gave it to Kari. "...call me."

Jo got out of the car. She was about to shut the door when she thought of something. She turned and leaned into the car.

"Actually," she said, "call me in twenty minutes, no matter what. I'll want a status report. And so will you."

Jo reached across Kari's lap and grabbed her gun from the glove compartment. She slammed the door shut and followed her quarry.

The motorcycle was still running. The weight of it was pressing the accelerator down, causing the bike to spin in circles, throwing mud everywhere.

The bike was a piece of evidence. Jo didn't want it running away. She keyed the ignition off before running into the trees.

This area had been clear-cut recently in the past. There was nothing here but saplings. There were thousands of them, growing as dense as the hairs on her head. Getting through them was a nightmare, especially in the dark.

She ran into wet, slippery trunks. Bouncing left and right like a pinball. Branches whipped her in the face. She assumed the kidnapper would have followed the path of least resistance... but there wasn't one. It was all bad. All nearly impossible to traverse at night.

She had no idea where he had gone.

It seemed like this forest would never end. But Jo abruptly broke out onto another dirt road. There was a more mature forest on the other side. Tall, majestic trees along gently sloping ground.

She saw the man running up the hill. His feet kept trying to slide out from under him. He wasn't making much progress.

Jo touched the butt of her gun. She could try and take a shot, but it didn't seem worth it. Recently, in Lapse, she managed to make a very difficult shot. A moving target. In the dark. In the forest.

But the conditions had been different. A bright moon reflecting off the snow on the ground. No rain. No mist.

With a sound like a growling beast, the rain increased in fury. It was pouring down with cold vengeance. The kidnapper was completely lost in sight.

Jo ran toward where she had last seen him, hiking up the hill.

TEN

Jo reached the summit of the hill and looked forward. The ground sloped down again at her feet, but the lay of the land ahead was a complete mystery. It was shrouded in darkness and a deepening fog.

She looked down. She spotted tracks in the mud. Two trenches side by side. The man had slipped as he was making his way down.

Jo followed the direction of the tracks. She moved too fast. A second later, her feet went out from under her. She slammed down onto her backside, sliding down the slope.

There was a bush to her right. She grabbed the spindly branches to stop herself. She stood up with a grunt and continued downward with greater care.

Through the swirling currents of rain, she caught a glimpse of something ahead. Lights glowing in the window of a house. It looked far away. A mile or so distant. But it was difficult to tell.

Either way, it drew her in. A beacon for wayward souls lost in the dark.

Maybe it felt the same to her quarry.

Jo hit the bottom of the hill. She put her foot down, expecting more slope. Instead, she hit flat ground. It was a jarring transition. Her teeth clicked together painfully.

Cursing, she broke into a jog. Somewhere up ahead, she heard something strange. A rattling, wobbling kind of sound.

She had an idea of what it might be. She moved slowly, holding out her hand. She felt something thin and metallic against her skin.

It was a fence. Thin wire strung between posts. There wasn't much wire there at all. Just a few strands. Not enough to keep anything in that wanted to get out.

Probably an electric fence. The rain must have shorted it out somewhere. Lucky me.

It would have been startling, getting zapped by something she couldn't even see yet.

Jo put her hand on top of the wire. She pressed down, testing its strength. It was very taut, like the string on a guitar.

She started to climb over carefully. She put her foot down on the other side. As she swung her other leg over, her weight settled on the wire for a second. It made a distinctive sound.

The same sound she had heard a moment ago, before she even knew the fence was there. It meant someone else had climbed over just a few seconds before.

Jo knew she was on the right track.

But she couldn't see anything other than the lights ahead of her. It was the only thing to navigate by. She ran toward them, stumbling on uneven ground.

She drew her pistol, getting it ready. It was possible she could run straight into the kidnapper without seeing him. If that happened, she needed to be ready.

As Jo ran blindly through the night, lightning flashed again. It was a much briefer display than before. But she caught sight of the man she was pursuing.

He was getting ahead of her. The gap was about a hundred feet. And growing. He was moving very fast.

Jo lined up a shot. The lightning faded, and she was blind again before she could aim. She kept running.

A large, dark shape loomed ahead of her. Jo dodged to the side, readying her gun to fire. The shape mooed at her. It was a cow, standing in the middle of the field. Dripping with rain and miserable.

Jo dodged around the huge animal. There were more cows, a small herd of them huddling together. They started walking toward Jo, assuming she was here to feed them.

Didn't have getting mauled by farmyard animals on my bingo card.

She left the cows behind. But her run-in with them had spiked her adrenaline. Her heart fluttered, feeling weak. She touched her chest, fearing the organ would give out on her.

It had been a while since her heart had been an issue. It wasn't hers to begin with. It had come from the chest of a dead killer. And now she had that heart in her. Pumping her blood. Powering her thoughts and movements.

Since day one, it had been giving her grief.

She had told Kari there was no time for pain. That rule applied to her as well. Killer's heart be damned. She was going to catch this guy.

ELEVEN

Jo was within a hundred yards of the house now. The back porch light was on. She watched as the kidnapper ran up the steps and pulled on the door. It opened without resistance.

These people lived in the middle of nowhere. They had no reason to keep their doors locked. Until now.

The man entered the house. He slammed the door shut behind him. Jo was close enough to hear the bang. She also heard the shouting voices that followed a few seconds later. They went from shocked to angry to terrified. An entire emotional journey took place as Jo was still covering the last fifty yards of the field.

She reached the back porch. She cleared all three steps in a single leap. Her heart kicked in her chest, unhappy with how she was exerting herself.

She tried to open the door. Unsurprisingly, the man had locked it. Jo jiggled the handle, testing its strength. Most modern doorknobs were weak. They could be knocked apart with a single heavy blow. This doorknob was not one of those. It was old heavy brass. Solid as a rock.

More screams from inside. A man's voice crying in pain. A woman screaming in fear. Pleading.

Jo used the butt of her handgun to smash the door's glass window. She rattled the gun around, knocking out the loose shards so she wouldn't slice her arm open. Once that was done, she reached through and unlocked the door.

The screaming stopped. The house was silent as Jo entered. She was in a mudroom off the kitchen. She moved through, following the kidnapper's dirty footprints.

They didn't go far. He had wiped most of the mud off on a rug inside the door. Whatever was left on his shoes faded away halfway across the kitchen.

Jo followed them as far as they went. She was standing between an ancient refrigerator and a sink that was big enough to take a bath in. The place was showing its age. The tile floor was cracked in places. The grout was crumbling. But it was all quite clean.

It was a shame to track more mud through the place, but Jo didn't have time to untie her shoes.

She stepped into the hallway, turning quickly from side to side. Covering her angles. To her left were a couple of rooms. A staircase leading to the second floor. To her right was a bathroom at the end of the hall. A small room. She could see the whole thing from where she was standing. There was no one inside.

She headed left. The first door she came to was wide open. The lights were off inside, but she could make out the shape of a dining table. A few chairs around it. Nothing was moving in there, either.

To be safe, Jo quickly flicked the light on and lunged inside, checking the corners.

No one there.

She was breathing heavily. Feeling paranoia and anxiety. Someone was in the house. A dangerous man. And there were at least two innocent people here as well.

Jo moved to the next room. And that was where they were.

It was a living room. The TV was turned on, but someone had muted it. The sofa was lying on its back, having been knocked over. An old woman on her knees, looking traumatized. Staring toward the two men standing by the window.

The man in front was the same age as the woman. He was wearing plaid pajamas. He had a long, scruffy beard.

The man behind him was younger and wearing a mask over his face. The kidnapper from the rest area. With one hand, he had a death grip on the farmer's shoulder. With the other, he held a knife to the man's throat.

The farmer was taller than the kidnapper. Wider, too. Jo still couldn't get a clean shot.

TWELVE

"I guess you can see what's going on here," the kidnapper said. He spoke in quick, snappy syllables. "I have two hostages. Or one, at least. So you shouldn't try anything."

The farmer's wife turned her wide eyes to Jo.

"Any other demands?" Jo asked.

"Yeah. Stop pointing that gun over here," the man replied.

Jo lowered her gun to a forty-five-degree angle. Aiming at a bare spot on the floor.

"Better," the kidnapper continued. "Man, this is a crazy situation. Really crazy!"

The hand that held the knife was shaking.

"I assume this is your first time trying anything like this," Jo said.

"You don't know that!" he snapped.

"I think I do. Especially now that you're being so defensive. Just watch. See this?" Jo slid her gun slowly back into its holster. "No one has to get hurt here. You aren't even in that much trouble. Not yet. If you hurt anyone, especially in front of me, things are going to get a lot worse for you."

The man glanced at the window beside him. He was on edge. Searching for a way out. Jo felt that if she gave him one, he'd take it with no hesitation. It meant he might get away. But at least the farmer and his wife would be safe.

"Who even are you?" the kidnapper asked.

"I showed you my ID back at the rest area. I'm an FBI agent."

He shook his head. "Yeah, sure. There was hardly any light there. I don't even know what I saw. How am I supposed to believe you?"

"I just watched you try and kidnap a woman a little while ago," Jo said with a sigh, "and now you want to act like you're being persecuted. Here, take another look."

She showed her FBI shield again. Holding it up high so everyone could see.

"I'm Agent Pullinger," she said. "And you need to start taking your situation very seriously."

"*Jo* Pullinger?" the kidnapper asked. "You're kind of famous. You work in Seattle, don't you?"

"I'm not sure how you would know that. But I'm an FBI agent. I work everywhere within the borders of this country. My power here is no less than it is in Seattle."

"Yeah, I know," he said. "That badge there might as well have magic powers. You can pretty much get anyone you meet to shut up."

"Excuse me," the farmer said, his eyes darting from side to side. "What's going on here? Are you going to let me go or what?"

"That depends on what *she* does," his captor replied. "Sorry, but it's going to have to be her that makes the next move. Because I have no idea what to do. I didn't expect any of this. I try and grab a girl at a quiet rest area in the middle of the night... and who should show up but a fed!"

He laughed. The farmer smiled a little. He was so confused that he forgot to be scared for a moment. He started to try and get away.

The kidnapper pressed down harder on the knife, drawing blood. Along with a yelp of pain.

"Don't make me cut you more, dude," he said. "I'm backed into a corner here. There's no telling what I'll do."

THIRTEEN

Jo took a step back. She was over the threshold of the door, halfway into the hall.

"Just stop," she said. "Don't hurt him anymore."

The masked man removed the pressure from the knife. He had made his point. The farmer stayed very still now.

"It's completely up to you what to do," Jo went on. "But I can see you're uncertain. I can give you some options, and you can pick which one you want to go with. How does that sound?"

The kidnapper gave it some thought.

"All right," he said doubtfully. "Give me the options."

"The first is the easiest and the least messy," Jo told him. "You can put that knife down and surrender yourself to me. You'll end up in police custody. I have things to do and places to be, so I'll be on my way as soon as you're in the back of a cruiser. You won't have to worry about the FBI coming down on you. We have bigger fish to fry."

"What'll happen to me?" he asked.

"You'll spend some time in jail waiting for your trial. I can't say for certain, but you'll likely spend a few years in prison."

He cringed. "Nah. I can't go to prison. No way. What are my other options?"

Jo smiled. "All the ones I have in mind end with you in jail. At least if they go according to plan."

"According to *your* plan."

"Right. The second option is you find a way to get out of this house. We continue the chase. You run. I follow. Eventually, I'll catch you."

"And then I'll be cuffed in a police cruiser," he said. "Unless I get away."

"Unless you get away," Jo agreed.

"Is that it? Just two options?"

Jo shook her head. "There's a third one. I signal the man you're holding hostage to dive forward. He's big and probably stronger than you. He can definitely break free, though he might get cut a bit in the process. As soon as I have a shot, I take it. I put you down. You either die or you spend some time in the hospital. And *then* you go to jail."

The farmer immediately began shaking. He was feeling the pressure. He definitely wasn't ready to do what Jo was suggesting. She hoped it wouldn't come to that, anyway.

"Huh..." the kidnapper replied, trying to adjust the mask without using his hands. "I'm thinking. Is there some kind of time limit here?"

"My patience," Jo said. "I already went through this same song and dance with some other kidnappers not so long ago. And I'm kind of sick of it."

"Then I guess I'll just go with the only option that gives me a chance. Option number two. I'll bet you're wondering how I plan on getting out of here. Well, I've got it all worked out. Here's how it'll go. You go out into the hallway. Shut the door and count to a hundred. Then you can come after me."

"What if I don't go?" Jo asked.

"Then we get to see how sharp this knife is," he growled. "I think it's pretty sharp."

Jo looked into the farmer's eyes. He didn't say anything, but she could feel him begging.

"Okay, you win," said Jo. "I'll do as you say."

She took another step backward, fully exiting the room. She grabbed the door handle and swung it shut. She started counting out loud.

"One... two... three... four..."

She heard heavy, stumbling footfalls. The farmer had been released. His wife let out a relieved gasp. Jo kept counting.

"Five... six... seven... eight... nine..."

Inside the room, the TV was unmuted. The volume was cranked up to mask the kidnapper's movements.

"Ten... eleven... twelve..."

She got to twenty before the wife called out, "He's gone!"

Jo stopped counting. She opened the door and went back inside. The old couple was sitting on the floor, holding each other.

"Quiet!" the farmer snapped at his wife. "He might come back."

His wife shook her head. "No. He's gone. And he's way too scared to ever come back here."

She caught Jo's eyes. Then she pointed toward an open window.

FOURTEEN

Jo bent down to look through the window. Wind-driven rain hit her in the face. She saw nothing but shadows. She knew she had to climb through, but she wasn't excited about it. Any sense of fun she had earlier was gone.

She put one leg through, straddling the sill. She shimmied toward the outside, preparing to pull her other leg through and drop down.

Her phone rang loudly. It had been twenty minutes, and Kari was calling her. Just as Jo had told her.

Crap.

She threw herself out of the window and hit the ground. She bent her knees to absorb the impact, then reached into her pocket. She pulled her phone out, hitting the red button on the screen. Trying to silence it.

It was too late. Her quarry already knew she was there.

Jo heard his feet squelching in the muck nearby. She looked up. There was a flash of motion. A shovel, swinging toward her head.

She threw herself to the ground. The shovel whisked past her scalp, hitting the wall of the house hard enough to crack one of the bricks.

Jo was flat on her back. She reached up, grabbing the handle of the shovel. Twisting to the side, she wrenched it out of his grasp.

She kept rolling, getting back to her feet. She reached for her gun. But she hadn't resecured her holster. The weapon was somewhere on the ground. And the masked man was getting away.

Jo went down on her knees, feeling around. She found the pistol and took off after him. She had been angry before, but now she was furious.

You tried to kill me. That was the biggest mistake of your life.

Blood pumped through her body. Adrenaline did its job, ridding her muscles of fatigue. But her heart started kicking again. Losing its rhythm and thumping painfully in her chest.

Jo made herself slow down. She breathed evenly, waiting for the spell to pass.

I haven't been sleeping much lately. Or eating very well. That's all it is. But the timing is terrible.

She reached the corner of the house. There was no sign of the kidnapper. Jo turned her phone's flashlight on and cast its glow into the night. It didn't reveal much to her at first.

Then she saw him. He was twenty feet away, darting out from behind the farmer's pickup truck. Running to Jo's right.

She fell to one knee and took three shots. None of them hit. The muzzle flash lit his progress across the yard. With each consecutive flash, he got further away until he was gone from sight, darting behind a toolshed.

FIFTEEN

The toolshed turned out to be just a small wing of a much bigger structure. A whole barn, vast and full of hiding places. Jo spent some time inside it, going from stall to stall. Checking all the nooks and crannies.

The barn brought memories of Lapse to mind. She had to investigate a barn there too.

At least then I had backup, she thought.

She was ready to shoot to kill. In her mind, the man had chosen the third option. The one where he ended up dead or in the hospital.

He wasn't in the barn. No wonder. He would have been a fool to hide there. And Jo had a feeling that he wasn't a fool.

She moved outside and continued searching the property. The rain was slowing down now. It seemed ready to stop at a moment's notice. The moon was peeking through thin clouds, providing enough light for Jo to catch any movement, but not enough to reveal the identity of all the objects surrounding her.

Her phone light was enough to identify most of them. They were all farming implements. Various plow and combine blades. Tractors and backhoes. Everything a person needed to run a modern operation.

Jo checked around each and every one of them. A painstaking process. As she performed this search, she had to contend with a nasty certainty that was growing inside her.

The man was already gone. He was a half mile away by now. Running for his life. If that was the case, she had no chance of finding him. He could have gone in any direction, and she was just one person.

If she still had hope of catching the man, she had to hope he was still here. As unlikely as that seemed. And she had to be thorough. To avoid a repeat situation, she set her phone to silent. Kari was probably getting worried, but she'd have to wait.

It didn't take long to search the rest of the property. Ten or fifteen minutes was all. The farm was an efficient operation. There was no excessive clutter, no extra outbuildings crammed full of junk.

Jo almost wished there was more to search. That way, she could postpone her inevitable conclusion.

I failed. I didn't catch him. He got away.

At least, it was only a reflection on herself. Kari would be fine. By now, she was at least with the police. He wouldn't be able to get to her again.

Jo checked a few final places. Behind a firewood pile. Under a tarp. There was no one in either spot.

It was time to give up and move on with her night.

SIXTEEN

Peter was about to die of exhaustion. He stopped to catch his breath. He fell to the ground, embracing the cold mud that waited there. It cooled his sweaty face. It sucked the heat out of his body, making him shiver.

He stayed that way for a minute. When his heart rate finally slowed down, he sat up and looked back the way he had come.

He could barely make out the lights of the farmhouse. He had made it at least a mile from the place, stumbling through the dark.

After those three gunshots that almost hit him, Agent Pullinger had lost sight of him. Peter made sure she wouldn't get another chance to put him down. He'd run faster than he ever had before.

Now he was here. There was no sign that Pullinger had followed him. Visibility was better now, and he didn't see any movement.

He got up and ran again. He moved slower now. It seemed safe to do so. He had time now. Time was all he had. He had no motorcycle. No car. No idea about where to go next.

At the edge of the farmer's field was another thicket of trees. Peter passed through it. His breathing was ragged, and he was clumsy. Sticks snapped loudly under his feet. He didn't care. He just wanted to be out of here.

There was a clearing in the woods. Another house stood in the middle of it. It was a huge log cabin. A mansion with a four-car garage. Someone wealthy lived there. The porch light was on, but everything else was dark. There wasn't even a dim TV light glowing in any of the windows.

The people who lived here were most likely fast asleep.

Peter saw the sign in the yard. Some local home security company. Trying to take one of the cars was out of the question, then. Maybe he could pull off the trick he tried to use on Kari earlier. He could ring the doorbell. Apologize for waking the person who answered the door. He could tell them his car had broken down. He needed a ride somewhere.

Would it work? Probably not. People were naturally suspicious of hooded young men who rang their doorbells in the middle of the night. They'd probably tell him to take a hike.

Damn people. Why do they have to be so smart?

Peter approached the house anyway. He was desperate for anything that could help him out.

He saw something leaning against the side of the garage. A bicycle that someone had left out. Not the best mode of transport, but better than his two feet. Better yet, it wasn't even locked up.

Peter hopped on and rolled down the driveway, heading into the unknown.

He had successfully evaded the FBI. The Federal Bureau of Investigation! That was something to be proud of.

But Peter could feel only shame and disappointment. He hadn't done the one thing he needed to do. He hadn't gotten the girl.

There was nothing to do now but search for his next opportunity.

He had no idea what his plan would be now, but he had to come up with one. And fast.

SEVENTEEN

After giving up on the hunt, Jo returned to the farmhouse.

She used the same entrance as before, the back door. When she got there, the farmer was standing inside. Surveying the shattered glass with a sorrowful look.

"I'm very sorry about that," Jo told him. She stood halfway up the steps, gripping the handrail. She was exhausted and unsteady.

"Fifty years," the man said. "That's how long I've lived here. Never had a problem until tonight."

Jo tried to smile. "My fault. I chased him, and this is where he ended up. But everything's going to be fine."

He nodded. "I've got insurance. Won't be any problem at all to fix this. Might take a while for the nightmares to go away, though."

Jo noticed the bandage on his neck. He had already been patched up. The bleeding seemed to have stopped. It was a shallow cut. Nothing life-threatening.

"Did you call the police?" Jo asked.

He nodded. "My wife did it straight away. Soon as you left. Should be here any minute now." He stared past Jo, into the distance. "Any minute."

He came back to himself, shaking his head. He opened the door.

"Come in," he said. "Cold out there. Wet, too."

Jo stepped past him. Her shoes crunched on broken glass. A second later, his wife arrived wielding a broom and dustpan. Shooing them out of the way.

"I'll stay with you both until the police get here," Jo went on. "Just a precaution. You're safe. That guy is long gone. If you'll excuse me..."

She went into the hall, pulling out her phone. She returned Kari's call.

"Hello?" a meek voice answered.

"This is Agent Pullinger, calling you back. Sorry, it took so long."

Kari sighed. "I was worried. I thought maybe..."

"He might have hurt me?" Jo suggested. "No. I'm fine. But he did get away. Are the police there?"

"They are," said Kari. "Only a couple at first. More just got here a minute ago, but they already left. They said something about a disturbance at the Brewster farm."

Jo laughed. "I guess that's where I am. I'm waiting on them now. I'll be back with you as soon as I can, all right?"

***

The cops arrived a couple of minutes later. Jo showed them around. The broken glass. The open window. The shovel that almost crushed her face in. She gave them her story and contact info. One of them, Officer Jeremy, offered to drive her back to her car.

He was a young guy. Scrawny. Wide eyes and a constant bewildered smile on his face. It was plain as day that he had no idea what he was doing... but he was happy to be doing it. Jo liked him.

They hadn't even reached the edge of the Brewster property before Officer Jeremy could no longer stand the silence in the car.

"That was some great thing you did," he said. "Saving that girl. You FBI people really are something special, huh?"

"We go through a lot of training," Jo agreed. "But that was all luck. If you'd been in my position, you would have done the same. Except you might have had your gun on you from the get-go. And maybe you would have snagged the guy."

"Oh, I don't know about that," Officer Jeremy chuckled. "Hey look, a cow. Huh. Guess we are on a farm, after all."

With only a few more short bursts of small talk, Officer Jeremy delivered her to her destination. Jo immediately got in her car.

"Seatbelt," she said, grunting while she spoke.

Kari quickly put her belt on. Jo turned around and headed down the frontage road. Looking for a way back onto the pavement.

"Were we supposed to just drive off like that?" Kari asked.

Jo turned up the heat. She hoped the noise would drown out the rattling that was coming from the car's undercarriage.

"These local guys have never dealt with this sort of thing before," Jo said. "They have no idea what they're doing, but I have faith they'll figure it out. The problem is, it'll take them a long time. I don't want to get stuck here. And I assume you don't, either."

Kari shrugged. "Officer Jeremy was kind of cute. I only got to see him for a couple of minutes."

"Don't worry, I'm sure you can look him up on Facebook." Jo found a way over the ditch. She drove out onto the main road and headed back toward the rest area. "I'm sure the cops already asked, but I wasn't there. Where are you headed?"

"Back home," Kari replied.

"Where's that?"

"Seattle."

Jo smiled. "Hey, me too. What were you doing in Oregon?"

"You first," Kari shot back. Jo gave her a stern look, and Kari relented. "Fine. I was visiting my grandma. She lived at this assisted living place in Eugene, and she isn't doing too well right now. Healthwise, I mean."

"Sorry to hear that," said Jo. "But isn't Eugene in the middle of the state?"

"Sort of. I have lots of time to get back, so I decided to take the road less traveled." Kari shrugged. "I guess the road less traveled is less traveled for reasons. One of them being that creepy kidnappers use it."

They arrived at the rest area. The crappy, dim light was still struggling for life. The lot was empty other than Kari's car. Jo doubted anyone else had been there.

Jo pulled up next to the other car. "There we go. Delivered, safe and sound. Hey, since you're in Seattle, too... why don't you give me your address? I can check on you in a couple of days. See how you're doing."

Kari smiled. "I'd like that. I already have your number. I'll text my address to you."

She waved goodbye as she climbed into her car.

EIGHTEEN

The SeaTac airport was a forlorn sight in the early morning. Bright lights illuminated the place like New Year's Eve. But there was nothing for them to shine on.

Other than a handful of cars in long-term parking, the lot was desolate. She saw a single traveler being dropped off at the front. Receiving hugs from his wife or mother. At this distance, Jo couldn't tell.

She knew how that man must feel. Tired. Strung out. Regretting the fact he wasn't still in bed. But looking forward to wrapping it all up so he could come home again. And hug the ones he loved.

Jo kept on driving. She gave the airport a farewell glance in her rearview mirror.

"See you again in a few hours," she said with a sigh.

***

The morning traffic was picking up as Jo entered the city proper. Newspapers were being delivered. Tired people were fetching their coffee. Jo drove through it all with a sense of purpose. The purpose of getting to her apartment was so she could crash.

It was getting harder and harder to keep her eyes open. She smacked herself in the face, blinking the sleep away.

Almost there, she thought.

It was strange to think that less than five hours ago, she had been chasing a would-be kidnapper across a cow field. Now she was in the big city. Huffing the scents of exhaust and briny ocean spray.

She reached her apartment at long last. It seemed like a year since she'd been there. Everything looked and felt different.

Jo slogged her way inside, locking the door and kicking her shoes off. She drank a glass of water. Rehydrating after getting blown on by her rental's heat vent all night.

She fell into bed. The first and last thing she thought of was the damage to her car. But she was too tired to be anxious. She was asleep before she knew it.

***

When she woke several hours later, Jo felt like she hadn't slept a wink. At the same time, she felt like a hundred years had passed. The sun was shining through the curtains. Turning her room into a hotbox. She was covered in sweat.

"I give it ten minutes, and it'll be raining again," she grumbled as she stumbled into the bathroom to brush her teeth.

Exactly ten minutes later, she was making her way outside. It wasn't raining yet, but the skies had suddenly turned gray.

The rain started when she was halfway back to SeaTac. It was pouring down in bucketloads as she ran inside the terminal. Too distracted with keeping herself dry to notice the yellow cab parked by the curb.

"Well, if ain't the other Jo!"

She turned to find the source of the voice. Joe, the cab driver, was standing just inside the door. His shoulders were speckled with rainwater. He was sipping a cup of coffee. There was a cane in his other hand.

"Joe!" she said enthusiastically. The old black man was the first friendly face she saw when she originally arrived in Seattle. He had driven her from the airport. "Last time I saw you..."

"Right after the hit and run that almost took my leg off," he said with good cheer.

"You're back on your feet already?" Jo asked.

He lifted his pant leg, showing a bandage wrapped around his ankle. "Doc says I'm good to start driving again. Called it a miraculous recovery. I got just enough strength to push down the gas pedal. Walking's still a challenge, though."

"It's only been a few weeks," Jo replied with a laugh. "Seems like you're doing great!"

"I sure can't complain." Joe sighed contentedly, looking around. "I love this place. Done lots of good business here over the years. What are you here about, Jo?"

Before she could answer, a shrill scream echoed across the terminal.

"*Auntie Jo!*"

Chrissy, Jo's seven-year-old niece, came sprinting from the baggage claim. Her father and mother were lagging behind, dragging their luggage. Kim had regained some of her deep color. Sam had gained the shade of a lobster from too much sun.

Jo squatted down, holding her arms wide. Chrissy flew into them. Jo lifted the girl high in the air, spinning around.

"Wee! This is fun!"

"Yeah, and *tiring*." Jo put her niece back down. "What did you eat on that trip, anyway? I swear you're twice as heavy."

Chrissy grinned. "Chicken nuggets. Lots of them. My mom and dad had fish every night. Gross."

Kim's shoes squeaked on the floor as she came to a stop. "She never runs out of energy!"

"No, she does not," Sam agreed. "I guess letting her have three boxes of apple juice on the flight wasn't the best idea. Speaking of which… Chrissy, are you sure you don't need to use the bathroom? Last chance before we get in the car."

Jo looked over to where Joe, the cab driver, had been. But he was gone. She saw him in the distance, chatting with someone else. He hadn't wanted to interfere with her family reunion and had excused himself.

One day I'll introduce him to the family, she thought.

She had been at his apartment before. It was packed to the brim with things Joe collected. Books and music records, mostly. Obviously, he enjoyed his hobbies. But he was such a sociable man, Jo thought he might be lonely.

She turned back to her family. They talked their way out the door. Jo told them not to mind the scuffed-up appearance of her car.

They decided they should all go out for dinner. Kim picked one of her favorite restaurants. Thirty seconds into the drive, Chrissy told them she had to pee.

NINETEEN

The next morning, Jo rose bright and early. She was still too wrecked from the ordeal in Lapse, followed by her run-in at the rest area, to do her usual run. She pumped a few sets of pushups, then some bodyweight squats. Enough to work up a sweat.

Then she showered. She felt hungry afterward, so she popped open the fridge. She saw her leftovers from dinner last night. Chicken alfredo. Delicious and served in enormous quantities.

Jo smiled as she remembered the night. Lots of laughter. Plenty of vacation stories from her family. A little too much wine. An enchanting evening overall.

She opted for a healthier breakfast of yogurt and fruit. She went out the door as soon as the food was down the hatch.

To her, the fact she was still excited to get to work seemed like a very good thing.

***

At her apartment, and everywhere else in Seattle, things felt different. She hadn't been gone that long. But enough had happened to her during that time to subtly change her perception of things.

However, the Seattle FBI field office felt the same as ever. It was hardly a warm building, architecturally speaking. It was a cold place. A few vast chambers. A lot of dimly lit hallways. Still, Jo felt a sense of coziness as soon as she stepped in.

Her apartment was just where she slept. This was her true home. The place she would be happy to never leave. As long as there was another case to get to.

And there pretty much always was.

Her first order of business was to get herself a cup of coffee from the breakroom. As soon as caffeine was acquired, she headed directly for her boss's office. Along the way, she was passed by several other agents as they sped through the halls, holding stacks of paperwork. As always, the place had the air of a library. Everyone was deep in concentration, working away in silence.

As usual, the door to her boss's office was shut. His title and name were stenciled on it in block letters.

SPECIAL AGENT IN CHARGE ROBERT GRANTHAM.

Jo knocked.

"Who is it?" a deep, gruff voice boomed.

"Agent Pullinger, sir," Jo called back.

"Pullinger! Get in here. Now."

Jo opened the door. She stepped in and shut it behind her. Her boss was sitting at his desk, peeling the paper off a blueberry muffin. Robert Grantham was a powerful man with a barrel chest. If Jo didn't know his true nature, she would have been terrified of him.

"Oh, you did it this time," he growled, licking crumbs off his thumb. "You're in deep trouble."

Jo took a seat, calmly folding one leg over the other. "Am I, sir? What did I do?'

"You were supposed to be on vacation, Pullinger. Rest and relaxation. So I'm wondering why my phone went off early yesterday morning, letting me know one of my agents was involved in an attempted kidnapping."

"Which agent was that, sir?" Jo asked with a smile.

He dropped his muffin with a dull *plop*. "Some hotshot named Johanna. Weird name. German, maybe."

"Swedish, actually. But I guess I am in trouble. You're using my full first name. I *was* on vacation, sir. But someone tried to grab a young woman pretty much right in front of me. I could have asked him to wait a couple of days until I was back on the clock, but I don't think he would have gone for it."

"Probably not. Did you eat yet?"

"I had a bite," said Jo.

"Then I'll have this muffin all to myself. Glad to see you got a cup of coffee, though. I would have thought the pot was empty."

"Does that mean McKinley's back in town?"

Grantham nodded. "He flew back from Boise on the first flight. I ordered him to take a little time off. But he showed up in the office yesterday morning. When I informed him he didn't need to be here, he told me he likes the coffee too much to stay away."

Jo drank from her cup and sighed. "It is good coffee, sir. The taxpayers' money isn't being wasted on that account."

"Good to hear. So why are you in my office?" Grantham demanded.

Jo shrugged. "I figured you'd want an update straight from me."

"Nope. Already got all the information I need. The kidnapper got away, but the victim is safe. Another good job."

"Could have been better," Jo sniffed.

"Could have been worse. Now get out of here. Go on. Let me eat my breakfast in peace." Grantham made shooing motions with his hand.

TWENTY

Jo gulped the rest of the coffee as she left Grantham's office. She headed back to the breakroom for a refill.

But she had to wait her turn. A tall, skinny man in his early thirties was already at the pot. As Jo watched, he filled his cup to the brim. Took a long drink. Then refilled it.

"Your tongue must be made of fiberglass," Jo commented.

Agent McKinley was so startled that he poured coffee on the front of his shirt. Jo grabbed a handful of napkins and held them out for him.

"My tongue might be," McKinley hissed in pain, "but my chest isn't. Ouch."

"Usually, it's not that easy to startle you," Jo said. "Are you on edge about something?"

"Five cups of coffee in the last hour. That's what I'm on the edge of." McKinley filled his cup back up. "How about you? First or second cup?"

"Second." Jo came in behind him, emptying the rest of the pot into her mug. "But I'm exhausted. I'm no Lewis McKinley, but I might go for a personal record in caffeine consumption today."

"I heard about what happened at that rest area," McKinley said. He grabbed the empty coffee pot and filled it at the water cooler to start a fresh batch. "Is that why you're tired?"

Jo shook her head. "I had to pick my family up from the airport. Lots of driving. I had time to stop at a hotel for a few hours, but I felt pretty wired. Just wanted to get back to Seattle. I guess chasing that guy in Oregon might have had something to do with that feeling."

They walked back toward their desks, nodding at other agents and support staff members as they passed.

"How was the rest of your drive?" McKinley asked.

"Boring. Which is just what Doctor Grantham had ordered. I did meet a guy."

"A guy?" McKinley asked.

"A truck driver. He was nice."

"A truck driver. Interesting." McKinley shrugged and took a drink of coffee. He tipped the cup all the way back. Already empty. "Boise was boring. Ford and I felt like third wheels. We were happy to get on the plane back here."

Bryan Ford. He had been one of the people with them in Lapse. But he wasn't FBI. Ford used to be a Seattle police detective before opening his own private investigation firm. Lately, he'd been doing contract work with the FBI. Mostly because he and Jo were good friends.

"Have you seen Ford since you landed?" Jo asked.

McKinley shook his head. "He went back to his job, and I went back to mine. He did say we should all get together for drinks sometime."

Jo grinned. "I'd like that. The three musketeers. How was Swann doing?"

"Fine, I think. You wouldn't know he'd been subjected to all that. He was strong. I think he'll be a good fit in Boise. Do you...?"

"Do I?" Jo asked. "Do I what?"

"Want to talk about it?" McKinley added slowly. "About Lapse? It was quite a wild experience."

They arrived at their desks. Jo plopped down in her chair and powered her desktop computer on. The thing made a grinding noise. The same thing it did every time it came on. She gave it a kick, and it went quiet.

"I need an upgrade," she said, sighing. "This machine's old enough to get a driver's license."

"You're exaggerating," McKinley replied. "That machine has an eight-core processor and sixteen gigs of RAM. It just needs a new intake fan. And you're dodging the question."

Jo gave him a sheepish smile. "Sorry. Yes, Lapse was wild. But it feels even wilder because it just happened. Once we get to the next wild case, it'll fade into the background. Hey, maybe I should at least get a new video card for this computer. That way, I can play games."

"Grantham would love that. We could set up a LAN party." McKinley tried to drink from his empty mug and frowned. "And now I have to wait for the next batch to finish brewing. So that's what I'll be doing for the next ten minutes, at least. Then I think I'll start working on my rubber band ball. What are your plans for the day?"

"Don't know." Jo logged into her computer and stared at her desktop wallpaper, a blue background with the FBI seal in the middle. "Guess I'll check my emails. See what I missed. Then I need to head out for a little while. I'd like to check up on Kari Cross."

"The girl you saved at the rest area the other night?" McKinley asked.

Jo nodded and opened her email account. It was looking like today would turn out to be a boring one.

TWENTY-ONE

The morning passed slowly. Jo nearly fell asleep reading her emails. A lot of them had to do with lab results from the Lapse case. DNA and other trace evidence. It would have been very interesting, except the case was already solved. There were no exciting revelations to be found.

She replied to the messages that required one. She thanked people for their diligent efforts. She got herself another cup of coffee. Along with a blueberry muffin. Her short meeting with Grantham had given her a craving.

It was approaching noon when she suddenly remembered Kari. She logged out of her computer and stood up, pulling her jacket on.

"Going out for lunch?" McKinley asked. He was literally bouncing in his chair, hopped up on caffeine. "Could you pick something up for me? I can give you cash."

"I was going to check on Kari, actually," Jo replied. She zipped up her jacket and pulled the hood up. Without looking outside or even checking her weather app, she knew it would be raining.

"Oh, yeah." McKinley slipped while trying to add another elastic to his rubber band ball. It flew off into the distance. "Oops. I'll get that later. Do you need me to look up her address?"

"No need. She texted it to me yesterday morning. Thanks, though. If you want, I'll bring a sandwich or something back for you."

"Nah, I'll just see what's in the break room."

"Probably a ton of sugar, and that's it," Jo told him.

McKinley shrugged. "Fine by me. I'll just get another cup of coffee to fight off the sugar crash. Have a fun time out there."

***

Jo walked out onto the sidewalk. There was an immediate pitter-patter against the top of her hood. She looked up long enough for a drop of rain to hit her in the eyeball.

"I knew it," she groaned, blinking away the rain. She ran to where her rental car was parked. She'd still been too afraid to take it to the local agency.

There's something else I can get done before coming back to the office.

She got in the car and pulled her hood back. Before heading out, she punched Kari's address into her phone. It was close by, in the Capitol Hill neighborhood of Seattle. GPS said it would take her ten minutes.

It actually took almost twenty. Lunchtime traffic being what it was.

Jo parked outside the house. She took a deep breath to get rid of her road rage. Then she got out. Rain splattered her scalp, and she yanked her hood back up with an angry groan.

For a moment, she stood on the sidewalk and stared at the house.

It wasn't large, but it was cute. A nice cool gray color. The front porch was well-decorated with plants and a comfy porch swing. It looked like the type of place a middle-class older couple might live.

But Jo had done some snooping on her computer that morning. Kari owned the place outright. No mortgage. And she lived here alone. A woman in her early twenties. Jo didn't know what Kari did for a living, but it must have been good.

Either that or her parents were rich.

There was another car parked at the curb outside the house. Jo recognized it from the rest area. It was Kari's.

"Guess she's home," Jo said to herself. "Good timing."

She approached the front door, reaching out to ring the bell. When she saw the door up close, she froze.

The door was shut. But the lock was scratched up and dented. And the wood near the latch was chewed up. Splintered and cracked.

Someone had recently broken into the house.

TWENTY-TWO

Dread crashed through Jo like a wave. A sense of fatalism and fear. She drew her sidearm and held her breath, her hand shaking as she reached for the door handle.

The door was unlocked. It swung ajar at her touch, revealing a tiny entry room that was just as lovely and well-appointed as the front porch.

Jo looked down. There were muddy prints across the floor, seemingly too large to belong to Kari. But the floor was carpet. No shoe impressions would be possible. A mineral analysis, maybe.

Her mind was already going through the procedures. She felt certain of what she would find as she ventured through the house, and it made her feel completely useless.

The muddy prints triggered a nauseating sense of déjà vu. Jo followed them down the hallway. Just as they had at the farmhouse, the prints faded away. By the time Jo reached the kitchen, they were gone.

She stepped onto the kitchen's tile floor. An acrid smell filled the space. She saw why a moment later. There was a coffee pot on the counter. The glass was completely black with burnt residue. Smoke was still curling out of it.

The pot was on. Someone had made a pot of coffee. Left it there long enough for the hotplate to evaporate everything.

Jo used the butt of her gun to turn the pot off. If it was left much longer, the carafe might explode. Maybe it would even start a fire.

Next to the burnt pot was a plate of food. Bacon and eggs. It was half-eaten. Cold. The fat on the bacon was congealed. But the food wasn't showing any signs of rot just yet.

She checked the sink next. There was no used coffee cup there or anywhere else in the kitchen.

As she was moving to check the rest of the house, Jo saw the table sitting in the corner of the kitchen. There were two chairs at it. Enough for Kari and one guest.

There wasn't much on the table. A napkin holder. A small succulent in a pot. And two other things that made Jo pause.

A phone and a set of car keys.

She took a step closer to get a better look. The keys were the same make as Kari's car. The phone was harder to identify. Jo had only seen it in the dark.

But she did remember something. When she dropped Kari back off at her car, Kari had checked her phone. Jo saw the wallpaper. It was a cute picture of a red panda.

Jo pushed the table with her thumb. It was enough of a jostle to make the phone wake up. She saw the very same picture of the red panda.

This was Kari's phone. And it was safe to assume these were Kari's car keys.

Jo realized she had been breathless since walking in. She had completely forgotten to announce herself.

"Kari, it's Agent Pullinger," she called. "Are you here?"

She prayed for a response. But there was none.

Jo searched the rest of the house.

There was no TV in the living room. But there was one in Kari's bedroom, and it was turned on.

There was also no sign of a wallet or purse anywhere.

Jo returned to the kitchen and crouched down, trying to map out a possible timeline.

With all the residue in the coffee pot, she could tell that Kari had made a full batch. And it wasn't one of those tiny coffee makers. It was a twelve-cup carafe.

How long would it take all of that to burn away? Quite a while.

But not long enough for the food to start rotting. Or attract any flies.

Jo theorized that Kari had been gone since yesterday morning. She must have gotten back to Seattle around the same time Jo did.

And she didn't even have time to eat her full breakfast before someone came for her.

TWENTY-THREE

Jo was still in the kitchen. Squatting, staring at the tile floor. Trying to process what was happening.

I promised her she was safe. The kidnapper got away, but there was no way he'd be coming back for her. It was just a random attack. Wasn't it?

She looked at the table. At Kari's phone. When she had jostled the table before, she had just been looking for the background image. She hadn't been searching for any other details.

Jo walked over and moved the table again. The phone lit up. Jo scanned the screen quickly. Checking for notifications. There were some emails, along with a text. The emails didn't concern Jo. The text did.

Text messages were the modern communication method of choice. They could be much more personal than emails. They could contain all kinds of information.

Jo wanted to get into that text message.

But she was alone. She had no gloves. No evidence bags. Nothing with which to process a potential crime scene.

She called Grantham.

"Agent Pullinger," his voice answered.

"Sir," said Jo, "I've got a situation here. I came to Capitol Hill to check on Kari Cross. She's not here. There are signs of a break-in. I think she's been taken."

There was a creaking sound. Grantham getting up from his chair. "Hold on. You're saying the girl that you saved from getting kidnapped in Oregon just got kidnapped from her house in Seattle?"

"Not quite *just*. Looks like she's been gone since yesterday."

Grantham sighed. "I guess this situation just got more interesting. What are you going to do?"

Jo didn't need to think for long. "I'm going to call Ford."

"That's fine with me. You two work well together. Keep me apprised of the situation. Get to work."

He hung up. Jo immediately called Bryan Ford's office.

A young woman answered. "Ford Investigative Solutions. Dessie speaking."

Dessie Archer. Ford's secretary.

"Hello, Dessie. This is Jo Pullinger."

"Oh!" Yet another creaking sound. Dessie leaning forward and concentrating. "Mr. Ford told me five minutes ago to tell any callers that he's in a meeting with a client. Even though I know he isn't. I'm sure he'll make an exception for you. Please hold."

There was a click. Classical music played over the line. After twenty seconds, Ford answered in his office.

"Jo," he said. "I was wondering when you'd start missing me."

"I'm not interrupting a meeting, am I?" Jo asked.

"No. Just me trying to get over a bad headache. Kelly and I hired a babysitter last night and went out for drinks. It got a little crazy."

"Not too dissimilar from the night I had."

"Last night, or the night before? I heard you had a thing in Oregon. Well, a smaller thing. Not the big thing we were both a part of in Lapse. You saved a young woman. How's she doing now?"

"That's why I'm calling," Jo replied, sighing. "I need your help. I'll text you the address. And if you could call that CSI team you know…"

"On it. I'll be there as soon as possible. And now I really won't be available to take any calls. Dessie'll be happy. She hates lying. See you in a bit."

Jo went out onto the porch to wait. The CSI team arrived first, driving a big white van. The first person to get out was a short guy with wispy blond hair. Jo had met him in Lapse, when he helped them process a different crime scene.

"Rupert," Jo said, waving.

"There you are," he replied in his English accent. "Ford didn't give us any info. Just said we'd better get here straight away. What seems to be the problem?"

Jo gave him the rundown as he and his team suited up in their coveralls and booties. Ford arrived as the CSI team was making their way inside. He parked his car across the street and walked over, massaging his temples.

Bryan Ford was in his early forties. To Jo, he seemed like the picture of an old-time detective. Tall and ruggedly handsome. The only thing missing was a fedora.

"Head still hurting?" Jo asked.

"Good to see you, too," he grumbled. "Popped a few aspirins. Starting to go away now. Although, I get the feeling it'll be back." He gestured at the house. "Nice little place. Is this where Kari lives?"

Jo nodded. "I gave Rupert the details already. I'll tell you on the drive."

"The drive?" He squinted at her. "You said you needed me here. Where are we going?"

"Back to the field office. I thought you'd get here way before Rupert. You were too slow."

He glared at her. "Fine. Who's driving?"

"You," said Jo. "I've still got my rental, and I'm putting way too many miles on it."

TWENTY-FOUR

Jo was sitting alone in the passenger seat of Ford's car. She twiddled her thumbs and watched rain streak down the window. The neon light of the convenience store shone through blurrily.

The door opened, and Ford got back inside. He popped open his freshly acquired energy drink and took a swig.

"Ah, that's the stuff," he said with a contented sigh, stuffing the can in his cup holder.

"Those things aren't very good for you," Jo pointed out.

"Well, when you feel the way I do right now, they taste like they are. Oh, here's this abomination."

He pulled something out of his coat pocket, wrapped in cellophane. It was a roast beef sandwich.

"Looks like someone sat on it," Ford said. "Or maybe used it to kick a field goal. But there you go."

"McKinley won't mind," Jo replied. "It's fuel. And a way to soak up the coffee in his stomach so he can drink more without dying."

"I don't think any amount of coffee could kill that kid." Ford pulled out into traffic and immediately started swearing. "You know, I'm not normally an angry driver. But those gin and tonics I had last night are still knocking around in my skull like bowling balls."

They made it to the field office in one piece. Ford tossed his empty energy drink can into the garbage as they walked in. Jo escorted him to McKinley's desk.

McKinley's rubber band ball was sitting to the side, forgotten but noticeably bigger than when Jo last saw it. McKinley was hunched toward his monitor, typing furiously and answering internal emails at an astonishing rate.

"Wow, very interesting toxicology report here," he said. "A man was poisoned with cyanide and arsenic at the same time. And if that wasn't enough, his murderer used a turkey baster to dump some antifreeze down his throat. Just in case being dead twice over wasn't enough."

Ford's eyes went wide. "Why aren't we working on *that* case?"

McKinley sent off his latest email and looked up. "Because his wife already confessed, and she'll spend the rest of her life in prison. But the test results only just came back. Is that for me?"

He accepted his squashed roast beef sandwich with a grateful nod. He unwrapped it and started eating. "Grantham let me know about Kari. I wanted to get through those emails fast so we could start working on her as soon as you got here. What do we know so far?"

"Other than what's at the scene?" Jo asked. "Not much. But Kari must have been targeted for a reason. The kidnapper's attempt at the rest area wasn't a random act like I thought. If we want to understand why he went after her, I think we need to learn more about Kari herself."

Ford wheeled Jo's chair over, then took one from a vacant desk. They sat down.

"The first thing I'd like to know," Jo said, "is how Kari afforded to buy out that house. Especially since she lives there by herself."

"I can find that out." McKinley cracked his knuckles and got to work. The first thing he came up with was a slew of enrollment paperwork from a local school. "Cornish College of the Arts. She just transferred there last summer. Before that, she was at the University of Washington."

"So she's an active student," Jo noted. "I assume she didn't buy her house with loan money."

McKinley shook his head and searched a bit more. "Here's the deed to her house. And the purchase agreement. The sellers wanted one and a quarter million. Kari offered a million in cash, and they took it."

"Cash?" Ford gasped. "Where'd she get *that* from?"

TWENTY-FIVE

"She bought a house for cash," Jo repeated. "A million-dollar sale. How old is she?"

"Twenty-three," McKinley replied. "I checked. Her birthday was two months ago."

"That's a lot of money. We need to see if it made a trail."

"Should be easy to find out. No need to get into any IRS files, hopefully..." McKinley worked his magic some more. Looking back through all records for Kari Cross, public and private. "All right. I think I solved the mystery. It looks like Kari's parents were owners of a very successful business."

"*Were*?" Jo asked.

"They died in a car crash. Here's the incident report. It was the other driver's fault, and Kari got a full life insurance payout. Along with inheritance and whatever else was in her parents' will. From what I can see, we're talking in the mid-eight-figure range. Somewhere around fifty million dollars."

Ford whistled. "Not bad. Sucks to lose your parents when you're still that young, but *still*. No ill-gotten gains here. And plenty of reasons for someone to want to kidnap her."

Jo nodded. "Her phone and keys were still in the house. But I couldn't find a purse or a wallet. The kidnapper must have it."

"Poor kid," Ford said with a sigh. "There are always vultures around to try and peck at what you've got. Sometimes one of them gets bold and tries to take even more. I think we can all agree that Kari is in a lot of trouble."

"Imminent danger," Jo echoed. "I hate to be a downer, but I'd be surprised if she's still alive. From what I saw at the house, her kidnapper was sloppy. Impulsive. Probably didn't have much of a plan, if any. A person like that..."

"He'd probably do something stupid," McKinley added. "Try and withdraw her money from an ATM. Maybe he tried to go to her bank. When that didn't work, he probably got scared."

The three of them fell silent. They were all imagining the same scenario. The kidnapper freaked out and decided to cover his tracks. That meant getting rid of Kari.

Jo thought the chances of finding her were good.

But finding her *alive* was a different matter.

"She told me she was visiting her grandmother in Eugene, Oregon," Jo said. "Her grandmother's health was deteriorating."

"That's unfortunate," McKinley said.

"It is, but it's not why I'm bringing it up. I'd like to know if Kari had any other connections. Her parents are deceased, we know that. But is there any other family?"

It took McKinley several minutes to check his sources.

"She was an only child," he said. "And her family tree is pretty sparse. Other than her grandmother, her closest living relative is a cousin in Alaska."

Jo nodded. "So there's no one in Seattle to worry about her. Maybe Kari was a loner. Maybe she thought keeping people at bay was in her best interest. A way to hide what she had. To protect her family's fortune. But someone found out about it anyway."

TWENTY-SIX

"All right, I know this is going to sound dumb," Ford said. "And it's not even something I'm considering. But let's just work our way through it. Do we know for a fact Kari is missing? That she didn't just have to leave abruptly?"

"So abruptly that she forgot to take her car?" Jo asked. "I can see that, if she had urgent business at the coffee shop one block over. So urgent that she also forgot the full pot she had already brewed at home."

"It's stupid," Ford said, sighing. "But maybe she was just very forgetful."

"To be *that* forgetful would require a medical condition of some kind," McKinley added. "I don't see anything in her file about that. The closest thing is a bad case of strep throat around Thanksgiving that caused her to take herself to the ER."

"Doesn't strep throat cause memory loss sometimes?" Ford asked hopefully. "All right. You got me. I really just want this kid to be all right. Isn't there some conceivable way...?"

"You're the detective," Jo said gently. "If you can't conceive a way other than some hitherto unseen case of strep throat-related memory loss, then there probably isn't one. She had a car, which she didn't bother taking with her. Also, she left her phone. What person in their early twenties leaves without their phone?"

"What person of any age, these days?" Ford agreed. "I hope Darrel can shed some light for us."

"Who's Darrel?" Jo asked.

"Darrel Hopkins. He's the technology expert on Rupert's team. He'll be able to get into Kari's phone no matter what kind of security she has on it."

McKinley sat back, taking another bite of his sandwich. "So, now we just wait to hear back. Unless you'd like to head back to Kari's place."

Jo shook her head. "I have faith in Rupert. And I don't want to get in his way. I'm sure there's something else useful I can spend my time on." She groaned, punching the arm of her chair. "She had a text on her phone. I just wish I knew what it said."

"It's probably nothing," Ford said. "Just a friend checking in with her."

I should have checked in, too, Jo thought. *I should have gone there yesterday. Now the kidnapper has had time to take her who-knows-where.*

"It had to be the same person," she hissed. "I stood right in front of him. I looked into his eyes. He's not going to be able to hide from me. If I see him, I'll know."

The same person, she thought. How could it not be? Two kidnapping attempts, not even twelve hours apart. One failed. One successful. One foiled because Jo had been there. One that succeeded because she wasn't.

This wasn't an ordinary case. This was personal. Jo felt completely responsible.

She *would* catch the person who did this. And she'd find Kari whether she was still breathing or not.

TWENTY-SEVEN

Ford's phone started buzzing. He took a look at the screen, then cursed and stood up.

"Sorry, it's one of my clients. I'd love to stay and help more with this, but I've got my own laundry list, and it's about a mile long. Rupert has your contact info, right?"

Jo nodded. "He should. Even if he doesn't, I'm not hard to find. Are you sure you can't stay?"

Ford sighed. "I'm sure. I hope Kari's alive and well. If this rabbit hole starts getting too deep and you need an extra pair of hands, call me. I'll work it out with Dessie, and I'll be there."

He answered his phone as he was walking away.

"Yes, Ms. Philips. I'm on my way there now to see if I can find out what your boyfriend spent your savings on... My guess, since you said he doesn't have a drinking problem? Sports betting."

McKinley cringed. "Sounds like a bad one. I'd rather deal with kidnapping. It's simpler than jilted love."

"But just as nasty," Jo replied. "McKinley, we've been shooting the breeze all morning, but I haven't asked the obvious question yet. How are you?"

McKinley shrugged and took another bite of his sandwich. "I assume you're talking about Lapse? I already went through a debriefing and a psychological evaluation. I did it right when I got back. It got my mind back on track. I'd recommend you to do it too, but I know what you'll say."

"I don't have time," Jo replied.

"Exactly."

"No, I mean, I really don't have time," Jo added. "Kari needs my help."

McKinley picked off a soggy piece of bread from his leg and tossed it in the trash. "You had time to ask how I was doing, but not time to look after yourself? I'm not a doctor, but I think you put too much pressure on yourself. You don't give yourself any leeway at all."

Jo waved her hands. "Hold on. Let me remind you of our dynamic here, McKinley. I'm the mentor. You're the protégé."

"I guess I forgot," said McKinley. "So, the protégé never questions anything the mentor says?"

"Not if the mentor is me. By the way, that sandwich looks disgusting."

"Tastes okay. Now you're changing the subject."

"And I'll change it right back. There are two reasons why I asked how you're doing. The first one is that I care about you. Second, I wanted to see where you were at. If I could count on your help on this case."

McKinley nodded. "You can. But I think I've had enough field work for now. I'd like to stay in the chair as much as I can this time."

"That's fine," Jo said. "The chair is where you do some of your best work. I just had to know you were behind me."

He smiled. "I always will be. Where else can I find a completely infallible mentor?"

"Damn straight." Jo grinned and nudged him on the arm. "But back to business. We've got Rupert gathering evidence for us at Kari's house. Let's hope whatever he finds can stand on its own, but I'd still like to find something to compare it to. It was the Oregon state police that helped me out when I foiled the first kidnapping attempt."

McKinley threw out the mushy heel of his sandwich. He scooted closer to his keyboard. "I'll get them to send over everything they have. I'm sure they're still in the middle of running tests, so it might take some time. What are you going to do?"

"What I'm good at." Jo stood up, pushing her chair back to her desk. And replacing the one Ford had taken for himself. "I'm going to scour Seattle and scoop up every last morsel of data I can find about Kari Cross."

TWENTY-EIGHT

Most of the homes along Bainbridge Island's Rockaway Beach were modestly sized. Their styles were eclectic, but their dimensions were about the same. Everyone had their narrow but luxuriantly expensive slice of the waterfront.

The exception was a mansion that took up as much room as four of its neighbors. It occupied a piece of land that jutted out a bit more. It was also a bit higher up, putting it in a commanding position.

A white van pulled up outside the mansion. It didn't look much different than the one driven by Rupert. But rather than being full of technicians and their gadgets, it was full of cleaning supplies. And there was only one person inside it.

Olga Aleksandrov parked the van outside the mansion's front gate and stepped out. She was slow in her movements. She was in no hurry to get inside the house. Every time she looked at the sprawling house, her stomach flipped.

So she looked at the city instead. Staring out over the roof of the mansion, she could make out Seattle in the distance. Sometimes it was good to look into the distance. For a moment, it made Olga's problems feel smaller.

A man approached the inside of the gate. He was tall and beefy. Dressed in a black suit. A few tattoos peeked out here and there. They were muddy and poorly done. To Olga, they looked like prison tattoos. Hints of a troubled past.

Though the present had its share of troubles as well.

"Ms. Aleksandrov," the guard said. "You should be inside already. My boss isn't paying you to daydream."

She made herself laugh, wiping a lock of blonde hair out of her eyes. When she spoke, her Russian accent was thick. "That's too bad. I am very good at it."

The guard gave her a serious look. He opened the gate for her and beckoned her in.

"Just have to grab some things," Olga said breathlessly.

She opened the back of the van. It was neatly organized but still just about overflowing. There was every cleaning chemical known to man inside. Every tool and apparatus you could ever need.

Olga knew exactly what she was here to clean. She grabbed the required items. She grabbed a few rags. A bucket. And a bottle of hydrogen peroxide. That should do the job. If she needed anything else, she could come back out for it.

She pranced over to the guard. "Ready."

He grunted impatiently, grabbing her arm and pulling her inside. He shut the gate and gestured toward the house. "You know the way by now."

He watched her go. When she was halfway to the house, he seemed to forget she existed. He wandered off into the yard with his arms crossed. Watching the perimeter of the grounds.

Olga felt out of place. She tugged nervously at her skirt as she walked up to the front door. A camera stared down at her. She tried to ignore it.

She rang the doorbell. She expected another guard to answer it. Another meathead who would take her to whatever mess she was here to clean.

Instead, the door was opened by the man who had hired her.

"Very nice to see you again," he said. "There's work to be done. Come with me."

TWENTY-NINE

Salvatore Russo had never been anything but kind to Olga. He was always a gentleman. Softspoken. Whenever she left for the day, he slipped her a huge wad of cash. In short, she had no reason to feel unsafe around him.

But when she looked into his cold eyes, she felt terrified anyway.

His eyes were glacier blue. They did not match his black hair and olive skin. He was as big and hairy as a bear.

Salvatore stepped aside, sweeping his arm to invite Olga inside. She entered the house tentatively. The foyer had been converted into something resembling an art museum. The walls were covered with rare paintings. The floor was lined with sculptures. Olga didn't know who had created any of these pieces. But she had no doubt they were very expensive.

"What would you like me to clean, Mr. Russo?" Olga squeaked.

"I told you the first dozen times you were here," he chuckled. "Call me Sal. That's what I tell people to call me, but only if I like 'em. Come on back, Olga. Follow me."

He led her into a hallway. They passed the kitchen. An old woman was inside, stirring a pot of sauce. It smelled wonderful. Olga usually loved Italian food, but the thought of eating now was repulsive.

She just wanted to get this done and go home. Hopefully, the big wad of cash would be enough to make her feel better. So far, it had been. It wasn't too hard to feel better when she was able to catch up on her bills and finally start sending money to her parents back home.

"Back here," Sal said. "The wine cellar."

Not the wine cellar again. Olga's heart sank.

There was a narrow doorway at the end of the hall. Sal opened it. A stone staircase led down into dusty shadows.

"After you," Sal said.

Olga swallowed hard and made her way down. There were tiny slot windows high on the walls of the cellar. They had stained glass in them. Multicolored light lay thick and heavy across the floor.

It was a big space. A vault full of cool, dry air. Most of it was full of shelves loaded with hundreds of wine bottles. There were also some huge wooden casks stacked along the outer walls.

"Did someone spill the wine?" Olga wondered aloud.

Sal laughed. "No. If they did, I'd kill 'em."

He kept walking. Olga followed him. They entered an area of long-term storage. The bottles here were ancient. Covered in cobwebs and dust so thick you couldn't read the labels.

"See this one?" Sal asked. He tapped the top of a bottle as they passed. "Worth as much as the average college tuition. Even if all my business ventures went kaput tomorrow, I'd be set. Just sell off a bottle once every few weeks and keep living the high life."

It was the same thing he had set the first time he took her down here. This time, though, he didn't give her a suspicious look. He no longer assumed she would try and steal anything. He trusted her.

Olga didn't know whether that was a good or bad thing.

"Now, let me remind you of our arrangement," Sal went on. "You remember? You clean things up, no questions asked. I pay you generously. When you leave, you forget everything you saw. Did you remember the peroxide?"

Olga showed him the bottle.

"Good," he said. "In here."

They entered a small room at the back of the cellar. It was empty except for a sink on the wall and a chair in the middle of the floor. The chair was lying on its back. There was a pool of blood underneath it. Speckles and trails of more blood splattered in other areas.

There was no sign of the person who had been in the chair. They had already been removed. Olga started sweating.

"I will get to work," she said.

"Good," Sal replied. "Come find me upstairs when you're done."

THIRTY

Sal left the room he called his abattoir. He stood outside for a moment. Watching Olga work. She got to it immediately. Sure, she made a few disgusted faces along the way. But she didn't waste time.

The Russian lady was a good worker. So far, she was passing every test. Sal wondered how long he ought to wait before giving her a promotion. He could always use more help with his side hustle. The one that necessitated beating people nearly to death. Or sometimes past it.

Not to mention he had way too many guys working for him. Sometimes a bit of feminine energy was refreshing.

He headed slowly out of the cellar. Along the way, he stopped at one of his less dusty shelves and looked through it. Searching for something to go with dinner. His aunt Carlotta was whipping up a nice, classic lasagna.

"Something red, I suppose," Sal muttered. He picked a bottle that looked nice and carried it with him.

Sal delivered the wine to the kitchen, setting it on the counter. He gave Carlotta a kiss on the cheek.

"Smells great, zia," he said. "I brought up a bottle to go with it."

She dipped a wooden spoon in the sauce and held it out to him. "Taste? Tell me if it needs anything."

He shook his head. "Come on, zia. I trust you. I know that sauce is already dynamite."

"Just *taste*," she insisted.

He sighed and ran his finger through the sauce. He gave it a lick. "Like I said. Dynamite. Just needs to simmer a bit longer."

"I know that," Carlotta grumbled. "I think it needs more garlic, though."

He kissed her other cheek. "Whatever you say. You know I'm gonna eat it either way."

There was a bathroom off the kitchen. Sal went in, used the toilet, and came back out. Only a few minutes had passed, but the bottle he'd brought from the cellar was already open. A quarter of it was gone.

Carlotta was still at the stove. There was no glass next to her.

Sal sighed and made his way to the sitting room. A man was lounging on the couch with his feet on the ottoman. He was scrawny and wore his dark hair in a ponytail. In his hand was a glass of red wine. He gave it a swirl, then took a dainty sip.

"That's my spot," Sal complained. "I always sit there."

The man stared at the TV and said nothing.

"Raul," Sal snapped. "Are you hearing me? That's my spot. And I specifically chose that wine to go with dinner. It's only noon now."

"Shut up, Salvatore," Raul said quietly. "I'm aware of what time it is."

Raul hadn't washed his hands. His knuckles were still caked with dried blood.

Sal gave in. He sat at the other end of the couch. As far from the hitman as he could get.

"You really did a number down there, you know," Sal said. "I told you to make the guy talk. You made it so he'll never talk again."

Raul stared at him. "Did I misunderstand the assignment? I thought my main objective was to remove a thorn from your side. I did that."

Sal withered. "I'll say. You did a bang-up job. Emphasis on *bang*. I got Olga down there cleaning it up. Don't sweat it, all right?"

Raul took another drink of wine. "Are you talking to yourself? Because you sweat more than anyone I've ever met."

Sal chuckled. He grabbed the front of his shirt and gave it a few shakes. Trying to air out his armpits. "Don't sweat the wine, either. I'll just send one of the boys down to grab another one. You know, maybe I'll even grab a glass for myself. Yeah. That sounds good."

He left the room, trying not to hurry.

In some ways, Raul was the best hiring choice Sal had ever made. He wanted ruthless and evil, and he'd gotten it. But sometimes the guy scared him.

THIRTY-ONE

Jo paused halfway up the steep hill to study what lay ahead. She was looking for the Cornish College of the Arts. If there was any doubt as to which building it was, those doubts were erased in a second. The word CORNISH was pasted on the side of it in giant white letters.

Her phone rang. She answered it.

"Agent Pullinger speaking."

"It's Rupert," a British voice replied. "So far, we aren't getting much at Kari's place. But we did manage to get into her phone."

"Anything?" Jo asked.

"Not much, I'm afraid. She did have a text message that reached her phone late yesterday morning. From a contact saved as Martin."

"What did it say?"

"I have the transcript here. I'll read it for you. It starts, 'Kari, is everything all right? Missed you this morning. You're never late, let alone absent. Call me.' And that's the end."

"No other messages?" Jo asked.

"Nothing that jumps out. Nothing much at all, really. It seems like Kari was in the habit of clearing out her texts on a regular basis. You could probably subpoena her service provider for a full history."

"If it's necessary," Jo said with a sigh. "Thank you very much, Rupert. Let me know if anything else jumps out at you."

Jo ended the call and went inside.

She expected the place to have a certain aesthetic. And she was dead on. The lobby was a tall room full of unfinished cement and exposed ductwork. The chairs in the waiting area covered the full spectrum of color.

There was only one other person in the lobby. A geeky girl sitting behind the reception desk. She had bangs and black-rimmed glasses. She and Jo stared at each other across the cool expanse of the lobby.

"Can I help you?" the receptionist called.

Jo smiled awkwardly and walked toward the desk. Her feet clicked on the floor. The sound echoed through the place.

"Yes," she said as she reached the desk. She showed her Bureau credentials. "I'm Agent Pullinger. I'm looking for information on a student."

"Oh." The receptionist sat straighter, affecting a professional posture. Her nametag said, "Ashley." "And who might you be looking for?"

Ashley reached out for her keyboard. Ready to start typing.

"Kari Cross," said Jo. "She's not in any kind of trouble."

Ashley typed the name in. "Not surprising. Kari's a good person. I hope she's all right. Is she?"

Jo didn't say anything. She waited patiently for Ashley to move on.

"Well, what do you want to know?" Ashley asked.

"To be honest, probably something that isn't in that computer," Jo replied. "How well do you know Kari?"

Ashley shrugged. "We talk sometimes. I wouldn't say we're close friends."

"Is there anyone here who could claim that title?" Jo asked hopefully.

"Uh, yeah…" Ashley turned, pointing down a hallway. "Professor Leone. I think he knows her pretty well. I'd ask him. I'd give you Kari's schedule, but it looks like she doesn't have any classes today."

Jo smiled. "That's all right. Is Leone one of her teachers?"

Ashley nodded. "I think she missed his class yesterday. That's not like her. Oh no, I bet she *is* in trouble. Is there anything I can do?"

"There is," Jo told her. "You can take a breath and go about your day as normal. You've been very helpful. I'll find you if I need anything else. Thank you."

She left the desk behind and followed the hallway. She found the door to a classroom with the professor's name on the wall. Along with the course he taught. MARTIN LEONE – PROFESSOR OF FILM.

The guy who texted her, Jo thought.

She was barely a couple of hours into her investigation, and things were already starting to move forward. It gave her a tiny extra shred of hope that she might find Kari alive.

THIRTY-TWO

There was a window beside Professor Leone's classroom door. Jo peeked inside. There were dozens of empty seats. A few spotlights on the ceiling, shining cones of light onto the floor. At the front, a man was sitting at a desk with poor posture, looking at something on his laptop.

Jo pulled the door open and stepped in. The classroom was cool and breezy. It smelled like paper and pen ink.

Professor Martin Leone looked up from his desk. He had shoulder-length hair in a ponytail. A neat goatee and mustache. Kind green eyes behind glasses. He was wearing a green turtleneck sweater that was spotted with coffee stains.

He stood up quickly, banging his knees on the desk.

"You're a cop," he said breathlessly.

Jo paused by the door. "Why do you ask? Do you have some reason to be afraid of cops?"

He chuckled a little. Shaking his head in a twitchy manner. "No. I mean, not for me. Definitely not. I've never done anything wrong."

Jo slowly nodded her head. "Uh-huh. I'm sure you haven't. I'm not a cop, though."

"Oh, thank god." He put a hand on his desk to steady himself.

Jo pulled out her ID. "I'm an FBI agent."

Martin let out a miserable moan and sat down fast. "FBI! Why are you here? What's going on?'

"I'll get to that. Just don't freak out on me. That's not useful for anything."

Jo walked the rest of the way to his desk. She sat on the corner of it. Looming over Leone. She put one hand on her hip, close to her gun. She had no idea what to expect from this guy.

"First of all," Jo said, "I'd like to know why you're so nervous. You haven't done anything wrong. Isn't that right?"

He nodded. "Yes. That's absolutely right. One hundred percent correct. I'd give you an A plus on that one." He picked up a pen and swished it through the air.

"Put that down," Jo ordered.

He dropped the pen on his desk and showed his hands.

"Good," Jo added. "Now answer the question, please."

"I'm worried about Kari Cross," said Martin. "She's a student of mine. A friend, too. She didn't come to class yesterday. And she hasn't answered my text."

Jo nodded. "Yes, we know she hasn't."

Martin groaned. "So, you are here about Kari. Is she all right?"

"I'll ask the questions," Jo said. "Can you tell me about your relationship with Kari?"

"Well..." Martin winced, pinching the bridge of his nose. "We met at a bookstore about two years ago. We hit it off and went out for drinks. That started a kind of romantic relationship."

"Kind of romantic?" Jo asked.

"I'm forty-two years old," Martin said. "Which means when we met, I was forty, and Kari was barely even old enough to go out for drinks. She told me right off the bat she was uncertain about the age difference. I guess I was too. But we had a bit of fun together."

"And then what?" Jo asked.

"She decided to transfer here, to Cornish," Martin went on. "Neither of us felt like navigating the ethics of a student-teacher romance, so we called an end to that part of our relationship. But we remained friends."

"I see. How well do you know Kari, then? How deep is your friendship?" Jo asked.

Martin shrugged. "I guess I know a good deal about her. I know she has more money than I'll ever see in my lifetime. She's just at college for the fun of it. So she has a purpose in life. A goal to shoot for, I guess. But that doesn't mean she took it less seriously. She's probably my most dependable student."

Jo nodded. "I see. So, ever since she missed class yesterday, you've been working yourself into a tizzy, worrying about her. When I came in, you recognized me as law enforcement."

"It's the way you hold yourself," Martin interjected. "You look tough. Like you could kick my butt with both arms tied behind your back. Which is why I'm telling you the absolute truth."

"You've been worried about Kari, and when I came in, you knew right away why I was here. That's the story you're going with?"

Martin looked uncertain at first. He fidgeted in his chair for a moment. Then he nodded.

"That's the truth," he said.

Jo stood up. "Thank you. I'll be in touch if I have more questions."

Could Martin Leone have something to do with Kari's disappearance? It was possible. When something like this happened, the culprit was, more often than not, a close friend or relative.

But a lot more digging needed to be done.

Jo left the classroom and headed for the lobby.

THIRTY-THREE

Peter nearly fell as he reached the sloped area of the sidewalk. He felt weak, and his bones hurt. He had never been so tired in his life.

This was what it was like, living life on the run. He had been running ever since he left that farmhouse in Oregon. He hoped it would be over soon, but he still had no idea how that was going to happen.

Until he figured that out, there were things he could do to make it feel better.

He entered the lobby of Cornish College. He recognized the receptionist. A pretty girl named Ashley. She was always nice.

Ashley smiled when she saw him. "Peter! Are you still thinking about signing up for classes? I have a few fresh brochures around here somewhere."

He leaned on the desk, putting on a charming smile. "Come on, Ashley. You know, I was just using that as a ruse so I could keep coming to see you."

"More like so you could keep seeing your friend Martin Leone," Ashley replied.

Peter shrugged. "Are you OK, Ashley? You look kind of freaked out."

Ashley leaned across the desk and spoke quietly. "Someone came to see Martin. An FBI lady. She's back there with him right now."

Peter's face fell. "An FBI lady?"

Ashley nodded. "It has something to do with Kari. I'm getting worried about her."

Peter recovered, plastering a smile back on his face. "I'm sure everything's fine. I came to talk to Martin about something, but I guess I'll wait for this FBI lady to leave. Do you mind?"

Ashley shook her head and gestured toward the colorful chairs in the waiting area.

Peter thanked her and went to sit down. The chairs looked ugly, but they were comfortable. Peter settled in, grabbing a magazine off the coffee table. It was about cars. He didn't know anything about cars, but he liked looking at the pictures.

He found a car he really liked. It was a bright red sports car. The make, model, and price were all listed. This particular car sold for over a quarter of a million dollars.

Maybe he'd be able to buy it one day. If he got through this without his uncle knowing anything, he could start thinking about what kind of life he wanted to make for himself. Even if all he could ever afford was a rusty beater, he'd be all right with that. As long as he got away with it.

Peter set the magazine down and waited.

He had chosen his seat deliberately. He had his back to the hallway that led to Martin's class. That way, the FBI lady wouldn't see his face. He could get a look at her as she walked by. She'd probably be too busy thinking about her next move. She'd have no idea he was watching.

After a minute, Peter heard clicking footsteps coming down the hall.

"Thanks again," a woman's voice said. "I have everything I need for now."

"Have a good day," Ashley called.

The FBI lady walked past Peter.

She was tall and athletic with blond hair. She wore a red coat that almost managed to hide the bulge of the sidearm on her hip.

She looked to her left. Directly at Peter.

He looked away. But not before noticing her eyes. They were a brilliant green color. The color of some venomous frog in the jungle, Peter thought.

She kept walking, and left the building.

Apparently, she hadn't recognized him. But he recognized her. It was Jo Pullinger, the semi-famous FBI agent. The same agent who had almost captured Peter in Oregon.

THIRTY-FOUR

Peter stood up from his chair. His eyes watched through the lobby's front windows. Following the progress of Agent Pullinger down the sidewalk. She put her hands in her pockets. The wind pulled her hair out behind her in a stream.

Then she was gone.

Peter took a deep breath and let it out slowly. The way his old therapist had taught him to do. The most basic trick for dealing with anxiety. But it worked a surprising amount of the time.

His first thought when he saw Pullinger was that she was onto him. She knew he was here. She knew exactly who he was.

Obviously, that wasn't the case. She had walked right out of the building without giving him a second look.

She knew Kari was missing. That wasn't a surprise at all. It was only a matter of time. And now Pullinger was simply going about the business of finding the missing person. That meant paying a visit to the college she attended.

It was standard operating procedure.

Peter was safe. For now.

He smiled, wiping sweat from his forehead. He walked down the hallway, giving Ashley a nod as he passed.

When he entered the classroom, he saw Martin lying face down on the floor. Groaning like he was in horrible pain.

Peter was used to Martin Leone being a bit of a drama queen. Martin was always overreacting to things. For once, though, the reaction seemed very proportional.

"Who's there now?" Martin moaned, looking up. "Oh. Hey, Peter."

He rolled onto his back and sat up with a grunt, laughing and straightening out his long hair.

"What's with you?" Peter asked. "Passing a kidney stone or something?"

"Did you see the lady in the red jacket walking out?" Martin asked.

He held out his hand. Peter grabbed it and helped him up.

"She's with the FBI," Martin went on. "She was asking about Kari. Wouldn't say what happened to her, though. I wonder if she's gotten herself into some kind of trouble."

"Kari?" Peter scoffed. "I guess I don't know her as well as you do. But from what you tell me, she's not the criminal type."

Martin turned away, pulling at his shirt like it was suffocating him. "What do you think is going on? Maybe I should go to her place. Check up on her. Yeah, that's a good idea. Kind of weird, maybe, since I'm one of her professors, but..."

"Gotta do what you gotta do," Peter replied.

Martin nodded. "Yeah. You haven't spoken to Kari lately, have you?"

"You know I haven't," Peter told him. "She seems like a cool person, but it was never going to happen. Thanks for trying to set me up with her, though. You're a good friend."

Martin gave him a shaky smile. "So are you. Sorry, I'm such a mess. Did you come here to ask me something?"

Peter nodded. He *had* come to ask Martin something. He wanted to know more about Kari's preferences. The things she enjoyed. What made her happy. Now that Martin knew she was in trouble, those questions would sound suspicious.

"I was walking past," Peter said. "Just thought I'd say hi. We haven't hung out in a while."

Martin sighed, touching a stack of papers on his desk. "No, I guess not. Always gets busy for me after winter break. Hopefully, we can go get a beer sometime soon."

"I'd like that." Peter stifled a yawn. "I'll get out of here now. Let you get back to whatever you were doing. See you later, Martin."

THIRTY-FIVE

As she left the lobby of Cornish College behind, Jo couldn't shake a weird feeling. Like she'd missed something. She looked back at the building once she reached the corner. Nothing particular jumped out at her.

Still, the feeling was there. Something was wrong, but she couldn't figure it out. Or even begin to make a guess.

I'm probably just weirded out by that Martin Leone guy, she thought. His demeanor could be explained by him being a concerned friend... or maybe a paranoid perpetrator. Someone who wasn't banking on running into an FBI agent today.

She'd have to check up on him. Or rather, she'd have to get McKinley to check up on him.

***

"Martin Leone?" McKinley asked.

Jo took a sip of her breakroom coffee. "*Professor* Martin Leone. He teaches a film class at Cornish. Kari's one of his students. They had a semi-romantic relationship in the past."

"Weird," McKinley said.

"To his credit," Jo continued, "he was more than happy to call it off once she transferred to his school. On paper, he seems like a normal guy with good manners. But you should have seen his face when I walked in. Maybe he's just melodramatic and cares about his friends. Or maybe he knows something."

"Maybe he *did* something," McKinley added. "But before I look into him... check this out. I got an email from a Sergeant Henderson from the Oregon state police. He sent over some high-res shots of shoe impressions found at the farmhouse."

McKinley opened the email attachments. They were high-quality photos. Taken from an exact top-down angle. Perfect lighting and visible detail.

"Henderson included some notes, too," McKinley said. "This specific photo is the best they have. It was found in some hard mud right outside the back door. They were able to get a very clear plaster mold. That's what you're looking at."

"They've got a good photographer," Jo commented. "I was afraid I might have to drive back down to Oregon to get what I need. Thank God for Sergeant Henderson. Do we know the shoes yet?"

McKinley nodded. "They're one of three different types of tennis shoe. All made by the same company. Unfortunately, they're pretty common. You can find them in just about any store that sells footwear."

"Not good," Jo grumbled. "Do we have anything to get happy about?"

McKinley used his mouse cursor, running it along the details of the impression. "We have some incidental marks here. A distinctive wear pattern."

Jo patted McKinley on the back. "That's good. Now we just need something to compare it to."

McKinley grinned, clicking another email. "Rupert just sent this over before you got here. Take a look." He opened the photo attachment. "Here's one of the muddy prints left at Kari's house. It's the least smudged of them all. You can just about make out some details here and there."

He shrank the image down. Then he dragged it over, placing it side by side with the photo sent by Sergeant Henderson.

"I see it," Jo said, pointing at a spot near the toe of each shoe impression. "Some scratches here. They're in the same spot. They look to be about the same size."

"But there's also this," said McKinley. He pointed to a large circular pattern in the Oregon image that didn't exist on the other shoe impression.

"Probably a small stone wedged in the shoe tread," Jo said. "We were running over some rough terrain that night."

McKinley sighed. "Good. That makes perfect sense. I was getting worried. But it looks like the evidence supports your theory. The same person is involved in both cases."

It was definitely something to get happy about. Shoe impressions were often weak evidence in the eyes of the court. They were difficult to reproduce, and they were less distinct than fingerprints. But here, she had two high-quality photos from two different crime scenes. And they looked like a match.

It was enough for Jo to know she was heading in the right direction.

THIRTY-SIX

"There's one more thing that came through from Oregon state police." McKinley closed the email attachments and clicked a different message in his inbox. "Sergeant Henderson sent it in a different email. Very efficient of him."

"I guess he has a new fanboy," Jo chuckled. "I'm sure he'd get a kick out of knowing an FBI agent is admiring his email skills. Maybe Henderson is Bureau material. If he ever feels like looking for new employment."

The second email from Henderson was text only. No attachments.

We looked over the motorcycle ridden by the suspect. It was scrubbed of all identifying characteristics. A highly professional job. There are probably industries out there with the sole purpose of providing vehicles to would-be criminals. I suppose this particular suspect took advantage of those services. The motorcycle could not be traced back to anyone. No DNA or fingerprints found. Great care was taken by the suspect.

"He said *probably*," Jo cooed. "How adorable. He's got a lot to learn if he ever wanted to join the FBI."

"It's a disappointing message," McKinley said. "The motorcycle was the best evidence we had. Now it doesn't even *count* as evidence. Where does this leave us?"

Jo grabbed McKinley's rubber band ball and gave it a test bounce on his desk. "With a slowly developing headache. And a quickly developing sense of alarm. We're dealing with someone who has connections and knowledge of how to pull off a crime. Far from the random attack I first assumed."

"Now we can say with a good degree of certainty," McKinley said with a sigh, leaning back in his chair. "The same person who tried to take Kari in Oregon tried again in Seattle. And succeeded. Does that mean he's local?"

"He might live in Seattle," Jo said. "That's what I need to find out. We can start by chasing the only suspect we currently have. Let's find out if Martin Leone left town recently. Maybe he visited Oregon."

McKinley was about to get to work. At that moment, a short red-haired woman poked her head around the nearby cubicle wall.

"Agent Larkin," Jo said. She was pleased with herself for remembering the name. It seemed like she spent all her time either in this corner with McKinley or running through the streets looking for the latest psychopath. There hadn't been much time for schmoozing since she transferred.

"Hello, Jo," Larkin said in a hurry. She smiled as her eyes moved to McKinley. "Hi, Lewis. How's it going? Working hard?"

McKinley looked uncomfortable. "Uh. Yeah. Just trying to figure out who kidnapped this person."

His eyes kept flicking toward Larkin. Each time they did, his pale cheeks seemed to get one shade redder.

McKinley's got a crush, Jo thought with a smile. *And it looks like Larkin does too. Do I need to play matchmaker here? Maybe I should check the employee handbook first...*

"Anyway," Larkin said, smoothing out a wrinkle on her shirt. "We're putting together a birthday surprise for the boss. I was tasked with collecting anyone who wanted to participate. So, here I am."

"Here you are," McKinley echoed in a dreamy voice.

"It's Grantham's birthday?" Jo asked.

Larkin nodded. "He never told any of us. Didn't want to make a fuss. Good thing we're smart and great at digging for information. Our party is agents only. The support staff, whom we've tipped off, will be giving him a card before the end of the day. So, are you in?"

"We'll look into Leone later," Jo said.

They followed Larkin to the breakroom. It was silent but full of agents, all waiting stoically. Arms crossed in front of them. Stern expressions on their faces. But they were all wearing cheap, cardboard party hats.

A cake sat on the table in the middle. There were numbered candles in it. Apparently, Grantham was turning sixty-three years old.

"Is he on his way?" Larkin whispered.

A dark-haired agent with a widow's peak nodded and giggled. "Yeah. I messaged him saying there was an urgent matter in the breakroom."

A booming sound echoed through the field office. Grantham arrived. Red in the face. He stomped into the breakroom. Looked around frantically and finally let out a huge sigh.

"You idiots," he said. "How did you find out it was my birthday?"

"We're the best at what we do," Larkin replied. "Is everybody ready?"

Someone lit the candles. McKinley tried to flee. Jo grabbed his arm and pulled him back.

"Nope," she said. "If I'm doing this, you're doing it too."

They sang happy birthday to Grantham. The birthday boy looked very pleased with himself.

THIRTY-SEVEN

"Good cake," Jo said.

"I made it myself," Larkin said, beaming. "From a box mix and a plastic jar of frosting. Do you think he's having a good time?"

She gestured to their boss. Grantham was currently shoveling in his third piece of cake and laughing at two agents who were engaged in an arm-wrestling competition.

"I'd say so," Jo replied. "Grantham can seem scary. But he's like a fun uncle. At least when he's not actively working."

Larkin didn't seem to hear anything she said. She was looking around the room. "I wonder where Lewis went?"

"McKinley's probably back at his desk, working away." Jo swallowed the last of her cake. She dropped her paper plate in the trash. "Speaking of which, I'd better get back to it. Thanks, though. This was a fun little diversion."

She left the breakroom, choosing a path that would bring her close to Grantham.

"Happy birthday, sir," she said as she walked by.

He nodded to her, raising his fork in thanks.

***

It would be a while before McKinley had any solid information on Leone. There wasn't much Jo could do to help him. And she was out of fresh ideas.

She went back to Kari's house. She parked up the street and walked the final block.

The little gray building was now festooned with crime scene tape. The doors and windows were blocked off. As Jo stood staring at the place, she heard a car door shut.

A cop had stepped out of his cruiser and was approaching her. "Excuse me, miss, but I don't like the way you're looking at that house. I don't care what you're selling. This is a crime scene. You'll have to keep walking."

Jo found her credentials and flashed them. "I'm with the Bureau. Agent Pullinger."

The cop was flustered. "Ah. Crap. Okay, yeah. You can be here. I, um..."

"You're watching the scene while Rupert's team is away?" Jo asked.

The cop nodded. "Yeah. They're having lunch. Just here to make sure no one tampers, you know."

Jo smiled. "Well, I'm about to tamper. But I'll keep it to a minimum. I promise."

The cop shrugged and walked slowly back to his car.

Jo ducked under the crime scene tape. She knew the front door would be accessible. The forced entry had destroyed the locking mechanism.

She pulled gloves on and entered the house. Shutting the door behind her. She didn't have anything to put on her feet, so she took her shoes off at the door. She padded into the house in just her socks.

Jo didn't plan on being here long. She just wanted to jog her memory. See if there was anything her subconscious had picked up on.

As she entered the kitchen, she remembered something.

The coffee pot.

It was turned off now. She had done that when she first came into the house. An effort to avoid burning the place down.

She had not taken a picture of the pot first. An oversight. But not one that mattered overly much. Because she remembered exactly what it looked like.

There were two green lights glowing on the coffee maker. One to show that it was on and actively brewing. One to show that the programming timer had been used. Someone had set the pot to brew at a specific time.

Before going to sleep after getting home from her long drive, Kari had set the coffee maker. That meant she didn't need to be there to turn it on. The coffee would have started brewing whether Kari was still in the house or not.

There was also the forced entry to consider. There was a good amount of damage to the door. The kidnapper had used something like a crowbar or hammer to get inside. That would have been a very conspicuous thing to do in the daylight. When the whole world could see.

When taken together, these two facts shifted the timeline Jo had in her head. It took the events even earlier. Kari had probably been taken in the predawn hours. Almost immediately after arriving home from her Oregon trip.

The kidnapper must have found an alternate means of driving to Seattle. He had made the trip quickly. Following closely behind.

Maybe he had even passed Jo on the highway. As they all headed north together. Part of the same twisted fate.

"He already knew where she lived," Jo said to herself. "He came directly here and grabbed her. Without wasting any time. Why did he want her so bad?"

THIRTY-EIGHT

Jo was still stewing over that question when she heard the vans pull up outside. The cop's voice rang out.

"There's someone in there. An FBI agent. Pullheimer, or something like that..."

"I see you've done an excellent job of keeping the riffraff out," Rupert's voice replied. "I shall recommend you for a medal of valor."

The door opened. Several men in plastic coveralls entered. Rupert was at the front. He rushed into the kitchen, holding out a pair of shoe covers.

"Look what the kitty-cat dragged in," he said. "Do you need these? Oh, you aren't wearing shoes. Thank the heavens for that."

"I'm not an amateur," Jo replied with a grunt. "Didn't you see the shoes inside the door?"

"No, actually. Blame the massive cheeseburger I just consumed. It's clouding my senses. Did you get what you came here for? Whatever that might be?"

"I think so," Jo told him. "But while I'm here..."

Rupert sighed. "This was all going to be in the report I will send later this afternoon. But I might as well tell you now. We found Kari's journal. She hasn't updated it in several months, but I believe the entries still hold important information."

"What do they say?" Jo asked.

Rupert looked at his team. "I'll talk to the good lady. You lot go back to work. Go on."

They dispersed through the house. Burping from their fast-food lunches.

"Kari was fond of traveling," Rupert said. "In earlier entries, she spoke of visiting faraway places. Tokyo, Cairo, Istanbul. But since she started taking school seriously, she's been limited to the local area."

"Lots to see around Seattle," Jo commented. "Not that I would know. Too busy."

"Yes, I know what you mean," Rupert said. "Kari wrote about some of her favorite places. She enjoyed the Hoh rainforest. I hope I'm saying that right, but somehow I doubt it. Anyway, she loved going there. She wrote of how mystical and magical the place was. The sort of things a young woman would write in her diary.

"She also wrote about Mount Rainier, Port Angeles, and plenty of other semi-local spots. But the one place that comes up in her writings again and again is Bainbridge Island."

"I haven't had the pleasure of visiting there yet," Jo said. "But it's close by. About a half-hour by ferry."

Rupert nodded. "It seemed for a stretch of four- or five months Kari was going there every chance she got. She wrote about how she was considering buying a house there. Living there full-time once she finished college. It was her dream place, quite literally."

"She dreamed about it?" Jo asked.

"Indeed. Very lovely dreams. She wrote that it seemed like the place she was destined for."

"What changed?"

Rupert frowned. "The last entry she wrote in her journal was a solemn one. And somehow frightening. She wrote in vague terms of running into 'a scary man' who made her feel 'in danger.' She didn't go into much detail, I'm afraid. But she ended the entry by saying she would no longer feel safe enough to visit Bainbridge Island."

Jo rubbed her chin. "A scary man. Could be the kidnapper. Or someone associated with him."

Rupert put up his hands. "My job is simply to report on the data. Your job is to interpret the data and act upon it. I hope I've given you something useful."

Jo nodded. "It's definitely something to think about, at least. Maybe I'll end up visiting Bainbridge Island at last."

THIRTY-NINE

"Is there anything else in the diary?" Jo asked. "Anything that mentions other people? Friends, enemies?"

Rupert shook his head. "Nothing that jumped out at me, no. But you may interpret things differently if you read her entries. We've already scanned every entry in the diary. Made high-resolution images. They'll be landing in your inbox shortly."

"Thank you very much." Jo stuck out her hand. Rupert gave it a firm shake. "I appreciate your efficiency. I'll get out of your way now."

Jo carried her shoes outside. She sat on the curb out front to put them on. She caught the cop from earlier watching her. Raising her hand, she waved at him. He returned the gesture in a halfhearted manner. He was probably still embarrassed.

Jo's phone dinged. By the sound, she knew it was her personal cell, which she kept in her right pocket. She pulled it out and checked the notification.

It was a text from her brother Sam.

We were planning a movie night. To catch up on some DVDs that came out while we were on vacation. I was wondering if you wanted to attend. Come over any time.

Jo smiled and typed her reply.

I'll be there!

She added a string of smiling emojis and tucked her phone back in her pocket. Getting back in her car, she drove away.

By now, she assumed McKinley would have some information on Leone.

But before heading to the field office, she stopped at a convenience store. She filled a basket with snacks. All the sweet and savory goodness you would need for a night of movie-watching.

***

Jo pulled off her coat and draped it over her desk chair. "Anything on Leone?"

McKinley was working on his rubber band ball again. He gave Jo an easy smile. "I was able to confirm with several of his colleagues. Leone has been teaching classes five days a week. The other two days, he went out for drinks with some of those same colleagues. The night you chased the kidnapper in Oregon, he was at a bar here in Seattle."

"You confirmed that with the employees of the bar?" Jo asked.

McKinley nodded. "He's a regular there. The waitstaff like him because he tips well. They remember him being there. He wasn't in Oregon that night."

Jo sighed. "I'm not surprised. He could still be involved, somehow. I'll have to keep tabs on him. Make sure he doesn't try and leave town before we wrap this case up."

McKinley frowned. "It doesn't feel like we're very close. Does it?"

"No. It doesn't. But we're moving forward. We just need that one lucky break."

Jo sat down at her desk and waited for Rupert's report to arrive.

The diary entries came first. And they turned out to be the closest thing to real evidence in the lot. Other than the one decent shoe print, there wasn't much.

Jo scrolled down to the last entry. It was dated a little over five months ago.

Maybe I'm just paranoid. When you come into a lot of money, maybe that tends to happen. You start to look over your shoulder. You think everyone's out to get you. Fairly innocuous interactions take on a sinister tone. Angry strangers yelling at you about your parking job start to look like people who want you dead.

Who am I writing this for? This whole journal, I mean. I thought at first I was writing it for myself. To look back at and get an idea of my mental state over the years. But perhaps that's not it.

Maybe I'm writing it for the person who finds my corpse floating in Puget Sound one of these days.

Either way, my ultimate safe haven has been corrupted. Went to Bainbridge again today. Ate Thai for lunch and took my customary walk along the marina. Some scary guy approached me. He said people like me should be careful where they walk. I don't know what that means.

I don't think I'm going to update this journal anymore. It's making me think too much about what's going on inside my head. Maybe that's a bad thing at this point in my life.

I just want to go with the flow. Like everyone else!

She finished the entry off with a few stickers. All of them depicted smiley faces. It was a happy way to end an otherwise solemn and dark entry. Jo thought it was rather more prescient than what Rupert had prepared her for.

Kari wrote about being found dead. Maybe it was just a normal thought for a young person going through a rough patch. Or maybe it was more than that.

A sign of what was yet to come. A message from the past to the future.

FORTY

Jo finished reading Kari's diary over for the fifth time. She rubbed her eyes and looked over at McKinley.

"Can I ask you something?" she said.

He pulled his eyes away from his screen. On it, there were several camera feeds. They showed various streets around Seattle. "Of course, Jo."

"Actually, I'll amend that," Jo added. "Can I ask you two something?"

He shrugged. "The answer's still yes."

"Okay. First of all, what are you doing there?" Jo pointed at his monitor.

"Oh." McKinley enlarged one of the feeds. It covered the whole screen. Nothing much was happening. Just a bunch of cars driving by. "I'm just thinking. Letting my mind wander and see where it lands. I like watching these traffic cams sometimes. It's soothing. Just watching the world go by. Knowing all of these people have their own problems that have nothing to do with mine. None of them even know I exist."

Jo nodded. "I like that answer. It's very McKinley. And it actually makes sense. When you arrive at the traffic-watching portion of the evening, does that means it's time to clock out?"

"Usually," said McKinley. "It means I'm at a dead end with whatever I'm doing. In this case, I'm at a dead end with Kari. Was that the other something you wanted to ask?"

"No. But it's close. I wanted to ask... do you think I have any hope of making more progress tonight? I'd like to think I could go out there right now and find Kari. Bring her home safe and sound. But it's not going to happen, and I know that. The best thing I can do is go to my brother's house, watch corny movies, and eat junk food. Right?"

McKinley shrugged. "If that's what will help you recharge and be ready for tomorrow. You can do whatever you want with your free time."

She smiled and stood up. "Thanks, McKinley. Do you want to come over? I'm sure they wouldn't mind if I brought company."

He shook his head. "No. I think I'll just sit here for a while."

"Maybe you can see if Agent Larkin is still here," Jo suggested.

McKinley was startled. "Huh?"

"Never mind." Jo grinned. "See you tomorrow."

***

"Auntie Jo!"

The shrill cry echoed through the neighborhood. Chrissy ran down the front walk and grappled onto Jo like a spider monkey.

"Hey, kid," Jo said, laughing. "It hasn't been *that* long since we saw each other."

"You're wearing the seashell necklace we got for you," Chrissy observed.

Jo nodded. "Yup. I found it in my pocket after we went out to eat. Thank you."

She lowered Chrissy to the floor, taking her hand. They walked into the house together. Jo plopped her bag of snack food onto the counter. Sam immediately started digging through it.

"Nice choices," he said with an approving nod. "These will pair well with the high-brow cinema we've chosen for the evening."

Kim washed her hands at the sink and brought over a giant bowl of guacamole. "Here you go, vultures. Freshly made. Dig in."

Jo ripped open a bag of tortilla chips. The bag was almost empty by the time they all made it into the living room.

The movie night was a smashing success. At least for the first ninety minutes. They picked an animated movie to watch first. Chrissy went from cheering at the final act to snoring as soon as the credits started to roll.

"She's still tired from traveling," Kim said. "Not this guy, though."

She held baby Jackson in her arms. His eyes were wide and fixed on the TV. Mesmerized.

"Already a cinephile at less than a year old," Sam said proudly. "Should I put in the next one?"

The second movie began. It was an action film. After the pulse-pounding opening scenes, it settled into a period of exposition and worldbuilding. Kim and the baby were asleep before the next big set piece.

"And then there were two," said Sam.

Jo nodded. "I should have known we'd last the longest. We're just too powerful."

Sam laughed and turned the volume down a few notches. "How's life? You looked a little strained when you walked in earlier. Usually, Chrissy can knock you out of that funk in an instant. It took a little longer this time."

"There's someone I'm worried about," Jo replied. "Someone who's missing. I feel a personal responsibility over them. That's all."

Sam nodded. "You're always welcome here, you know. We've had some difficult conversations in the past, but you're my sister. I always want you to be part of my life. And the kids, too."

He was referring to past incidents. Jo's working life bleeding into her personal life with nearly disastrous results.

"I'm really grateful for you and Kim," said Jo. "If it wasn't for you guys... well, I don't want to think about what life would be like."

Her phone rang loudly. She pulled it out to silence it. The number on the screen was unfamiliar. But something told her it might be important.

FORTY-ONE

"Sorry, I need to take this," Jo said.

Baby Jackson had been woken by the ringing. He was fidgeting. Letting out little angry grunts. Any second now, he'd burst into full-on crying. Jo carefully scooped him out of his sleeping mother's arms.

Carrying the baby in one arm, she quickly exited the living room. She found her way through the dark house. Pulled open the sliding glass door and stepped into the backyard. The air was cool and smelled slightly of car exhaust. The grass was dewy, soaking into her socks.

Jo shut the door and looked out across the yard. There had been good times here. Cookouts. Games. But it was all overshadowed in her mind by a single incident.

Less than a month ago, her life had been turned upside down by a psychopath named Graff. He was obsessed with Jo... and, by extension, her family as well. At one point, he came here, to her brother's house. He had almost kidnapped the baby.

Jo held the boy closer, kissing the top of his head. His wispy hair tickled her nose. He was content now, reaching up to play with her necklace.

She took a deep breath. Composed herself. Then she answered the phone. For the first time, she noticed it was her work phone. Maybe that was the cue her subconscious had picked up on. The reason it told her the call was important.

"Hello?" she said.

"Um… is this Agent Pullinger?" asked a young man. His voice shook. He was nervous.

"This is," Jo confirmed. "Can I ask who's calling?"

Inside her head, she said a prayer. She hoped the call was bringing good news about Kari.

"You might not believe me," the man continued. "I know. I sound like an anxious wreck right now. I probably seemed a lot more confident the last time we spoke. I guess that was the adrenaline."

Jo's heart thumped in her chest. She sat down on the edge of the patio, not caring about the puddle that soaked into the seat of her pants.

"Who is this?" she demanded. "If I don't get a clear answer right now, I'm hanging up."

"Yeah, I guess you wouldn't recognize my voice. Not like we know each other that well. I'm the guy you chased down in Oregon."

Jo let out her breath. The voice did sound right. She couldn't be sure. Just like she couldn't be sure about the two shoe impressions. But to her ears, it was a match.

"How do I know it's really you?" she asked.

The man laughed. "I knew you'd ask something like that. I've been looking at the police reports that came out about our scuffle. None of them mention you very much. They don't say anything about when I almost hit you in the face with that shovel."

Jo's heart was racing. Not out of fear but out of excitement. This was the guy. He had made contact. Getting Kari back had just gotten slightly more possible.

"I need to ask about Kari," Jo said.

"Kari Cross. Yeah."

"Did you take her?" Jo asked.

"Yes. I did."

"Is she alive?"

"Of course she is. Remember, I had a knife. I used it to hold that old guy hostage."

"The farmer," said Jo.

"Right. When I tried to grab Kari at that rest area, I didn't have a knife in my hands. If I wanted her dead, I could have stabbed her a bunch of times before you ever got out of the bathroom. But I didn't. I never even took my knife out."

"So, you don't want her dead," Jo said.

"Nope. Not at all."

"So you wouldn't be opposed to letting her go," Jo quickly added. "I'm an FBI agent. I have plenty of resources at my disposal. We could set up the release at a safe place and time. Kari could go free, and no one would ever know who kidnapped her."

He scoffed. "Yeah, right. Because I'm a total moron. Don't worry about Kari. I didn't even call to talk to you about her."

"Then why did you call?" Jo asked.

"Because I felt bad. I haven't been able to sleep much. Every time I close my eyes, I see the different ways things could have gone. I almost killed you, Agent Pullinger. That's what's been bothering me."

"With that shovel?" Jo asked. "I dodged it. I was never going to let it hit me."

"Well, I still wanted to apologize. Which probably doesn't mean much to you. So I wanted to make a bigger gesture, too. To put things right, you know. You should drop by Kari's place. I left something for you there, just now."

FORTY-TWO

"Are you there now?" Jo asked. "Are you still at Kari's house?"

"I left before I called you," the kidnapper answered. "I'm probably half a mile away now. By the time you get there, I'll be much farther. I'm not trying to get caught. But I am trying to make things right. You'll see."

It sounded like he was trying to wrap up the call.

"Wait!" Jo snapped. "I'm trying to make things right, too. We can do it together. Partners."

"No way. You'll just arrest me."

"Only if you let me," said Jo. "You've been staying hidden so far. I'm sure there's a way we can save Kari that will allow you to keep running. We can talk about it."

"Yeah, I'll just stay on the line while you drive back to your field office so you can run a trace on me. Well, I'm already a couple of steps ahead of you. I don't want you to be my enemy, Agent Pullinger, but I guess that's the way things go. Cops and robbers. Bye."

Jo knew there was no hope of keeping him on the line. She said nothing. The call ended. She pulled up her caller ID and studied the number.

It was unfamiliar for a good reason. The area code was strange. It wasn't from Seattle or any of its surrounding areas. She knew the kidnapper had his resources. The ability to get a motorcycle with no identifying characteristics.

The phone was most likely a burner. Nothing traceable. By now, he'd probably chucked it down a storm drain. She texted it to McKinley anyway, figuring he'd still be awake. Her suspicion was confirmed a moment later, when he replied.

What's this?

She answered. *The kidnapper called me. This number's probably a dead end. Can you check it out anyway? Or forward it to someone who can, if you're not still at the office.*

His answer was short and punchy. *On it.*

She put her phone away. The baby was still playing with her necklace. She bounced him gently, her mind wandering.

The kidnapper had sounded ordinary. Friendly, almost. Maybe it was just an act. Maybe he had set up a trap for her at Kari's house. He was clever enough for it. And smart enough to find her phone number.

Either way, she was going back to Kari's. She had to know what the kidnapper had left for her. But it would be too dangerous to go alone.

Her phone rang again. This time, it was McKinley.

She answered it. "So, you are still at the office."

"I took a nap in the breakroom," he said defensively. "It was completely unplanned, but sometimes those are the best naps. I have an answer for you on that phone number."

"That was quick," said Jo.

"That's usually the case with answers you don't want. The number's registered to someone named John Smith. The area code is for central Kansas."

"So, just as much of a dead end as I thought."

"Yes. I can't even track the phone. Which means it's been turned off and probably dismantled. Disposed of."

"Yeah, that was my thought. Thanks for trying, though. Don't you have a bed at home, McKinley?'

"Yeah. And not much else. But I guess I should head there anyway. See you tomorrow."

They hung up. Jo went back inside. She entered the living room slowly, careful not to make too much noise. Kim was firmly back in dreamland, but Sam was still awake. Munching his way through a pack of frosted oatmeal cookies.

"Careful," said Jo. "You'll get heartburn."

"Everything OK?" he asked.

She nodded. "So far, so good. But I need to go. Sorry."

He shrugged. "As far as Chrissy's concerned, you were here all night. That's all I care about. Go on and catch some bad guys."

"That's the hope," Jo said with a sigh.

She handed Baby Jackson over to his father. With a wave of her hand, she left the house.

FORTY-THREE

Jo shut the front door of her brother's house. She found the spare key he had given her. She used it to lock the door. As soon as she heard the click, she felt better. Kari wasn't safe, but at least Jo's family was.

She checked the time. It was almost eleven. Fairly late by most people's standards. But for a person in law enforcement, it might as well be noon.

Just as she knew McKinley would still be awake, she knew the same about Bryan Ford. She was so confident about it that she didn't even text him first. She just called his cell.

She chewed her lip anxiously as she waited for him to answer. She was hyper-aware of every wasted second. The sooner they got to Kari's house, the sooner they could start planning their next move.

"You've reached Bryan Ford," Ford said into her ear. "I can't come to the phone right now..."

There was nothing else. Jo waited for several seconds. Planning out what she would say when she heard the beep.

"Oh, wait," Ford suddenly added. "I actually can come to the phone right now. Would you look at that? Hm... or can I?"

Jo narrowed her eyes in confusion. "Is this some kind of joke answering machine message? Not very professional, Ford."

"Can't be a professional all the time," Ford said. "Life would get too boring."

Jo sighed. "Ford! Are you serious? I just stood here for thirty seconds like an idiot, waiting to leave a message."

"Really?" he replied with a laugh. "I wish I was there to see it. Come on. I've wanted to pull that gag on you for a while. Guess it's late enough, *and* I'm loopy enough. And you called. Couldn't resist. I hope you're not calling about anything important, or else I'd feel like a jerk."

"It's eleven o'clock," said Jo. "Why else would I be calling?"

"I dunno. We are friends, after all. Maybe you just wanted to check in."

"Well... are you busy right now?" Jo asked.

"In general? Yes," Ford replied. "I'm in my home office right now. Burning the midnight oil. Or I guess the pre-midnight oil. Trying to catch up on paperwork. Which is incredibly boring, so if you need me for something..."

"Kari Cross's house," Jo said. "Be there as soon as you can. Hopefully, it's sooner than before."

"Hey, I'm good to go. No more headaches. I'll be fast, I promise. I could use a bit of excitement. Just have to give Kelly a kiss and promise her I'm not doing anything too crazy."

"I haven't given you the craziness level yet," Jo reminded him.

"Yeah, I know. Keep it that way. Then I don't have to lie. See you soon."

FORTY-FOUR

Jo got in her car and headed out. It was approaching half past eleven, and traffic was no longer a concern. She blew through a few yellow lights and a couple of reds. When she reached Kari's house, she didn't see Ford's car anywhere.

She parked by the curb a couple of houses down and watched. There was still a police cruiser parked outside the crime scene. Jo watched it for a while. She was trying to determine if there was an officer inside it.

Finally, she got out of her car and approached the cruiser. She got close enough to get a good look in the side mirror. The driver's seat was empty.

A moment later, a flashlight beam shone across the sidewalk. The officer arrived, moving lackadaisically. When he saw Jo, his demeanor changed. He stiffened up, shining his light into her face.

"Can I help you?" he barked.

"FBI," Jo said, showing her ID. "You were tasked with watching a crime scene. If you had to step out of your vehicle, you should have radioed for temporary backup."

"Says who?" he demanded.

"Common sense," Jo replied. "And pride in your work. Maybe you don't have any of that, though."

He shrugged, lowering his light. "I just had to take a leak. I was barely gone a minute."

Jo checked her watch. "I've been here for almost five. You were gone from your post the whole time."

"I was at the corner, behind a tree," he said defensively. "I could still see the house just fine. No one came."

Someone did, Jo thought.

The kidnapper. He had been here. He had left something for her to find. Now that she had seen the bang-up job the lookout was doing, she could believe it. There were definite holes in the defense here.

"I'm going to need your name and badge number," Jo said. "Your superiors should know the weak job you're doing. I have a lot of respect for the Seattle PD, and I take their reputation seriously."

The cop groaned like a reprimanded child. He rattled off his number and name.

"All right, Officer Teller," said Jo. "I'll consider letting you off easy if you can answer this question honestly. Is it possible that someone was able to enter the house without your knowledge?"

He shrugged. "Maybe. But not through the front. I've been watching. Even while I was down the street. I promise."

Jo nodded. "All right. Please try and do better in the future. Thanks for your time."

She left him standing there with his mouth hanging open. Jo waited outside the house and watched the night go by. Eventually, after a couple of minutes, Officer Teller got back in his car. He watched the crime scene like a hawk from then on.

Ford arrived. He pulled up behind the cruiser. Officer Teller gave Jo a questioning look. She gave him the thumbs up to let him know the newcomer was with her.

Ford got out. His tall, thin frame was draped with an oversized trench coat. The tails furled out behind him as he hurried over to Jo.

"Am I late again?" he asked. "It was my daughter's fault this time. She woke up just as I was about to leave. I had to read her a story. She wanted to read it to me, actually, but then I knew she'd be up all night showing off her reading skills."

Jo laughed. "It's fine, Ford. Officer Teller's been doing an almost decent job of watching the scene."

"Oh?" Ford looked over at the cop car. "Never heard of an Officer Teller. He looks like a kid. Must be new. Anyway, what are we doing here? I'm always down for some excitement, but I'm not sure how exciting it is to stand on a sidewalk in the cold."

"I got a call from Kari's kidnapper," Jo told him. "He was here. Just a little while ago."

FORTY-FIVE

"The kidnapper called you?" Ford asked. The wind blew. His coattails made a snapping sound. "How do you know it was him?"

"He gave me a detail that hasn't been publicly released," said Jo. "Some articles mentioned the presence of an FBI agent, but none of them had my name. And none of them featured any statements made by me. But he knew I was the one who was there. And he mentioned the part where he almost killed me."

"He almost killed you?" Ford demanded.

"With a shovel."

"That does it," Ford said with a grunt. "This guy's dead as soon as I get my hands on him."

"As soon as we get our hands on Kari," Jo reminded him.

"Right. Which brings us back to the present time. I still don't know why we're here."

"The kidnapper told me he left something for me to find," Jo went on. "You're here for backup."

Ford nodded. "I'll watch your back, Jo."

"Good. I'd like to check inside first. If he screwed with the crime scene at all, we need to know. I'm pretty sure Rupert has already gotten everything out of there, but better safe than sorry."

"So we just... go in?" Ford asked. "We should at least take our shoes off first."

Jo grinned. "Of course. That's the least we can do."

They shucked their shoes at the door and pushed it shut behind them. It didn't latch, but the deformed wood did a good enough job of holding it.

Jo turned on her flashlight. Ford pulled out a flashlight of his own and joined its beam with hers. The two shafts of light crisscrossed through the entryway.

"I see some powder on the walls and floor," Ford observed. "Rupert's team is checking for tracks and prints. Does anything look different to you?"

Jo shook her head. She led the way down the hall. They moved slowly. Shining their lights over everything.

"I'm not seeing anything," Ford said.

"Me neither," Jo said, sighing. "I was hoping it might be something obvious. But now I'm thinking he might have left something very tiny and subtle. Or maybe he wasn't here at all."

"He could just be wasting your time," Ford agreed. "Did he tell you anything more? Anything about what he was leaving for you?"

"An apology," said Jo. She took a step into the kitchen and looked around. "He said he was sorry for trying to hurt me."

Ford laughed. "What is it about you that attracts all these weirdos, Jo?"

"I don't know," Jo confessed. "When I first entered the house, there was a plate of half-eaten food on the counter. Rupert's team took it away. I thought it was Kari's breakfast. But my new theory holds that the kidnapper entered while Kari was still asleep."

"So, you think he stopped to get a snack while he was here?" Ford asked.

"Maybe."

"Yup. Sounds like a weirdo. But that's good for us. Could be some DNA on that plate. Is anything different in here?"

"By now, I know this room by heart," said Jo. "No. Nothing's different. Officer Teller said there's no way anyone could have entered by the front of the house. If he can be trusted, that means…"

"If the kidnapper was here," said Ford, "he would have had to come in through the back."

"Or he didn't come inside at all," Jo added.

"The backyard?" Ford asked.

Jo nodded.

They moved in that direction.

FORTY-SIX

They were standing in the hall at the back of the house, looking around. There was a bathroom to their left. Kari's room was to the right. Looking into the latter, Jo had an eerie feeling. The bed was empty but unmade. Like Kari had just been in it a moment ago. Like she had jumped out when she heard them come in and hid somewhere.

"No back door," Ford observed. "Seems like a code violation. What are you supposed to do if there's a fire?"

"Jump out one of the windows, maybe." Jo gestured into the bedroom. "Nice big one in there."

"Is that how we're getting to the backyard?" Ford asked with a grin. "Are we jumping through a window, cowboy style? Because *that* would be exciting."

Jo laughed. "No need to be dramatic. There aren't even any banditos chasing us. We'll just use the front door and walk around."

"Boring," Ford grumbled. "But fair. Ever since that night in Lapse, my hips have been aching. Must be getting old."

"Getting old?" Jo asked. "You've *been* old, my friend."

They headed for the front door. Moving single file through the dark house.

"You don't have to remind me," Ford replied. "But with age comes wisdom. And wisdom says we should have gone through the window."

"Is Wisdom the name of the devil on your shoulder?" Jo asked. "Hey, that reminds me of a joke. But I'll tell it to you later."

They went out the front door and put their shoes back on. The police cruiser was empty yet again. Officer Teller was nowhere to be seen.

"I guess I'll be reporting him after all," Jo said. "Pretty bold of him to leave again when he knows I'm still here. Should we split up? Both go around one side of the house?"

"No way. Why would I want to miss out on your lovely company? I'll lead the way."

Ford hopped off the front porch. He walked around the corner of the house. Jo followed him. They moved slowly. Looking at everything.

There wasn't much to see. Kari kept the outside of her house as orderly as the inside. Her garbage and recycling bins were neatly spaced and perfectly straight. The AC unit, no longer in use due to the cold weather, was covered with a tarp that had been staked into the ground.

"Nice little place," Ford whispered. "I hope we can find Kari and get her back here. She deserves a peaceful life."

"You don't even know her, Ford," said Jo. "But of course, you would say that. You're a sweetheart."

"Yeah, I know," he said with a grunt. "If we catch the bad guy, don't tell him that. He'll expect me to go easy."

It didn't take long for them to reach the backyard. It was separated from the neighbors by a waist-high picket fence. In total area, it wasn't much bigger than the kitchen. You could walk across it in five or six steps.

Jo let her flashlight beam trail across the back wall of the house. She immediately saw something that did not belong. She aimed the light at it. It was a shovel, leaning against the foundation.

"There we go," Jo said.

"That?" Ford asked. "I know the kidnapper almost brained you with one of those. But most homeowners own a shovel. What's special about this one? Wait a second... is that blood?"

A message had been written across the blade of the shovel in a red medium. Jo knelt beside the shovel and sniffed at it.

"Lipstick," she said. "Probably one of Kari's tubes, if I had to guess."

"What does it say?" Ford asked.

Jo leaned back to get the whole message. The kidnapper had lousy penmanship. Combined with his choice of using greasy lipstick, it was difficult to decipher.

Thankfully, it was only a few words.

"*No hard feelings*," Jo read. She pointed right below the words, where a smiley face had been drawn. "This is getting complicated, Ford. Because I actually believe he's sorry."

"A nice-guy kidnapper," Ford said. "Seems like we're looking for a walking oxymoron."

FORTY-SEVEN

"I told you we should have taken that way," Ford said. He pointed at the bedroom window. "We would have come out right next to this shovel. No wasted time. See? Wisdom."

Jo took a step back. Studying the shovel from a distance. "Why would he bother leaving this? It's a potential source of evidence. He might have shot himself in the foot, all for a simple apology."

"There are two ways it might make sense," Ford told her. "One, he's a lunatic looking for a laugh."

"He didn't sound crazy on the phone," Jo said. "He sounded weirdly normal."

"Two," Ford added, "he's a socially awkward dork with good intentions. He thinks he's going to get away with all of this. He wants to look like a good guy. He believes he *is* a good guy. Hence the apologetic gesture. This explanation allows the shovel to make sense."

"But not the kidnapping," said Jo. "How can you kidnap a woman with good intentions? It doesn't make any sense. So maybe the truth is a melding of both explanations. He believes he's a good guy because he's actually a lunatic. But still... there has to be a motive behind all this."

Ford pointed his foot at the shovel. "You want to bag this monstrosity? I've got some trash bags in my car. Can't promise the beautifully scrawled message won't get damaged in transit, though."

"Go get a bag," Jo replied. "I'll take some pictures."

He nodded and exited the backyard. Jo pulled out her phone. She made sure the flash was on and took three photos of the shovel. One from straight on. The other two from oblique angles.

Some of the shots came out blurry. She had to redo them. By the time she was finished, she heard a rustling sound. Ford appeared, waving a black trash bag in his hands.

He held it open while Jo carefully lowered the shovel in. He pulled the drawstring shut and lightly knotted it.

"Good to go," he said. "Think we'll get anything from it?"

Jo shook her head. "He was careful not to leave prints on the motorcycle in Oregon. I doubt he left anything on this shovel, either."

They heard the hum of an engine out on the street. The sigh of tires slowing to a stop on the damp pavement. The engine cut out. A car door opened and shut.

Jo and Ford instinctively flattened themselves against the wall. Listening closely.

"The kidnapper?" Ford whispered.

Jo pulled out her sidearm. "One way to find out. We can't count on Officer Teller to let us know. This time, I'll lead."

They turned their flashlights off. With Jo in front, they rushed along the side of the house. As they approached the front, they heard someone's anxious ramblings.

"No way... this can't be right... please, don't let it be true..."

Jo paused. She signaled Ford to stand down. She recognized the voice and was pretty sure he wasn't a threat.

She let her sidearm hang at her side. She marched into the open, startling the man who was loitering on the front walk.

Professor Martin Leone nearly jumped out of his skin. "Oh, crap! It's you. Agent Pullinger. What are you doing here?"

"Performing some follow-up tasks," Jo said. "Now you tell me."

Leone looked past her. At Ford. He licked his lips nervously and stared at the house.

"Sorry," he said. "I saw the cop car. But I thought it would still be OK to look at the house from back here. I just came to check up on Kari. But I guess there was no need. She isn't here, is she?"

"It'll be in the news soon," Jo told him. "So there's no harm in telling you. Kari's missing. We're here to make sure we don't miss a single detail."

"You're going to find her, right?" Leone asked.

"We're going to do everything we can," was all Jo could think to say.

He accepted her answer. Nodding, he backed up until he was on the sidewalk. "Again... I'm sorry."

"So am I," Jo replied. "Before you go, I want to ask you one more time. Can you think of anyone who would want to harm Kari in any way?"

Leone shook his head. "No one. Kari's too nice to have enemies. It had to be someone who was after her money. Am I free to go?"

"Yes, but make sure you stay available," Jo told him.

He hurried away. He got back in his car and left.

"Officer Teller still isn't back," Ford pointed out. "I'll call for a replacement. I can stay and wait, if you want me to." Jo shook her head.

"Go home, Bryan. Be with your family. I'll stay. You can put that bag in my car."

She used her fob to pop her trunk open.

"Still driving the rental?" Ford asked.

Jo shrugged. "I keep forgetting to return it. But I remember now that I got the full coverage insurance, so I should be fine."

"Lucky you." Ford smirked as he walked away.

"Lucky me," Jo echoed, staring up at the stars.

FORTY-EIGHT

A row of bushes separated Kari's front yard from her neighbor's. They were dense and leafy. Perfect for hiding behind.

Raul situated himself just right. He was able to watch the proceedings through a small gap in the foliage. He watched Leone approach the house and start tearing at his long hair. Crying about Kari.

Then he watched the woman and the tall man coming out from the backyard. Raul had no idea who they were. But Leone gave it away when he called her Agent Pullinger.

She was FBI. That was troubling. An extra piece of complication that Raul wasn't thrilled about. He had dealt with the feds before. He knew he could beat them. But it was generally a good idea to avoid them as often as possible.

Maybe he could still manage that.

So, the woman was FBI. But who was the man she was with? Logic would suggest he was a partner. A fellow member of the Bureau. But he didn't come across like a fed.

More mysteries to unravel, Raul thought with a smile.

The professor left. The tall man called for a replacement lookout. Apparently, he had contacts in the Seattle PD. The way he talked, it was clear he knew what he was doing. A detective? It was common for FBI agents to enlist some lower-level help on cases like these.

Raul would identify the man as soon as he could. That way, he knew which door to kick down if it came to that.

Once the phone call ended, the tall man left. He detoured to Pullinger's car and dropped a garbage bag into her trunk. He closed the trunk and departed. When he was gone, Pullinger sat on the steps of the house. Waiting patiently.

Raul followed suit. He lay as still as a stone. He knew how to be patient. He could lay there for a million years if need be. And when the time came to act, he would spring to his feet and go about it. As fresh as a daisy.

But Raul was not perfect. He would never claim to be. Sometimes, he made mistakes. Such as the mistake he had made ten minutes earlier. He accidentally knelt on a twig, snapping it loudly.

Officer Teller had come over to investigate.

Officer Teller was still here. He was inside the neighbor's trash barrel. He would most likely be found within the hour as soon as his replacement realized something was wrong. It might take longer, though. The trash barrel wouldn't be the first place anyone looked.

Plenty of time to get away.

The new cop car arrived. Pullinger got off the steps. She went to meet the lookout.

Raul had his chance. He hurried away, dashing through a few more yards. He reached his car, parked three streets over, and got inside. As soon as the door was shut, he relaxed.

He drove away. Following the speed limit exactly. He had to make a phone call soon. But there was time to enjoy a bit of music. In Seattle, there was an 80s station that Raul enjoyed. He turned it on and let the retro vibes wash over him.

He let the first song end. He had tuned in halfway through it. A second song began to play. He listened to the full thing. Once it ended, he was ready to make the call.

Raul turned the music down. He called his boss's number.

"Yeah?" Sal demanded. "Did you get the job done?"

"Kari has already been taken," Raul replied. "The house is now a crime scene."

"Someone beat us to it," Sal said, sighing. "I knew we shouldn't have waited. That's what I get for having a heart. Or whatever's left of one. Somebody's got her, and it ain't me."

"I wonder who it could be?" Raul mused.

"Yeah, yeah," Sal said, sighing again. "This pains me greatly. It really does. But I've got a business, and no one messes with it. You know what to do, Raul."

"I'll start tying up the loose ends," Raul said. "And sewing shut the mouths of every possible witness."

"Perfect. That's why I hired you. Is there anything else you need to tell me?'

"One thing. The FBI is already involved. I don't know why they were so quick to jump in on this case, but I'll find out."

FORTY-NINE

Martin Leone drove around the city. He didn't want to be anywhere. His mind was haunted by visions of Kari Cross. The memories. The moments he would never be able to relive. Even if she was still alive, and Agent Pullinger saved her...

He and Kari had no future together. But he still loved her. And he couldn't stop thinking about her. He imagined Kari in a cold, dark place. In pain, suffering more than a wonderful person like her should ever suffer.

The idea that Kari was already dead occurred to him. Maybe that would be best. For her. But he was selfish. He wanted her to come back. He at least wanted to see her again. Talk to her. See her smile.

Leone got tired. He had no choice but to return home. He drove back to his townhouse. It was a few blocks away from Cornish College. A conveniently short commute. Sometimes he wondered why he even owned a car. It cost him money. The only reliable thing about it was that it broke exactly twice per year.

But it came in handy on nights like these. When he just wanted to drive.

He parked outside the townhouse and opened his door. He stuck one leg out and sat there for a while. An unmoving blob of inertia. He had no energy left. No enthusiasm for anything.

And I still have to teach tomorrow, he thought with a wave of panic. He had no idea how he was going to get through it. But he'd find a way. As long as he kept his eyes away from the empty chair where Kari usually sat, maybe he would be okay.

Finally, he got out of his car. Shuffling up the sidewalk like a drunk, he struggled to pull his keys from his pocket. He tried to unlock the door. He fumbled the keys. They clattered to the ground.

Cursing, he bent down to grab the keys.

There was a weird sound. Like a whistle that traveled through the air. Something hit the door. *Thud.*

Leone looked up. There was a hole in the door. He could see the wood fibers, shredded and smoking.

"Huh?" he said.

It took him too long to process what he was seeing. He stood straight up and looked over his shoulder. He thought he saw someone moving in an alley across the street. A shadow.

Suddenly, he realized what had caused the hole in the door. A bullet. Someone had shot at him with a silenced weapon. If he hadn't bent down, that bullet would have gone through his head.

Maybe I should run, he thought.

The next shot came before he could move. It hit him in the forehead. It happened fast. He had no time for another thought. If he did, it probably would have been of Kari.

Leone was dead before he hit the ground.

The shadow in the alley lingered for a moment. Admiring its handiwork. Then it hurried away. Got into a car a few blocks away and drove off listening to 80s music.

FIFTY

A blaring sound woke Jo from a dream about Ted, the truck driver. She stared at her ceiling, wondering what was going on. Was the world ending? Was there a tornado on its way, ready to uproot her apartment and throw it into the sky?

No. It was just her alarm, coming from her phone. She rolled over to turn it off. She stared at her screen for a moment. It was 5:30 AM.

Why did I even turn that alarm on? Oh yeah. I was feeling disciplined last night and decided I should go for a run before work.

She had gotten home last night around 1 AM. She didn't fall asleep until almost an hour later. Despite knowing she would get less than four hours of sleep. Past Jo thought this whole alarm business was a good idea. Present Jo hated past Jo with the heat of a thousand suns.

Present Jo lay in bed for another five minutes. Trying to make her mind up. To run or not to run?

To run, she thought.

Maybe present Jo hated herself a little bit, too.

She checked the weather. It was currently 47 degrees outside. But it wasn't raining. That was a bonus. Jo went to her kitchen. She chugged a glass of water and splashed some more on her face. Instead of waking her up, the cold splash just made her angrier.

Her dream had been a good one. Not only was she with Ted, having a lovely time, but she'd just gotten news from McKinley. The kidnapper was caught, and Kari was free. Everything was right and nothing hurt.

As she got dressed, Jo flexed her arms and kicked her legs around. Too many long nights. Too much pavement. It all settled into her joints, making her stiff. Every year, it took just a bit longer to get moving, for everything to start working. She was still young enough. And fit, despite the surgery scar on her chest.

But eventually, she'd have to start doing things that would make her feel old. Chiropractor visits. Deep tissue massages. Or maybe they would actually make her feel young. Put a spring back in her step that she didn't even know was missing.

Jo opened the GPS app on her phone. She hit start as she pulled her front door shut behind her. It was a slog to start. Her ankles hurt. Her breathing and her heartbeat seemingly refused to sync up. She felt winded immediately.

She felt like giving up. But after less than a quarter mile, everything changed. It always did. Her body finally accepted what she was demanding from it. She settled into a fluid gait. A steady pace. She ignored the cold air and focused on the simple and natural mechanics of running.

It was a beautiful thing. A break from worrying about people who needed her help.

It didn't last long. She was barely into her second mile when her phone rang. She looked at the contact name. It was McKinley. Her heart skipped a beat. Hope surged through her. Maybe her dream would prove to be prophetic.

Maybe Kari had been found. That news was sure to put a spring in Jo's step. Forget the chiropractor and the masseuse.

"Please tell me you have good news," Jo answered.

"Unfortunately not," McKinley spoke through a yawn.

"What is it?" Jo asked.

"Professor Martin Leone. He was found dead outside his townhouse a couple of hours ago. Police have been at the scene."

Jo's heart skipped another beat. This time, it was despair she felt. "Where's his body now?"

"The medical examiner." McKinley tried to stifle another yawn and failed.

"Don't tell me you're still at the office," Jo said.

"No. I'm at home. Couldn't sleep, so I was messing around on my laptop. That's how I heard the news."

"Then you should try and get some more rest. But first, send me Leone's address. I'll check his place out, then pay a visit to the coroner. I'll update you later."

FIFTY-ONE

There was no time for a shower. Jo changed her clothes quickly and slapped on some deodorant. She kept a jug of iced coffee in her fridge. After pouring some into a travel cup, she was out the door.

She punched Leone's address into her GPS. The route took her into the vicinity of Cornish College. When she pulled up in front of the townhouse, she recognized Leone's car from the night before.

It looked sad, sitting there. Like a dog waiting for its owner, who would never return.

Police lights were flashing. Plastic sheets had been strung up, blocking the view of Leone's front door. An officer was standing on the sidewalk with his hands on his hips. Looking stern. Ready to turn away any potential gawkers.

Jo took out her ID before she even walked up. No use in wasting time.

"Agent Pullinger, FBI," she said.

"Officer Getty," said the cop. "Can I help you with something?"

"I need to get inside and check out Leone's home," Jo explained.

"What for? Everything happened out here. There's nothing in the place that'll interest you," Getty said.

"That's for me to decide." Jo kept her ID out. "But thanks for your help."

Getty stepped aside. Jo headed up the front walk. She ducked in behind the plastic sheeting. Showing her ID to the two officers who were standing beyond it.

"This is where he was found?" she asked.

Neither of the cops answered. They didn't need to. The porch in front of Leone's door was covered in blood. Jo noticed a hole in the door.

"Bullet?" she asked, pointing.

The older cop with the mustache answered. "First shot missed. Second one hit just fine."

"Caliber?"

"You sure are in a hurry this morning," he answered, smirking. "Yeah. Nine millimeter. Nothing special."

Jo nodded. "I'd like to get inside. Is the door unlocked?"

"Nope. The victim didn't quite manage to get it open. However..." The mustached cop leaned over the porch railing. He gestured to an open window. "We managed to wiggle this window open. No use climbing in and getting yourself all dirty, Agent. Didn't Getty tell you there's nothing in there?"

"He did," Jo said.

She didn't elaborate further. She left the porch and climbed through the window. It was a small place. More of a studio apartment than a proper townhome. There was one light on. A weak bulb in the stove hood. It was enough to give her an idea of the place.

It was a sloppy bachelor pad. Leone made no real effort to keep it clean. There were empty beer bottles and snack wrappers on the coffee table.

Other than the junk, the place was consistently decorated. Leone had a thing for aviation. There were posters of different fighter planes on the walls. Models he had built filling a couple of bookcases.

It was always interesting to get a picture of people. To try and inhabit their minds for a bit. But none of this seemed useful. Jo already had a pretty good idea of why Leone was dead.

He knew something. Something that someone dangerous didn't want him to know.

Unfortunately, he hadn't shared that knowledge. And Jo was left to sift through the wreckage.

She used her flashlight to illuminate her path. She didn't linger for long. The place was a pigsty. It smelled bad. In the end, she admitted that the officers outside were right.

There was nothing to see here.

She climbed back out of the window with a chagrined smile on her face. Ready to crack some jokes with the cops.

Something must have just come through the radio. The cops on the porch looked worried. Getty had abandoned his post in favor of pacing up and down the sidewalk.

"What's going on?" Jo asked.

The mustached cop gave her a sorrowful frown. "A friend of Getty's. Officer Teller. He was just found dead, right by that missing girl's place."

Jo had to pause and catch her breath. Things had just gotten very interesting.

FIFTY-TWO

Professor Leone was already dead. He wasn't getting any deader. And the longer the medical examiner spent with the body, the more they would be able to tell Jo when she got there.

For now, she could put herself to better use elsewhere.

She drove to Kari's home. It was starting to become a familiar route. Each time she saw the little house, she fell in love with it. It was a nice place, despite the horrors that surrounded it lately.

The police were outside in full force. Swarming the street. Turning the predawn shadow into New Year's Eve with their flashing lights. She held her badge in front of her like a crucifix. Fighting her way through the crowd.

She finally reached the heart of the matter. It was taking place in the side yard of Kari's closest neighbor. Several officers were standing around a large garbage can. They kept their distance, staring at it solemnly.

One man stood directly beside the can. But he refused to touch it. He looked uncomfortable.

"Who's in charge here?" Jo asked.

The guy by the can looked up at her. "I guess I am. I'm Sergeant Cohen."

"Agent Pullinger," Jo said. "I was just here last night, following up on the Kari Cross investigation. I spoke with Officer Teller. I thought…"

She didn't finish her sentence. She was going to tell them about how she reprimanded Teller. It didn't seem like an important fact now.

"Well," Cohen said with a sigh, "want to take a look? Help yourself. Here are some gloves."

She donned the gloves and reached for the garbage can lid. Everyone shrunk back, averting their eyes. It gave Jo a sick feeling.

She slowly opened the can and looked inside. With all the strobe lights on the street and the sun just starting to rise, it was easy to see.

Jo expected something gruesome. A blood bath. A mangled and nearly unrecognizable body.

Teller had been shoved into the can butt-first. His legs and arms were extended above him. There was a look of fear and pain frozen on his face. The body was pristine. He had been dispatched quickly and cleanly.

"His head has a slight twist," Jo observed. "I'm guessing a broken neck."

"That's what we thought," Cohen wheezed. He pressed a hand to his stomach and breathed deeply. "If I didn't feel so sick, I'd be angrier than hell. Whoever did this is going to pay severely."

"That's the goal," Jo replied. She shut the garbage can's lid. "I don't know who did it, but I think they were busy last night. You all know about Martin Leone?"

"The professor who got shot outside his house?" Cohen asked. "You think the same guy did both of 'em?"

Jo nodded. "Keep your eyes and ears open, gentlemen. And if you hear or see anything, please contact me. We'll catch this killer."

She left them to their work. She had her own job to do.

Jo thought about Teller as she got in her car. She felt ashamed for yelling at him, but maybe it was what he needed. Maybe he would have gone on to be a great cop. An asset to the Seattle PD. Now, no one would ever know.

Her mind turned to Teller's killer. He must have been lurking in the side yard. Listening and watching. Was it Kari's kidnapper? Jo couldn't believe that. The young guy who had drawn an apology onto a shovel with lipstick could not be the stone-cold killer of two men.

If she was dealing with two different perpetrators, then what in the world was going on here?

FIFTY-THREE

Jo's footsteps echoed in the back halls of the medical examiner's office. She stared up at the white tiled ceilings. Breathing in the cold, conditioned air. The stinging smell of formaldehyde drifted through an opening door.

A woman in a smock and mask stepped out.

"Are you the FBI agent?" she asked.

Jo nodded and showed her ID. Her elbow was getting sore from swinging it out so much. "I'm Jo Pullinger."

"Good to meet you. Come right in here."

She followed the woman into a small room. Jo took off her jacket and scrubbed her hands and forearms clean at a huge sink. She put on a white apron, along with gloves, a mask, and a hairnet. Finally, she followed the coroner into the next room.

"I didn't catch your name," Jo said.

"Oh, I'm Stella Reese. I'm new here. Transferred just recently from the Ada County office. That's in Boise, Idaho."

"Funny. I recently almost got murdered while driving a fellow agent out there. Small world."

Professor Leone was laid out on a metal table. He was nude, showing every square inch of waxy, pale skin. Jo walked up to the body slowly, studying Leone's face. It was always strange. The difference in a body when the lights went out.

"It's easy to see how he died," Jo said.

Stella nodded. "Gunshot in the middle of the forehead. And I really do mean the *middle*. I measured. Laser accuracy. Angle was pretty much straight. If anything, it was slightly upward. The shooter might have been a lot shorter than Leone. But the more likely explanation is he was at a lower elevation."

Jo nodded. She was dealing with a guy who could hit any target he wanted, even with a nine millimeter pistol. Who could dispatch a police officer twenty feet away from an FBI agent without her knowledge. Who could slip away into the night, leaving no trace.

"Have you ever seen anything like this before?" Jo asked.

"In Boise? Absolutely not," Stella replied with a laugh. "We don't get many trained hitmen out that way."

"Trained hitmen? That's an interesting choice of words," Jo remarked.

Stella pointed to a table by the wall. There was a computer there. On the screen, there was a freeze frame from a CCTV camera.

"Go hit the spacebar," Stella said.

Jo went and hit the button. The video played. She recognized the front porch of Leone's townhouse. So far, no blood had been shed.

"You might have to skip ahead," Stella advised. "The action starts at about two minutes."

Jo scrubbed to the two-minute mark.

Leone arrived. He came up the front walk, wavering from side to side.

"He looks intoxicated," Jo said.

"No alcohol was found in his system," said Stella. "No drugs, either."

Jo nodded, looking closer. The expression of anguish was plain on Leone's face as he approached his front door. He was thinking of Kari. The stumbling was likely just caused by emotional exhaustion.

Leone tried to unlock his door. He dropped his keys. As soon as he bent over, the first shot came. The CCTV footage had no sound, but the cloud of wood dust from the door gave it away.

Leone stood up and looked behind him. He was experiencing a moment of confusion. It was late at night. He was preoccupied with dark thoughts already. And, like most people, he didn't expect to get shot at. It took him a long time to figure out what was happening.

It was understandable. And tragic. Because the second shot came fast and hit its mark. Right in the middle of Leone's forehead.

"Laser accuracy," Stella said again.

Jo nodded. "The first shot missing was a fluke. If Leone had been a bit luckier, it would have given him a chance to get away. I see what you mean though, Stella. This killer knows what he's doing."

The footage went on for another five minutes. Leone lay on the porch, seeping blood. Nothing else happened. No one moved. The killer didn't bother to come over. He probably knew there was a camera. And he also knew Leone was dead.

This is a guy who isn't used to missing, Jo thought.

Even if Leone had escaped the porch and made a run for safety, he wouldn't have made it far. He wouldn't have survived the night.

The only question was, who would the hitman go for next?

FIFTY-FOUR

On her way to the field office, Jo found herself glancing at the rearview mirror. Checking for anyone who might be following. She didn't realize she was doing it at first. A subconscious move.

She had no idea who the killer was. No idea what he looked like. Or if it was even a "he" at all. It could be anyone. What set an excellent killer apart from a good one was their ability to blend in. To go unnoticed. To slip in and out of a place, leaving no trace in the memory of anyone.

She watched pedestrians. The pretty girl who was in too big of a hurry; she tripped, and spilled her coffee. The nice man in his fifties who stopped to help her. He looked like a father. Someone who was nurturing and kind.

A killer? Maybe. Jo didn't know what to think.

Perhaps the kidnapper and the killer were one and the same. The young man sounded so normal over the phone. But that could be just another form of camouflage. A way of blending in.

She checked to make sure her doors were locked when she had to stop at a red light. The city was full of strangers. Any one of them could pull a gun on her. She'd be dead before she could ever call for help. Or warn her colleagues that death was coming.

The killer was there last night. At Kari's house. Watching from the neighbor's yard. He must have overheard her conversation with Leone. He knew the FBI was involved, and he knew the name of the agent who was working the case.

She could well be his next target.

She was relieved when she entered the field office. As soon as the door shut behind her, she felt safe.

McKinley was at his desk. He beckoned her over.

"Take a look at this," he said. "The camera at Leone's front door wasn't the only one that witnessed the incident. There's an ATM at the convenience store on the corner that saw it too. And one of the neighbors has a doorbell camera."

Jo pulled her chair over and sat down. McKinley showed her the ATM footage first. It was at an extreme angle. She could barely make out Leone's front door at the edge of the frame. Leone showed up. The whole scene played out again. The first shot. The confused look. The second shot.

The death.

Time passed. Nothing moved.

"It just goes on like that," McKinley said. "No motion until a car drove by ten minutes later and saw Leone lying there. There were three people in the car. Three sisters. One of them is getting married, and they were on their way back from the bachelorette party."

"Bad way to end the night," Jo said. "But I guess it makes it more memorable. What about the other feed?"

McKinley pulled up the doorbell camera footage. It was across the street from Leone and a couple of doors down. It was much closer than the ATM. And the angle was almost straight on.

Leone's car pulled up. He got out. He tried to open his door. He failed. He died.

Again, nothing moved.

Just to prove a point, McKinley scrubbed the footage forward. He reached the part where the three sisters arrived. The car screeched to a stop. Frantic motion was seen inside the car.

"They're freaking out a bit right here," said McKinley. "They eventually come to their senses and call the cops. They park a little way up the street and wait for help."

"And then there's plenty of movement," Jo added. "But nothing until the sisters show up. So there aren't many places the killer could have shot from. Or ways he could have escaped. I'll have to go back and check the scene out again."

McKinley put his computer to sleep and stood up. He put his jacket on.

"I'll come with you," he said.

Jo smiled. "I thought you wanted to stick to desk duty on this one."

He shrugged. "That hasn't changed. I could use some air. A bite to eat wouldn't be bad either."

FIFTY-FIVE

Leone's townhouse was an entirely different place now. The sun was out. Traffic was flowing freely past the crime scene. Officer Getty was still standing guard. He looked like a sad bulldog.

Jo and McKinley parked at the convenience store. She glanced at the ATM as they walked by. The little camera was barely visible. But it saw everything.

Not quite everything, Jo thought.

They approached Getty. He gave them a nod.

"Agent Pullinger, hello again," he mumbled.

"I'm Agent McKinley," McKinley said.

Getty nodded again. He grunted something that sounded like, "Good to meet you."

"Any news about Teller?" Jo asked.

Getty shook his head. "Nothing. They're still combing the yard over there. Last I heard, the homeowners are on vacation and can't be contacted. But I doubt that hinders our investigation much." Getty jerked a thumb at Leone's door. "I bet it's just like here. Everything happened outside."

Jo nodded in response. She looked around. Scanning the scene. The street was lined with similar townhouses. Other than the convenience store, every structure she saw was residential.

There were certainly plenty of windows. A sniper could have hidden in any of them. Waiting. Watching for his target. Plenty of time to aim, no worry about being seen. Not in the dead of night, by a guy whose eyes were probably blurry with tears.

Except the angle of the shot precluded this idea. The shooter had been at a lower elevation. Leone had been killed while standing on his porch. It looked to be roughly three feet higher than street level.

So, the killer had been in the street.

But that was also impossible. One or both of the cameras would have seen him.

Jo looked past the street. She looked at the sidewalk on the other side.

"The shot was straight-on," she told McKinley. "The shooter had to have been standing pretty much directly across. Which leaves that alleyway as the only possibility I can see."

She pointed. McKinley looked. The alley was about six feet wide. It ran between two separate townhouse structures. There were recycling bins and dumpsters inside it. As far as alleyways went, it was clean.

"It would be pretty dark in there at night," Jo said. "Wouldn't it?"

"Black as a coal miner's throat," Getty replied. "I was standing here for a long time before the sun came up. I must have stared into that alley for ten minutes straight. Couldn't see anything."

"No cameras either, I suspect," Jo went on. "No one bothers watching an alleyway. No one's concerned about trash getting stolen. Come on, McKinley."

They crossed the street, darting between passing cars.

Jo positioned herself inside the mouth of the alleyway. She faced Leone's door and raised her hand, as though she were holding a pistol. She stuck her thumb up. Lined the tip of it up with Leone's door.

"Angle definitely seems right," she said. "Let's look for bullet casings."

They scoured the ground. They went to their hands and knees, checking under dumpsters. They even shined their lights into a storm drain grate.

"Nothing," said McKinley. "I wonder if the police were able to recover any. Let me go ask."

He ran back across the street, his gangly legs striking the ground awkwardly. He spoke with Getty for a moment, then came back.

"They checked the alleyway out as soon as they got here," said McKinley.

"Sometimes you can't get better than a beat cop's intuition," Jo snorted. "Did they find anything?"

"Not a thing. The killer must have taken his empties with him."

"Not surprising, given the picture we have of this shooter so far," said Jo. "Very meticulous. A professional. I don't like what I'm seeing."

"Neither do I," McKinley agreed. "We're getting into some kind of mess here. Again."

"Ready to get back to your desk yet?" Jo asked with a grin. "Or do you want to help me knock on some doors and look for witnesses?"

"Sounds fairly safe," he said with a sigh. "Lead the way."

FIFTY-SIX

Olga Aleksandrov parked her van outside the mansion. She watched through the window as seagulls floated in the air. They were coasting on an updraft. An ocean wind. They hung suspended. Unmoving, other than a slight tilt to their wings now and then.

Olga wished to be as free as those birds.

She turned her eyes to the house. The great, big, monstrous house. She used to think it was beautiful. She would be jealous of her boss's good fortune when she came here. Now she thought it was completely ugly.

Especially since it was bereft of the one person who made it tolerable.

She wiped tears from her eyes. Turning on her phone, she stared at the lock screen. It showed a photo of her parents. Their smiling faces.

"I don't know why it's so hard for me today," she said. "Last time, I was strong. This time... I will try. Yes, I will do my best. For you. So that you can come here, and we can all be free together."

She put her phone in her purse and got out of the van.

The same ogre-like guard was at the gate to greet her.

"Ms. Aleksandrov," he said with a grunt. "You always make me wait for you. I hate waiting."

Olga's fear and sadness turned to anger in a flash.

"And I hate the mean way you always greet me," she snapped. "I miss Philip."

The guard laughed. "Philip was a weakling."

"He was nice," she said. "That doesn't make him weak. He was a much better guard than you. Much more loyal."

"Oh yeah? Then why isn't he here right now? Oh, right. He decided he didn't want 'blood money' anymore. Even though it spends just the same as any other kind. Just get in here and stop wasting my time."

He opened the gate for her. Olga lugged her cleaning supplies inside.

When she got her task list this morning, she was relieved to see that "slip and slide sanitation" wasn't on it. It was a euphemism for blood. She was carrying no hydrogen peroxide today.

Just like last time, her boss was there to greet her. But Salvatore Russo wasn't in nearly as good a mood. He looked tired and spoke in a snippy way.

"Olga, good morning," he grumbled. "Come inside. Just normal cleaning today. Nothing in the cellar."

He waved her past and shut the door behind her. As soon as they were both inside, he started to walk away.

"Mr. Russo?" Olga said.

He looked at her. "For the last time, woman. Just call me Sal."

Olga laughed nervously. "If I may ask... where has Peter been? I have not seen him in a long time."

Sal's face went red. He started to shake. Finally, he took a deep breath and calmed down. He gave Olga a smile.

"You and my nephew get along well," he said. "I hear you even get ice cream together sometimes."

Olga nodded. "I don't want to be bold, but he's almost like a son to me. I love him so."

"That's good." Sal patted her arm. "You're family, Olga. I think I told you that last time you were here. Don't bother yourself about Peter. He and I just had a disagreement about some business, is all. Go ahead and do your work."

He left her there, slamming a door shut behind him.

Olga trembled as she went about her tasks. She was afraid she had made her boss mad.

Just as long she didn't run into Raul, she decided she would be fine.

FIFTY-SEVEN

Peter was doing his best to act casual. He strolled along the street with his hands in his pockets. He was wearing a hoodie, trying to hide his face.

He passed by a café with an outdoor seating area. There was a man at a table, reading a newspaper. He had dark hair in a ponytail. Peter's heart raced when he saw the man.

But it wasn't who he thought it was. This guy was younger and pudgier. He looked like a human instead of a ravenous wolf.

Peter kept going. He resisted the urge to keep looking over his shoulder. If someone *was* watching him, he didn't want to make himself look more suspicious.

You're paranoid, he told himself. *Yeah. Paranoid. The highly trained and sociopathic hitman who works for your uncle definitely won't be able to find you. No way. Stop worrying.*

He started to worry about four times worse than before.

The clothing shop was where he remembered it. A boutique that sold nice things for an affordable price. And since Peter only felt safe using cash, affordable was what he needed.

When he walked inside, the girl behind the counter smiled and said hello. She was pretty. Normally, Peter would stop to flirt with her a bit. Probably unsuccessfully. He wasn't bad looking himself, but his social skills weren't up to par.

He smiled at the girl and walked by. The store was called a boutique, which meant it pretty much only had women's clothing. That was fine for Peter's needs.

He moved up and down the aisles and racks. Pulling out shirts and pants and jackets and holding them up. Trying to imagine Kari in them. Kari was a beautiful person, and he thought she would look good in anything.

The problem was the size. He had no idea what size she was. He looked over at the girl by the counter again. She looked to be about the same height and weight as Kari.

Peter took a few garments up to the counter.

"Ready to check out?" she asked. Her nametag said *Lindsay*.

"Not quite," Peter replied. "I'm trying to buy a gift for someone. But I couldn't think of a sneaky way of asking her size."

"Oh..." Lindsay rubbed her chin. "Well, you could try and get access to her closet. Take a picture of a few tags and bring them back to me."

Peter shook his head. "That would work, but I want to surprise her today. I don't really have time. You actually look like you have the same build as her. Would any of this stuff fit you?"

Lindsay smiled and pulled the garments toward her. She looked at the tags. She held them up against her body, turning to look into a mirror.

"You made some lucky picks," she said. "These would all fit me just fine. As long as she's about my size, you should be golden."

Peter smiled and pulled out his wallet. A minute later, he was walking out of the store with a bag of clothes in hand.

Maybe these will make her happy, he thought. *Or at least they'll show her that I'm not trying to hurt her.*

***

It was a long walk back to Peter's hiding place. His feet were killing him, and he was thirsty and hungry. But food and drink would have to wait.

He was in a rundown neighborhood. The crime rate in these parts had always been bad, but it had gotten worse in recent years. A lot of houses had been trashed. Windows were boarded up. The abandoned places weren't so abandoned, though. They were occupied by homeless people and squatters.

But there was one house in particular that they were smart enough to stay away from. Its roof was in the end stages of total collapse. Black mold covered the walls. Sheets of red paper had been taped all over the outside. One word was visible on each of them: CONDEMNED.

It was far from glamorous, but it was a place to hide where Peter could be sure he wouldn't be disturbed.

FIFTY-EIGHT

Peter looked around. Making sure no one was watching. The street was desolate. Quiet. At night, it was a different story. Last night, there had been some kind of party out there. Lots of drinking. Loud voices. Someone had gotten hurt, and the police were called.

It was noon now. Peter still had many hours before the nightlife kicked into high gear. But he still moved quickly on his way inside.

The front part of the house was inaccessible. Mostly because the second floor had fallen into it. At the back, things were still fairly open. Peter was able to climb in through a window. He strolled across the floor. Kicking used needles out of his way. Along with other garbage, he didn't want to know the origin of.

He shoved the basement door open, then pushed it shut behind him. He went downstairs. Halfway down, he knocked on the wall. Making a pattern of sound. It was the secret code he had told Kari about. That way, she would know it was him.

He found her in the back corner of the basement. Behind the crumbling walls of a laundry room. She was chained to a radiator in the corner, her mouth covered with a gag. Peter cringed when he saw her.

It never got easier. He felt terrible for what he was doing. What he was putting her through. He wanted to tell her why he was doing it all. But the less she knew, the better it would be. For her, not him.

That was how love worked. Love was selfless. It was about taking care of someone, whether they knew it or not. It wasn't about taking credit.

It was the hardest thing he had ever done, being her villain. Knowing she would always hate him and fear him.

He sat cross-legged on the floor next to her. She was lying on a self-inflating mat that Peter had stolen from someone's garage. The kind used for camping.

"I'd like to take that gag off," Peter said. "As long as we still have an agreement. You won't scream, right?"

She nodded. Her eyes were smeared with mascara, but they were dry. She had no tears left. She had cried them all out already.

Peter pulled her gag down.

"That thing *reeks*," Kari said. "Where'd you get it from? Can I get a new one, please?"

Peter nodded. "Sure. Sorry. I'll find one for you when I go back out."

He looked behind them. There was a shelf in the laundry room that used to be used for detergent and fabric softener. Peter had turned it into a pantry.

"We still have plenty of water," he said. "But we need food. I'll have to get that too."

She glanced at his pocket. "How much money do you have left?"

"About fifty bucks," he said.

"That's not enough. We can get more. Just take me to an ATM. I can pull out as much money as we need."

Peter smiled. "Sorry, but that's not going to work. I don't really feel like getting caught when I'm this close."

"This close to what, exactly?" Kari demanded.

His smile failed. "I'm not going to tell you. If I have it my way, you'll never know. That way, you can go on with your life like nothing ever happened. Like your parents would have wanted."

Her nose wrinkled. "Don't talk about my parents."

"Sorry," he said again. To change the subject, he pulled the new clothes out of the bag. "See? I bought these for you. I'm pretty sure they fit. If you want, I can help you try them on."

She looked away. "No thanks."

"Well…" Peter's heart sank. He dropped the clothes back in the bag. "Do you want anything to eat?"

She didn't say anything.

He was surprised he had gotten any words out of her. She had been giving him the silent treatment for the most part.

The best he could do was give her access to food. She could eat it if she wanted. He dragged over a box of granola bars and set it by the bed. Along with a jug of water.

"There you go," he said. "I'm going to find us more food. I'll be back before it gets dark. I promise."

He left her there. He was relieved when she was no longer in his sight. He could pretend like none of it was happening.

Peter tried to be confident around Kari. He didn't want to scare her more than she was already. But he didn't actually feel confident.

The whole plan was going off the rails. If it had ever been on rails in the first place.

FIFTY-NINE

Jo and McKinley canvassed the neighborhood. They knocked at every door in a three-block radius. It took them all morning. And it turned out to be fruitless. The shooting happened too late at night. No one was awake. No one reported any strange noises.

"Could have been a silenced weapon," Jo suggested as they walked back toward the alley. "They usually still make a good bit of noise. But it can easily be attributed to a car door shutting or a trash can falling over. Something mundane."

"No one would remember a sound like that," McKinley said with a sigh. "Even if they did, we wouldn't be any further along. We already know a person stood in the alleyway and fired two shots. He picked up his bullet casings and ran. It took ten minutes for Leone's body to be discovered. A person can get to a lot of places in ten minutes."

"But," Jo said, "he would still have to follow a particular path. Once he exited the alleyway, he could have made a few different choices for where to go next. But the alley is a chokepoint. We checked the mouth of it for casings. Now we need to scour the rest of it. I hope you're not too hungry."

McKinley's stomach growled right on cue. "I'll survive. Let's do it."

They started at one end of the alley and worked their way down. They moved as slowly as sloths, checking every inch of the place. They were lucky it was so clean. It didn't take as long as they feared.

"Nothing, once again," McKinley said. "I'm sensing a pattern here."

Jo sighed. "All right. Let's get some lunch."

They were about to leave the alley when Jo noticed something small and white, sticking out between the wheels of a trash can. She had seen it before, but she took it for a straw wrapper. Now, she realized it was something else.

She used a pen from her pocket to pick the thing up.

"What is it?" McKinley asked.

"A hair tie," she said.

He shrugged. "It's probably been here for a while."

"No. It's not dirty. It's not even wet. Even though it was raining yesterday. It hasn't been here long at all." She moved it close to her nose and sniffed. "Still smells like shampoo."

"So, our shooter likes to wear their hair in a ponytail?" McKinley asked.

"Maybe," Jo replied. "This makes it more likely to be a female shooter. But it's hardly a clincher. A lot of guys have long hair these days. And when you're trying to do some precision shooting, it's a good idea to keep the hair out of your eyes."

She carried the hair tie to her car. She bagged it up and put it next to the shovel.

"Got a lot of stuff to turn in," McKinley said.

"I'll do it after we eat," Jo said. "I'm starving."

***

Jo thought back to her dream. She remembered Ted's sweet smile. His kind, comforting voice. His trucker hat.

She had his number. She thought about calling him right now. But that was just her loneliness talking. She had too much work ahead of her to be thinking about men. Unless Ted was her shooter or kidnapper, she couldn't be thinking about him right now.

But that didn't do a very good job of stopping her.

"Jo," McKinley said.

His voice startled her. She came back to reality. There was a bowl of chili in front of her, getting cold. She stirred it a bit and took a bite.

"Are you all right?" McKinley asked. "You looked like you were lost in your head for a moment."

"I was," Jo said. "And for once, my head was a nice place to be lost in."

He smiled. "Want to share what you were thinking about?"

"Not even a little bit," she told him. "This chili is pretty good, though. Very warming."

Just like my daydreams.

They finished their lunches. And their coffees. Jo insisted on paying. McKinley didn't put up too much of a fuss about it. Ordinary social decorum dictated that he should fight her over who paid the bill. He didn't.

That was what Jo liked about him. He didn't care too much about trying to be someone else. He was happy just being McKinley.

Nice thoughts filled Jo with a warm and fuzzy feeling.

It all changed as they stepped out of the diner.

SIXTY

McKinley's phone rang. He pulled it out casually. As soon as he saw the name, he went stiff. Jo leaned in to check who was calling.

Agent Larkin.

"Uh-oh," Jo said. "Now you remember what it was like in high school, trying to ask your crush to the prom."

In keeping with the vision she had of a teenage McKinley, he groaned and rolled his eyes at her. She half-expected him to yell, *Mom, get out of my room!*

He answered the phone. It took him two or three seconds to say anything. Finally, he cleared his throat. "This is Agent McKinley. Yes, I can hear you. Um... how's it going? I mean, what can I help you with? Oh. Hold on, let me put you on speakerphone."

He hit the button and held his phone out. They got in the car and shut the doors.

"Agent Larkin," Jo said. "This is Agent Pullinger. Go ahead."

"Yeah, something just came through the wire on the Kari Cross case," Larkin said. "She was visiting her sick grandma, correct?"

"That's why she was in Oregon," Jo confirmed.

"Well, she was in a nursing home, ill but stable. She took a sudden turn for the worse just three hours after you saved Kari at the rest area.

She was transferred to the hospital immediately. I'm sorry to say she passed away this morning."

Jo and McKinley stared at each other.

"I'm sorry too," said Jo. "Any word on how she died?"

"She was dealing with a host of health problems. We're still waiting on the details. But we know she went peacefully. She also had no idea her granddaughter was missing. She was in a coma for most of her hospital stay."

"I'm not sure if that's a blessing or a tragedy," Jo said, chewing her lip. "Thanks for letting us know, Larkin."

"Not a problem," she said. "I'll let you two get back to it. Buh-bye."

McKinley put his phone away.

"She says 'buh-bye' to end a call," Jo said. "That's very sweet. Don't you think?'

McKinley turned the radio on. "Hmm. Wonder if there's anything good on the rock station?"

"Fine, fine. I won't tease you anymore." Jo turned the radio off. She drove out of the parking lot. "I don't know what to make of the grandmother's death. Do you?'

McKinley shook his head. "My logical brain is telling me it has nothing to do with anything. But I have a feeling."

"I do, too," said Jo. "There's some kind of connection here. The timing is strange."

"What now?" McKinley asked.

Jo shrugged. "I'll think about that while I digest. There must be something we're missing."

McKinley looked around. "Is this still the rental car?"

She smiled sheepishly. "Maybe."

"Jo, I know exactly what we're doing next. We're returning this thing."

"Not with evidence in the back, we're not," said Jo. "I'll take you back to the office. You can bring the evidence in. I'll take my car to the lot. Promise."

McKinley nodded. "I'll ask Grantham to send a ride for you."

"Good. We have a plan now. It has nothing to do with solving the case, but at least it's something."

They high-fived and turned the radio back on.

SIXTY-ONE

Jo dropped McKinley off at the office. She looked up the local car rental place and drove there. For some reason, she felt more anxious doing this than she did when she was being shot at. It was like going to the dentist. No matter how old she got, certain things always scared her.

But everything went well. Jo had to pay extra for the number of miles she had put on the car. A mechanic working at the place took one look at the undercarriage and gave her a nod. The damage was superficial. The insurance she'd bought would more than cover it.

"All right, then," Jo said to the kind folks at the agency. "Thank you very much. And have a lovely day."

When she reached the parking lot, two black cars with tinted windows were waiting. A man in a suit was standing beside each of them. One of them handed her a set of keys. Both men got into one car and drove away.

"And thank you, too," Jo said to no one.

She got in her car and started driving. She didn't know where she was going. She didn't know if she was going anywhere at all or just enjoying the smooth feel of the car.

Suddenly, she was pulling into a public parking lot that was familiar. It was the same place she parked for her first visit to Cornish College.

"Guess I'm back," she mused. "Following a hunch, I didn't even know I had. Let's go."

She climbed up the steep sidewalk. She took her time. Feeling the effects of the morning run and her lack of sleep. She tried to figure out why she was there. Maybe her subconscious was telling her that Leone was more involved than she thought. She assumed he was just a witness, but what if he was directly engaged in the whole thing?

She shook her head. Dispelling the idea. It didn't work. Leone was an afterthought. A quick little mess to be cleaned. He knew something that put him in the crosshairs. Jo had to figure out what that something was.

This was where Leone worked. This was the place he spent the most time. Other than lazing around in his townhouse, drinking beer and munching on cheese puffs.

If the secret was anywhere, it would be here.

The same girl as before was at the reception desk. Her nametag was loose. Hanging down, unreadable. It didn't matter. Jo remembered.

"Ashley, hi," Jo said.

The girl looked bored when Jo first came in. But she smiled now, her mood changing.

"Agent Pullinger!" she said. "I looked you up after you were here. I saw the thing about the Bridgeton Ripper. And that guy you worked with."

"Martin Rhodes," Jo said with a wistful smile.

Ashley nodded. "That's a pretty hardcore story. You're super tough."

"That's what I had to tell myself to get out of bed this morning," Jo replied. "Thank you for saying so, Ashley. I'm thanking a lot of people today, aren't I?"

"Huh?" Ashley asked.

"Don't worry about it. I assume you heard about Professor Leone?"

Ashley's mood changed for the second time. The joyful smile sank into a sad frown.

"Yeah," she replied. "That's really crazy. And tragic. Professor Leone was a nice guy. Kind of melodramatic, but everyone liked him. He cared about people. Who do you think would want a guy like that dead?"

"That's what I'm going to find out," said Jo. "I was wondering if you had any inklings. Any ideas or memories you'd like to share with me? Anything about Leone that could be even remotely helpful."

"Hmmm." Ashley glanced around. "Well, I know his favorite salad dressing was thousand island. He always went and got a salad for lunch. He came into the lobby with a packet of dressing held between his teeth. Pretty much every day."

"That might be *too* remote," said Jo.

"Oh," Ashley said, disappointed. "Sorry, but I don't think there's much I can give you."

Jo smiled. "That's all right. Have a good day, Ashley."

She started to walk away.

"Wait!" Ashley called. "He had another visitor the day you came. Actually, it was right after you were here."

Jo looked back. "Do you know who the visitor was?"

Ashley nodded. "He's a friend of the professor. A kid named Peter."

"Last name?" Jo asked.

"Sorry. I don't know."

Jo looked up. She counted three security cameras just from where she was standing. She pointed at one of them. "Is the footage from these stored on the premises?"

"Off-site," said Ashley. "We have a server somewhere, I think. I'm not sure."

Jo thanked the receptionist again before leaving.

SIXTY-TWO

"McKinley," Jo said into her phone. "I've got something."

"Where are you?" McKinley asked.

"In traffic," Jo replied with a sigh, tapping her steering wheel. "On 9th Avenue. Hey, there's a coffee shop called Grumpy Bean. Sounds like you before you have your first cup. Anyway, I've got a whole ocean of brake lights in front of me. It's going to be a minute before I get back."

"No rush," McKinley said calmly. "I've never heard of Grumpy Bean..."

"Don't even think about it," Jo replied. "I'm not stopping. I'm heading straight back to your desk. By the time I get there, I'd like to see the security camera footage from the Cornish College lobby."

"Timeframe?" McKinley asked.

"When I visited. Someone else came to see Leone right after me. You can check the printout on my desk. It's my ongoing report for the Kari Cross case. It should have the time you're looking for on it."

"All right. I'll work on that. See you when you get here."

Jo hung up and focused on controlling her urge to drive onto the sidewalk. Her phone rang. Ford was calling her.

"What's up?" she asked.

"Not much," said Ford. "I'm out chasing leads, but I just keep hitting dead ends. I'm in a slump, and I need some cheering up."

"Can't help you with that," Jo replied. "I just found a promising lead of my own."

"Well, good luck with that. But you owe me a joke. Remember? Last night, you said you'd tell me a joke. You never did."

"I remember," said Jo. "And I've got some time, so here goes. A guy decides to visit his grandfather one weekend."

"It's pretty good so far," said Ford. "How old is the grandfather?"

"Pretty old. It doesn't matter. Anyway, the guy visits his grandfather. It's just the two of them and the grandfather's dog. They sit down for dinner. The young guy notices the plates don't look very clean. There's a kind of film on them."

"Yummy," Ford said.

"He asks his grandfather about the dirty dishes. The grandfather says, 'They're as clean as cold water can get them.'"

"Oof. Well, he's doing his best."

"So, the young guy shrugs and finishes eating. When the plates are empty, the grandfather puts them on the floor. 'Come here, Cold Water,' he calls. The dog runs over and licks them clean."

Ford burst out laughing. "That's not bad, Jo. I'll have to tell Kelly and Hazel that one. It'll make Kelly gag, but Hazel's gonna love it."

"Feel better now?" Jo asked.

"Yup. A lot better. Thanks. If you'll excuse me, I just saw a wayward ex-husband I've been looking for. Time to get some child support payments rolling again. Talk to you later."

***

McKinley was ready by the time she reached his station. He had the footage pulled up and paused. It was from a camera directly behind the reception desk. Aimed down at a steep angle. In the freeze frame, Jo could see the top of Ashley's head as she worked at her computer.

"It was easy to find these files," McKinley said. "Not very secure. Just sitting on a server that's used by a hundred other buildings. I've got it set right before you walk in."

"Nice." Jo pulled her chair over and plopped down. "Let's go."

McKinley hit the play button. Jo watched herself walk up to the desk.

"Is that really what I look like from above?" she hissed.

"You look great, Jo," McKinley said.

"Don't let Larkin hear you say that," Jo advised. "She'll get jealous."

He winced. "Can we just get back to the video?"

Onscreen, Jo and Ashley spoke. Jo veered off to the side, disappearing. On her way to see Leone in his classroom.

"I haven't watched this far yet," said McKinley. "I was waiting for you."

"Like it's a blockbuster movie with a twist ending," Jo replied. "I guess it feels that way, doesn't it? It's exciting."

Another person arrived at the desk a couple of minutes later. He was a young man. A bit above average height. Dark hair, pale skin. He was fairly handsome.

He and Ashley spoke. By their body language, it was clear they knew each other. But maybe not very well. There was a stiff and awkward aspect to both of them, though they smiled and laughed.

The young man left, stepping away from the desk.

"Follow him," Jo urged.

SIXTY-THREE

McKinley switched to a different video file. They were all the same length. They were synced up. He only had to skip to the right time-stamp.

The second camera was in the waiting area. The young man entered the frame. He sat down and grabbed a magazine. He looked nervous at first. Bouncing his leg and glancing around. But he got immersed in the magazine and settled down.

"Here you come," McKinley said, pointing at the edge of the screen.

Jo appeared, walking past the sitting area. She looked at the young man briefly. Just taking in her surroundings. But the effect on the man was profound. His mouth fell open. His eyes followed Jo across the lobby.

"Seems like you're the last person he wanted to see," McKinley said.

Jo nodded. "He recognizes me. From where, though? Could be our kidnapper. Or the man who killed Leone. Maybe both. Can we get a better view of his face?"

"Maybe," said McKinley.

He swapped between camera feeds at a frantic pace. Scrubbing back and forth through the footage. They found a frame where the young man was looking up. Maybe he was searching for cameras. Maybe he was just studying the ceiling.

Either way, they got a clear image of his face.

"I can run recognition software on this," McKinley said excitedly.

He hit the print screen button on his keyboard and copied the captured image into a program. He hit the start button. The computer went to work, running calculations on the young man's face. Cross-referencing a boatload of numbers with other faces in the database.

"Will this find him?" Jo asked. "Even if he doesn't have a criminal record?"

McKinley nodded. "This searches way more than just inmate files. It looks through all records. Even if this guy has a state ID and nothing else…"

A dialog box popped up onscreen: MATCH FOUND.

"…it will find him," McKinley finished.

"Way to speak it into existence," Jo said. "That's the power of positive thinking."

McKinley clicked the OK button. A scanned image of a Washington state driver's license appeared.

"That's him," Jo said. "Peter Russo. Address is 5120 Rockaway Beach Road. Bainbridge Island. Which is the place Kari loved to visit. Before someone scared her away. I'm sensing a decent connection here."

"This kid doesn't look very scary," McKinley pointed out.

Jo nodded. "I need to make a quick call."

She found the number for the Cornish front desk. Ashley answered.

"This is Agent Pullinger," Jo said. "Just a quick follow-up. Can you tell me about Peter? How well do you know him?"

"Oh, not super well," Ashley replied. "I only talk to him when he comes to see Professor Leone. But sometimes, the professor is in the middle of a lecture, so Peter kind of hangs out. He seems nice."

"Nice?" Jo asked.

"Yeah. Just like a normal guy. Kind of flirty but not pushy. You know?"

"I suppose so. Has he ever said or done anything that made you feel a little scared? Did Leone ever mention anything like that to you?"

"Hmmm... nope!" Ashley said brightly. "I think Peter's just a friendly guy. Nothing weird about him."

"Okay. Thanks again for your time."

"So it probably wasn't him who confronted Kari on Bainbridge Island," McKinley said.

Jo stared at the image on his screen. The license photo of Peter Russo. She thought back to the night in Oregon. The farmhouse. She had stared straight into the eyes of the kidnapper. Did they match?

Sure. Peter also had brown eyes. The most common eye color in the world. Not much help there.

She turned her attention to Peter's height and weight. His license said he was 5'10" and 175 pounds. That matched as well. But these were pretty average measurements. They could describe millions of people.

"I can see the wheels turning in your head, Jo," said McKinley. "Don't worry. Because I know Peter's family. The address and the last name match."

Jo perked up. "Who are they? Important people?"

"You could say that," McKinley replied.

SIXTY-FOUR

McKinley opened his web browser and typed out a URL. It took him to a clean but generic corporate website. The banner image showed a smiling man operating a forklift. The name of the company stood next to the forklift in bold, shiny letters. RUSSO SHIPPING INC.

"Have you spent much time at the Seattle waterfront?" McKinley asked.

"Other than to get some fish and chips?" Jo replied. "No, I guess not. Somehow my cases haven't taken me out there. So far."

"So you haven't been to the Smith Cove Waterway or any of the piers around there," McKinley went on. "There's a cruise ship moored up there sometimes. A lot of container ships. You can go stand on Pier 90 any day of the week and see the name RUSSO stenciled on a boat. Sometimes more than one. They're a worldwide organization."

"So, who's Peter?" Jo asked. "The son of the owner?"

McKinley shook his head. "The nephew. Let's go over here."

There was a button near the top of the page. ABOUT US. McKinley clicked it. It took him to a page that showed headshots and short bios about the key people at the company.

The first person on the list was a guy in middle age. He had dark skin and jet-black hair, slicked back. His eyes were a pale blue color. They didn't match the rest of his appearance at all.

Jo read the biography.

Salvatore Russo is the CEO and founder of Russo Shipping Inc. From a young age, he was always interested in shipping. He has always wondered how things get from point A to point B. Now he has the answers. Not only that but he's figured out how to move things with the utmost efficiency and security.

Jo chuckled. "It's a sales pitch disguised as a feel-good get-to-know-the-family page. So, this is Peter's uncle?"

McKinley nodded. "Peter's parents died when he was a kid. His uncle took him in."

"Fascinating stuff," Jo said. "But how do you know all this? Is it one of your hobbies to research shipping companies?"

"It's the hobby of the FBI, actually," McKinley responded.

He closed out of the web browser and started searching through files on the local network. He found the file on Salvatore Russo quickly.

"Russo Shipping has been investigated plenty in the past," McKinley went on. "Not just by us, but by agencies around the world. The CIA, Interpol, the NCA... the list goes on. No charges have ever been brought against Salvatore or the company as a whole, but there's been a lot of suspicion of illegal activity."

"Drug trafficking?" Jo offered.

"That would be the main concern, yes," McKinley agreed. "But there was an informant a few years back. He told an Interpol agent that he saw a cache of firearms being loaded onto a Russo ship. The informant ended up dead a week after that."

"Probably not a coincidence," said Jo. "So, we have Peter Russo, who matches what I remember about the kidnapper. He's the nephew of Salvatore, who owns an international shipping company that has been suspected of criminal actions by intelligence and law enforcement agencies around the world."

"That's the gist of it," said McKinley.

Jo smiled. "This is looking good. What's the latest on Russo Shipping?"

McKinley scrolled through the files. "There hasn't been anything for over a year. Either Salvatore has been keeping his nose clean, or he got better at avoiding suspicion. Not long before you transferred here, Grantham was thinking about putting together a task force to get to the bottom of things with Russo. I considered asking for a place on that task force."

"So you had to do your research," said Jo. "Which is what you excel at, McKinley. If there is a connection here, which is a reasonable assumption, we just might be able to put Salvatore Russo out of business."

SIXTY-FIVE

"The address for Peter," Jo said, "what was it again?"

"5120 Rockaway Beach," McKinley answered.

"Is that also where Salvatore lives?" Jo asked.

"Yes. It's a large house. I guess you would call it a mansion. As long as he isn't currently traveling, that's where Salvatore will be."

"Great. I'm going to need a phone number."

McKinley smirked. "I'll send it your way."

Jo scooted her chair back to her desk. She logged back into her computer. There was already an instant message from McKinley waiting for her.

She dialed the number using her desk phone. She put the handset against her ear and waited. With her free time, she pulled at some loose laminate on the corner of her desk. It had started as a tiny bit of peeling material. Through her anxious picking, it was now a huge scar.

"This is Salvatore Russo," a deep voice answered. "I recognize your number. Part of it, anyway. Is the FBI about to start harassing me again?"

Jo smiled to herself. She was pretty sure Salvatore was a bad guy. And it felt good to make bad guys sweat.

"I'm Agent Pullinger, Mr. Russo."

"Call me Sal," he replied with a grunt.

"All right, Sal. The first thing I'll say is, I don't actually want to start harassing you. And this has nothing to do with any investigations the FBI may have carried out in the past."

"Good," he said. "My ships are clean. Always have been. Always will be. About time you goons realized that. How can I help you then, Agent? What was it? Pullinger?"

"That's right," said Jo. "The business I have shouldn't be discussed over the phone. Do you think we could meet somewhere and talk?"

Sal let out a sigh. "I guess I could have an open spot in my calendar. What venue did you have in mind?"

"Somewhere we can both feel comfortable. In Seattle."

"All right. I was going into the city for a business meeting anyway. I'm a busy man, Agent Pullinger. Unfortunately, I won't be able to dedicate much time to our conversation. But I'll try and answer your questions."

"Very good, Mr. Russo," said Jo. "Perhaps you'd be willing to stop by the FBI office? We could talk here."

He scoffed to show what he thought of that idea. "Nah. I'm not too keen on that. How about Ivar's? The place of Pier 54."

"You know, I was just thinking about fish and chips a little while ago," Jo said with a laugh. "I'd be happy to meet you there."

"An hour from now?" Sal asked.

Jo checked the time. "Yes, that works for me. I'll see you then. Thanks very much for your time."

She hung up. Turning to McKinley, she pumped her arm in triumph. "Score! That was easier than I expected it to be."

"He's been quite amenable to our requests in the past," McKinley replied. "Do you want some backup on this one?"

She thought about it. Ivar's was a famous fish and chips place. There were always tons of people there. And the area it resided in was busy as well. It was right by the ferry terminal.

It should be a perfectly safe place for a meeting. Even if Salvatore Russo turned out to be the evilest man on the planet.

"I can handle it," she said. "Want me to bring you back anything?"

McKinley rubbed his hands together. "Cod. Three pieces. No... *four* pieces. Yes, that should do it."

He reached into his wallet and handed her a twenty-dollar bill.

"I wouldn't mind a coffee to go either," he said. "You can keep whatever change you get back."

Jo took the money. "You're a great partner, McKinley. I mean that. I hope the fish isn't cold by the time I get it back."

He shrugged. "I've eaten it straight out of the fridge at two AM. Don't worry about it."

SIXTY-SIX

When it came to recognizing Sal Russo in the crowd, Jo wasn't worried. She only had to look for his eyes. She remembered watching a documentary about Iceland. There were places there where you could walk into a tunnel. Under a glacier. You could look up through layers of ice that had been there for millennia.

The color of those glaciers was an otherworldly blue. The same color as Sal's eyes. She almost wondered if they were contacts. A way to set himself out from others in the business. To make his face stick in the minds of his customers. A funny idea. But she wasn't going to ask him about that.

She had no idea how dangerous he was. Not yet.

She arrived at the intersection of Alaskan Way and Madison Street. A ferry was just arriving from Bainbridge Island. The prow was full of passengers. Kids clung to the railing, watching with open mouths as the boat approached its dock.

Jo took a right turn and immediately arrived in front of Ivar's. It was a walk-up counter under a roof. An open area full of smells. Fried fish and malt vinegar. Tartar sauce and saltwater. A strong hint of exhaust fumes.

She entered the overhang and looked around. A half dozen people were waiting for their orders. None of them was Sal.

Jo went outside. There was a separate dining area, enclosed behind glass walls. Sal wasn't in there, either.

Which left only one place. Jo walked between the walk-up counter and the dining area. She came out onto a small boardwalk platform. There were benches and picnic tables here. The railings around the boardwalk were speckled with seagull droppings.

This was where you came if you wanted to take part in a local tradition. Several people were at the railing. Tossing pieces of their french fries into the water. A mass of seagulls was waiting below, ready to scoop up their treats.

Sal was not at the railing. He was sitting by himself on a bench, picking at a paper tray of fried clams.

"Mr. Russo?" Jo said.

He looked up with those cold eyes. "Agent Pullinger, I presume."

She showed him her ID. He leaned forward to study it.

"Very shiny," he said, taking a bite of clams. "You must polish it on a routine basis. Care to sit down?"

He scooted to the side. Giving her space on his bench. Instead, Jo sat at the nearest picnic table. Facing Sal. Their knees almost touching.

He looked at her suspiciously. "What's this all about, Agent Pullinger? You said on the phone it wasn't about my work. But I know how you fibbies work. Always bending the truth. You got a nice badge there, but my taxes are what pay your salary. Remember that."

He pointed at her with a stubby-fingered hand. She studied it. The fingers were hairy. He wore a couple of rings. One of them was a class ring from whatever college he went to. His hands were clean. Free from scars and scratches.

He must delegate his dirty work to someone else, Jo thought.

"I wasn't lying," Jo replied. "I want to ask you about your nephew, Peter."

Sal sat back. He set his clams to the side. "What about him?"

"Have you spoken to him recently?" Jo asked.

Sal shrugged. "To tell you the truth... no. Peter's a troublemaker. I never know what he's up to. And he doesn't tell me anything. You believe that? Me!" He knocked himself in the chest with both hands. "The man who raised him after his parents kicked the bucket!"

"How did they die, if I might ask?" said Jo.

He waved a hand. "Ah, that's ancient history. Tragic stuff. Helena got sick. Cancer. After she went, my brother Anthony couldn't take being alone. He drove himself into a tree at ninety miles an hour. Thankfully, he had the good sense to drop his boy off at my place first. He was always smart, my brother. But troubled. Just like Peter."

"What do you mean by troubled?" asked Jo.

"I mean, they have their demons." Sal swirled a hand beside his head. "It's something in their brains, I guess. Must be hereditary. Peter's always been difficult to keep under control. But you still haven't told me why you're so interested in him."

"I haven't decided if I should or not," Jo answered. "But I have another question. Do you know a young woman by the name of Kari Cross?"

SIXTY-SEVEN

As soon as Jo dropped the Kari bomb, she saw the battle raging in Sal's eyes. It was quick. Before she knew it, it was over. But it had been there. An inner turmoil. A hard decision in progress.

"Who?" Sal asked.

"Kari Cross," Jo repeated. "Does the name ring a bell?"

Sal took a bite of food and shook his head. "Nope. Not really. Should it?"

"Her name has been in the news," Jo said. "Especially this morning."

"Oh! Yeah, that missing girl. Tough break. She had everything in the world, and I guess someone wanted to take it from her. You can never be too careful out here, isn't that right, Agent Pullinger?"

She smiled. "I couldn't agree more, Mr. Russo."

He popped a few more clams into his mouth. Then he looked at the time. He slapped his knees and stood up. "I'd best be going now. Got business to attend to, sorry to say. Here's my card."

He wiped the grease off his hands with a napkin. Then he reached into his breast pocket and handed her a card.

"Call me anytime, day or night, rain or shine," he said with a friendly smile. "I didn't get where I am today by being difficult. I've got nothing to hide from the FBI. You could even swing by my casa sometime."

Jo took the card. "Thanks for your time, Mr. Russo."

"Call me Sal," he told her. "I won't tell you again."

He offered his hand. They shook. Sal made his way off the board-walk, waggling his fingers goodbye.

Jo waited until he was out of sight. She went into the overhang, loitering by the walk-up counter. She watched Sal strolling along the sidewalk. He had a disgusted look on his face. He dropped his half-eaten tray of clams into the trash.

A car pulled up at the curb. He quickly got into the backseat. It sped away recklessly. Making every other car on the road honk at it.

Where are you off to in such a hurry, Sal? Or maybe you're just in a hurry to get away from me?

He knew something about Kari. There was a connection. Something between them. Something involving his nephew, Peter.

Jo mulled it over in her mind as she ordered her food. And McKinley's. She wasn't hungry, but she could feel her blood sugar dropping. She would need all the energy she could get to find the bottom of this rabbit hole.

SIXTY-EIGHT

Sal loved food. Mostly he liked fresh Italian cooking. His aunt's lasagna was good. Her panzanella was always a warm burst of nostalgia for his childhood.

But his tastes ranged much further than that. He loved Japanese food especially. When you got the good stuff, there was nothing tastier. You could eat and eat without getting too full.

He also had a soft spot for fried food. He was American, after all. Ivar's was a staple in his diet. He got it pretty much every time he came to the city. Usually, he went for the calamari. Today he'd decided on clams.

It's not that the clams were bad. They were delicious, actually. If he was in the right mood, he would have put away two trays. Easy. But his appetite half died when he got the call from the FBI agent.

It died the rest of the way the second she started asking her questions.

Sal tossed out the rest of the clams. He had tunnel vision. He just wanted to get to his car and get out of there. It took a lot to rattle Sal.

But he was good and rattled.

He pulled the rear door open and threw himself onto the cool leather seat. His normal city driver, a guy named Bjorn, was behind the wheel.

"Drive," Sal ordered as he slammed his door shut.

"Where to, sir?" Bjorn asked.

"Don't care. Just get me away from here. For god's sake, go!"

Bjorn stepped on it. He nearly hit three different cars as he made his way onto the street. A chorus of horns rang out behind them. People were mad. Sal didn't care.

"Keep stepping on it," Sal said with a grunt. "Remember, your kid has braces because of me. If you get a ticket, I'll pay for that too."

Bjorn nodded. He was a good driver. He was also a good listener. He did what he was told.

But Sal didn't know him that well. They hardly ever talked. He didn't trust Bjorn completely.

There was a button on his door, next to the window controls. Sal hit it. A soundproof divider slid up, separating the front and rear seats. Bjorn wouldn't hear anything Sal said while it was up.

Sal wiped the sweat off his hands. He grabbed his phone and called Raul.

"Yes?" Raul answered.

"Where are you now?" Sal asked.

"Searching for Peter," Raul replied. "Would you like me to divert to a different task?"

"No, definitely not. You gotta find the kid, pronto. We need to clean this mess up. The FBI lady you saw at Kari's house... what did you say her name was?"

"Pullinger," said Raul.

Sal felt cold and hot at the same time. "That's what I thought. She and I just had a little talk. She doesn't know anything yet, but I get a feeling she's a tenacious one. She ain't gonna look away so easy. Not like all the other feds I've dealt with."

"You sound frightened," said Raul calmly. "There is no reason for that. You have had many dealings with the FBI in the past."

"But this is different. Back then, they were investigating dubious claims about cargo holds. Now they're investigating my nephew. They're investigating *me*. You better work fast, Raul."

"There's only so much I can do, Sal. I'm not a superhuman."

"Yeah, yeah. Don't get your knickers in a twist, Raul."

"An ironic statement for you to make at the present time."

"Whatever," said Sal. "I've got a plan that'll help us get Peter. So listen up."

SIXTY-NINE

Jo ate half of her fish and chips on the way to the office. She carried the rest inside with her. There were longing sniffs and jealous stares from everyone she passed.

"Got your cod, McKinley," she called out as she approached her desk. "And it's still warm."

But he wasn't at his station. She set his tray down by his keyboard. She draped a napkin over the top to try and keep some heat in.

Sitting at her desk, she stared at his empty seat. She wondered if McKinley was at home for a change. After eating a few more fries, she decided there was no use waiting.

"I'll have to do my own research for once," she said with a smile.

So far, they had looked into both Sal and Kari separately. Now it was time to put the two together. There had to be some kind of connection.

She started by looking at Kari again. She found all the same information as before. Her parents' death, her inheritance, buying a house for cash, attending school in Seattle. The only job she'd ever had was at an ice cream stand when she was in high school. No connection there.

Next, she dug into Kari's parents. And that was where she unearthed a bombshell.

McKinley showed up while Jo was still intently researching. Without a word, he grabbed his fish and chips and brought his chair over.

"This is a role reversal," he quipped.

"Shut up," Jo snapped. "Actually, don't. You can give me whatever input you have. Because this is all starting to make sense."

"Is it?" McKinley asked.

"Well... not quite," Jo admitted. "But listen to this. I've managed to dig up the full life and times of Grant Cross and Melissa Cross, née Townsend."

"Kari's parents," McKinley said.

Jo nodded. "Correct."

"It wasn't a question. I remember their names from our previous research."

"Of course you do. But I'll be you didn't know this." She used her cursor to highlight a passage in a magazine article. "The happy couple started a corporation called Brickwall Group. Named for where they met, a brick structure on the University of Washington campus."

"I didn't know that second part," said McKinley. "Sounds romantic."

"They were a power couple," Jo added. "Do you know what Brickwall Group did?"

McKinley dunked a piece of cod into tartar sauce and took a bite. "They were a manufacturing company. They made everything from gardening tools to basic medical supplies. Surgical masks and stuff. They had offices and plants in a few different countries."

"Did you know who one of their major shipping partners was?" Jo asked.

"I'm going to guess Russo Shipping Incorporated," said McKinley. "But we've already established that it's a huge company. It might just be a coincidence."

Jo popped her last french fry into her mouth. "There's a connection between the Russo family and Kari. But you're right. The fact that Brickwall used Russo Shipping might just be a lovely little coincidence."

McKinley eyed her suspiciously. "You're using your smartass tone again. That means you have something else to tell me."

Jo grinned. "Get ready. We're about to go on a little journey."

SEVENTY

Jo found images from a different article. This one was from a newspaper rather than a magazine, but it was still full color.

"*The Bainbridge Island Review*," McKinley read. "There it is again. Bainbridge Island."

The article was from twenty years in the past. The headline read *Local Businesspeople Flock to the Farmer's Market*.

The main photo in the article showed a street lined with stands and tent canopies. A great deal of produce was on display, including a giant pumpkin. But Jo was more interested in the three people standing in the foreground.

From the left, the first was a man with dark brown hair. He wore glasses with circular lenses and a stiffly starched dress shirt. All in all, he looked like a geek.

The next person was a woman. She was of average height. Dark hair and green eyes. She seemed very familiar.

"She looks exactly like Kari," Jo whispered.

"These two are Grant and Melissa?" McKinley said.

Jo didn't answer. She was waiting for him to make the full connection.

The third person was another man. He was shorter than Grant but densely built. His dark hair was slicked back. Icy blue eyes stared at the camera. Salvatore Russo hadn't changed much over the years. His belly was more prominent now, but that was all.

"That's him," McKinley gasped. "That's Salvatore."

Jo nodded. She scrolled down, letting him see the caption. *From right to left – Salvatore Russo, CEO of Russo Shipping Inc. – Melissa and Grant Cross, owners of Brickwall Group.*

"So they did know each other," McKinley said. "It wasn't just a coincidental business transaction."

"Nope," Jo confirmed. "And the evidence goes deeper. I scraped through old versions of the Russo Shipping website and found something interesting."

She clicked another tab on her browser. It took her to an archived version of the website. There were broken images and hyperlinks that led nowhere, but the pictures she cared about were still visible.

"There used to be a subsection to the 'about us' page," said Jo. "It had pictures of Sal and his exploits around the world. I guess he used to be even braggier than he is now."

She scrolled through shots of young Sal doing the requisite rich-guy things. Climbing Everest. Walking along the Great Wall of China. Scuba diving in the Maldives. They all showed Sal alone or among people that Jo didn't recognize. Locals or other wealthy tourists.

When she found the image she was after, she stopped and let McKinley have a look.

In this shot, Sal was lounging on the deck of a yacht. He was wearing an unbuttoned Hawaiian shirt. Holding a tropical beverage. And he wasn't alone. Two other people were with him.

"It's Grant and Melissa again," McKinley said. "This is amazing, Jo. Not sure why I didn't think of checking old versions of the site. The fact that these pictures are still visible must mean they're still stored on the website's server. I wonder what else might still be there?"

"You can check that out in a little bit," Jo told him. "There are two more pictures you need to see."

She scrolled until she found them. The first was Sal, Melissa, and Grant standing on a pier, all holding up fish they had caught. The second showed them sitting on a private jet. But it wasn't under the context of business. They were dressed casually and drinking alcoholic beverages.

Jo put her cursor over the image. She waited. After a few seconds, the filename popped up. *Sal among friends.*

"We can say with a high degree of certainty now," Jo said. "Not only did Sal know Kari's parents, he was close with them. They went on trips together. I'll bet they hung out as often as they could."

"And now Sal's nephew may have kidnapped their daughter," McKinley added. "I have a feeling there's a lot more to find. We just need to keep looking."

SEVENTY-ONE

"This is far as I've gotten," Jo told McKinley. "When I got back from my meeting with Sal, I saw you weren't here..."

McKinley saw the giddy smile on her face.

"You forget how much fun research can be," he said. "Are we calling him Sal now? Not Salvatore? How did the meeting go, by the way?"

"He insisted." Jo shrugged. "And it went... all right. I think. Sal seems like a perfect gentleman. He's got a silver tongue. If I wasn't looking for the signs of a bad man, I would have thought he was a good one. You should have seen what happened when I mentioned Kari's name."

"Did he lose his cool?" McKinley asked.

"In a manner of speaking. I could tell he was making a lot of quick decisions and calculations. He looked like his brain might overheat. He recovered fast, but I saw his poker face fail. And he knows I saw it."

"So, this Sal guy certainly knows something," said McKinley. "Which increases the odds that his nephew is also involved."

"And the odds were already getting high," Jo agreed. "We have a tangible connection between the Crosses and the Russos now. But we still don't know *why* any of this is happening."

"I have an idea," said McKinley. He kicked his wheeled chair back to his desk. Taking his fish and chips with him. "We keep talking about Brickwall Group in the past tense. I wonder why."

"I know why *I* am," said Jo. "While I was doing my research just now, I saw that the company was dissolved a few years back."

McKinley nodded. He went typing away at his computer. Taking bites of food now and then. Finally, he beckoned Jo over.

"Brickwall Group was dissolved about three and a half years ago," he said. "Just a couple of months after Grant and Melissa died in the car accident. The decision to dissolve the company was an interesting one. Brickwall Group was still extremely lucrative. In fact, the last fiscal quarter they had was their best one ever."

"So, why shoot a cash cow in the head?" Jo asked. "The motivation has to be something other than money."

"I'd say so," McKinley agreed. "The decision to end the business would have fallen to its owner. The person who had the most power. And after Grant and Melissa died, their will and testament transferred those powers to..."

"Kari Cross," said Jo. "Their daughter."

McKinley grinned, taking a celebratory bite of fish. "Kari's the one who decided to dissolve Brickwall Group. And I have the full details of the procedure here. It looks like she went about it in a kindhearted way. After selling off most of the company's assets, she used the money from those sales to pay one last healthy bonus check to all the people who were losing their jobs."

"She wouldn't have needed all that money," said Jo. "From her parent's inheritance, she would have already had enough to live on forever. She just didn't want the hassle. She tried to make a clean break."

"She did her best," said McKinley. "The severance checks were paid out. Everyone went their separate ways. I don't think any of the previous employees of Brickwall Group would be mad enough to kidnap Kari. Especially not after more than three years have passed."

Jo nodded. "If we're going with the dissolution of the company as a motive, we would need to look at someone with a better reason for being mad at Kari."

"That brings us to Russo Shipping," McKinley added. "The company used by Brickwall Group for at least ninety percent of their shipping needs."

SEVENTY-TWO

"Let's lay this theory out," Jo said. "Kari shuts down Brickwall Group. This creates a big loss of business for Sal. Sal gets mad and decides to get even. But for some reason, he waits three and a half years to do it."

"And he uses his nephew," McKinley said. "I suppose it doesn't make a lot of sense. Do you want any of these fries?"

Jo shook her head. "It makes almost zero sense at the moment. The only thing I can buy is that Sal would be mad at Kari. Not only was Brickwall a moneymaker for him, but he was also friends with the owners. It could be a personal loss as well as a financial one."

McKinley was out of fish. But he still had tartar sauce left. He dunked his fries in it and munched them down.

"We just need to lay the rest of the groundwork," he said. "Clear away the fog. This *has* to be some way of getting back at Kari. Right?"

"It's at least the most likely explanation," Jo replied. "We're down to basic facts, here. I'd say we're onto something."

***

Jo and McKinley continued researching for the rest of the workday and beyond. Jo stayed later than she usually did. Drinking coffee and poring through old records. Hoping to find something that would bring the whole mystery together.

She didn't. And she started to get tired. The coffee wasn't doing the trick anymore. At about seven PM, she'd finally had enough.

"I'm going home, kid," she said to McKinley.

He sat back, rubbing his face. "Yeah, I'll probably head out too. I need to sleep on this. Maybe one of us will wake up with an epiphany."

"Maybe." Jo touched his shoulder. "Have a good night. Thanks for beating your head against the wall with me."

"That's what I'm paid for," he quipped.

Jo grabbed her coat and stepped away. Despite his words, McKinley remained at his desk. Knowing him, Jo decided he'd be there for another hour or two. He had a bone, and he wouldn't stop chewing it. Not until his eyes started closing of their own accord.

Jo headed home. It was a peaceful drive. Mostly devoid of traffic. The whole way, she was thinking about what she had in her freezer. A box of shrimp eggrolls, along with a bag of orange chicken. It would make a nice inauthentic Chinese meal. The dinner of champions.

She parked her car. Got out and walked up to her apartment door. She reached out with her key. Slid it into the lock.

She had no idea someone was already waiting inside. There were no cues for her subconscious to pick up on. Her intruder had made a clean entry. She yawned as she went inside. Her eyes squeezed shut.

The only thing running through her mind was the hot shower she would take while her food was in the oven.

A man sat on her living room chair, watching her come in.

SEVENTY-THREE

"What a day," Jo said with a sigh. She shut her door. Turned the dead-bolt. "Hmmm... do I still have that bottle of Riesling in the fridge?"

A glass of chilled white wine. A steaming hot shower. Right now, nothing sounded better. Other than finding Kari and catching the kidnapper, of course.

She hung her keys up by the door. Taking her jacket off, she dropped it on a hook. As Jo turned away from the door, she saw something startling.

On her kitchen counter, there was a framed photo of her and her late father. The living room was around the corner. A light was on in there. A floor lamp. She always left it turned on, for security purposes.

Now the light was reflecting on the glass over the photo. In that light, she could see a man sitting in her chair. The same chair she lounged in when she watched trashy TV late at night.

He was watching her. Staring at her in the reflection. She could only see his eyes. The rest of his face was covered with a black ski mask.

Jo froze. Her blood turned to ice water. She didn't know whether to run back outside or reach for her gun.

She decided to go for her gun.

He saw her do it.

"Do not," he ordered. His voice boomed around the corner. "I know where your family lives, Johanna Pullinger. Your brother and his wife. Their two beautiful children. I know they have been in danger before. A direct result of your line of work. But I promise they have never before been in *my* kind of danger."

He spoke with an accent. Something from Central America, maybe.

Jo lifted her hands. She held them out. Making sure he saw.

"Good," he said. "There is a table there. Just inside the door. I want you to place your gun on the table. Slowly."

Jo unsnapped her holster from her hip and set it on the table beside her. At the same time, she ran some calculations. Her apartment wasn't large. He could jump out of that chair and reach her in just a few seconds.

But he didn't have to reach her. He just had to get around the corner. Then he could shoot her. That would take only a second. Jo didn't see a gun but knew he must have one.

It might have been enough time to disengage the deadbolt and get out of the door. But she wasn't willing to gamble on it.

If all he wanted was to kill her, he could have been waiting just inside the door. Or outside. He could shoot her before she even knew he was there.

"What do you want?" Jo asked.

"To talk," he replied. "The gun is now safely stowed. You may enter the living room now."

Jo left her gun behind. It felt like leaving a part of her soul. She looked at the picture of her father as she passed. Seeking strength from him, as she had so many times in the past.

As always, it worked. She marched into the living room.

The man with the dark eyes gestured to another chair. "Sit down. Please."

Jo took a seat.

"Comfortable?" the man asked.

Jo shrugged. "This is the guest chair. I didn't splurge on it. You're sitting in *my* chair. That's the comfortable one."

He laughed. "You are a strong-willed person. I know little about you, but already you have my admiration. You would make a good quarry. A wonderful adversary."

"But you're not hunting me now," Jo said.

"No, I am not," he agreed. "Let us get to business, shall we?"

SEVENTY-FOUR

The man spoke about getting down to business. But he went silent after that. He looked around the apartment. Nodding at some things. Clicking his tongue at others. Judging Jo's choice of furniture and décor.

"You like sunflowers," he said finally. "And the color purple. That is what I am seeing."

"What I'm seeing is a guy with a lot of nerve," Jo fired back. "Am I supposed to figure out what you wanted to talk about? Or are you going to let me know?"

"You already know, Agent Pullinger," he said.

"No, I don't," she replied. Even though she was certain, she did.

He smiled. Crossing one leg over the other. That's when Jo saw his gun. A silenced 9mm pistol, tucked under his thigh.

"I am not a gentleman," he said. "My own mother would despise me, if she were still alive. I am not civilized, either. I am a predatory creature. A lion, escaped from the zoo. Like that lion, I hunt with purpose. Never do I kill anyone impulsively. But I enjoy every kill I make."

"You seem to think highly of yourself," said Jo.

"I simply know what I am." He shrugged, unfolding his legs. Covering the gun up again. "My name is Raul. I can tell you that because I am not afraid of you. Nor am I worried that the FBI can touch me. If I ever go down, it will be of my accord. It will be caused by a failing on my part."

"Then I wish you the worst of luck," said Jo.

On paper, she thought everything Raul said might seem comical. A small man desperately trying to sound scary. But listening to his voice, looking into his eyes, she believed it all. She knew he was exactly what he claimed to be.

An apex predator.

She tried not to show her trepidation. Getting out of this situation alive would require that she maintain her poise at all times. She had to be very careful.

Raul's mood changed. His voice dropped to a growling register. "You will tell me what I want to know. At the very least, you will answer my questions honestly. I will know if you are lying."

"You might not," said Jo. "My FBI training included courses on interrogation. Both as the interrogator and the one being interrogated. I know how to lie pretty well."

"Are you trying to taunt me?" he asked.

"No. I just want to make sure we both understand the situation. There's no room for any kind of misunderstanding."

He nodded. "How pragmatic of you. You saw my handiwork with Professor Leone. But he was an easy target. I have killed much more dangerous men in the past. Lords and barons. Presidents and their lovers."

"Are you freelance?" Jo asked. "Or are you working for somebody at the moment?"

"I will ask the questions now," he hissed. "You are looking for two people now. One of them is Kari Cross. The other is Peter Russo. I am also looking for these people. You will tell me where they are."

"That's an easy one," said Jo. "I have no idea where they are. If I did, I wouldn't still be looking."

"But you have leads," he went on. "You must know something. You only have to tell me what that something is. As soon as you do, I will leave. You will not be harmed."

"I don't know anything," Jo replied. "Not about where Kari and Peter are. I figured out that Peter is involved. That's all."

He clicked his tongue again. "That's not all. You are lying. Tell me everything. Or else my next stop will be your brother's house."

SEVENTY-FIVE

Jo's heart fluttered. She felt faint. There was an urge to press a hand to her chest. But she didn't want to look weak in front of this person.

He pulled his gun out. Pointed it at her face.

"Tell me," he said.

Jo took a deep breath. "I know Kari's parents were friends with Salvatore Russo. There's a connection that goes back decades. But I haven't made sense of any of it yet. I have no idea why Kari was kidnapped."

Raul smiled. He lowered his weapon.

"I see you are being truthful," he said. "Perhaps we will meet again soon, Agent Pullinger. There is no need to worry about your family. You can see I am being truthful as well."

She nodded. "No need to worry."

"Not at this moment, at least," he said. "Do not move until I am gone. Maybe you will wait even longer, if you're as smart as I believe."

Those were his last words. He got up and left the apartment in a hurry.

Jo stayed in her seat. She stared at the empty chair. At the impression left by Raul. The stuffing in the chair slowly reinflated. Taking its original shape. The impression was gone.

It took only ten seconds. In that short time, Jo ran through it all in her mind. If she chased after Raul, it was possible he would shoot her. But she wasn't thinking about that. She was thinking about Sam, Kim and the kids.

If it had only been Jo, she would have gone after him in a heartbeat. As soon as she heard the door shut, she would have been on her feet.

But her fear for her family made her hesitate.

If she let Raul go, he would keep his promise. Her family would be safe. At least until Jo gave him another reason to target them.

If she gave chase, one of two things would happen. She might fail, and he would get away. In that case, he would hunt her family in retaliation.

Or she would succeed. She would catch Raul and put him out of commission. He would never be a threat again.

Every second that passed, the chances of the second option happening shrank away. The chances she would fail went higher.

Jo silenced her fears. After the ten seconds went by, she stood up and ran for the door.

Her gun was still on the table. She grabbed it. Pulled it out of the holster as she opened the door.

Cold night air rushed in, swirling around her. A car drove by. The LED headlights were obnoxiously bright. Lighting everything up. Jo shaded her eyes and tried to get a look at the driver. It was a woman in her mid-twenties. Not the guy she was after.

Jo saw no sign of Raul.

Thinking better of the whole thing, she went back inside and called Grantham.

"Pullinger," he said. "What is it?"

"I was just paid a visit by the man who shot Professor Leone," she said. "His name is Raul. He spoke with a Central American accent. He's thinly built, about five-eight in height. I believe he has long hair and wears it in a ponytail."

"Okay. I'll make sure the right people are put on the task of finding him. Is he there now?'

"No, sir. He got away."

"All right. I can hear the worry in your voice, Jo. Are you safe? Do you need me to send someone to you?"

"I'm safe," she confirmed. "I don't need backup. But I'm not sure I want to sleep at my apartment tonight."

"Then get a hotel," Grantham advised. "And don't hesitate to contact me if you need anything. I don't care if you wake me out of a dead sleep. Even if I'm right in the middle of my favorite dream."

"I appreciate that, sir. Thank you. But I think I'll be fine until tomorrow."

SEVENTY-SIX

Raul moved fast. He slipped out through Agent Pullinger's door. He shut the door softly behind him. Then he sprinted across the road. Slipping into the shadows between two buildings. He crouched behind a parked car and waited. Dropping to his belly, he peered under the car to watch the street.

Bright headlights flooded the street. Raul squinted as they sliced past him.

Agent Pullinger's door opened again. She took a step out. Her right hand was behind her back. Hiding her gun from any civilians who might be in the area. Her eyes flicked from side to side. Scanning the street.

Raul smiled. She had come after him almost immediately. A small delay. There was plenty of intelligence in her. She was thoughtful. Like Raul, she was deliberate in her actions.

But she was not a coward. Not like so many law enforcement agents Raul had faced in his years. Perhaps, at last, he had found a proper enemy. Someone he could have some real fun with.

Pullinger proved her intellect once again as she stepped back inside, shutting the door. She decided not to chase after him. A smart idea. It would not end well for her. Or her loved ones.

Raul waited a moment. Once the car with the bright lights was gone, he stood up and walked away.

When he reached the next street, he pulled his mask off and shoved it into his pocket. He reached into his jacket, sliding his pistol into a shoulder holster. He turned his jacket inside out and put it back on. It was reversible and looked good either way he wore it.

Two more streets over, Raul found his car. It was parked outside a very busy bar. No one would notice it or remember it the next day.

He drove away and called his boss.

"Raul!" Sal exclaimed. "Perfect timing. I've got news, and I was waiting until you called back to give it to you. But first..."

"The meeting with Agent Pullinger went well," said Raul. "She has made the connection between you and the Cross family."

Sal sighed. "That was inevitable. I wish it took her a little longer, but still. I ain't worried. Anything else?"

"She doesn't know where Kari or Peter are. And I have put the fear in her. She will be more hesitant going forward. Perhaps she will even lose her nerve and give up the chase. If not..."

"You'll take her out," said Sal. "There's no need to go after those kids, Raul. That was just a threat, right?"

"I will follow your orders," Raul replied.

"Good," Sal said, relieved. "Now, back to what I was talking about. Remember the plan I told you about earlier? The one that'll help us get Peter?"

"It wasn't much of a plan," Raul replied with a grunt. "You wanted to wait for Peter to make contact."

"It was a backup, all right? Something to bank on in case you couldn't track him down. I'm sure you could, if you had another day or two. No question about it. But there's no need. He called me just a little while ago."

"How did he make the call?" Raul asked.

"He borrowed a stranger's cell phone. I already checked out the number. Anyway, Peter had a moment of weakness. I believe he's starting to doubt whatever idiotic plan he came up with. He wants to meet with me. Talk things through. He gave me a time and a place."

Raul laughed. "Excellent. Give the details to me, Sal. I'll be there to pick him up."

SEVENTY-SEVEN

Jo did not sleep well. The first night in a new spot was never restful. Not even when it was a cozy hotel less than five blocks from her apartment.

She tossed and turned. Waking often to check the time. Trying to determine when to call it quits on this whole trying-to-sleep thing. Once five o'clock hit, she decided that was enough.

She showered. Scrubbing herself with one of those puny hotel soap bars. She scrubbed longer than usual, scraping at her skin until it turned red. Trying to wash away the memory of last night.

It didn't work. By the time she got out of the shower, she felt clean but just as confused as before. She took her time getting dressed. There was no rush. At the earliest, Grantham usually got to work at around six.

She waited until a quarter past. Then she finally headed out. No need to stop for breakfast. Her stomach was already in knots, thinking about what she was about to do. Her parents had always told her it wasn't shameful to quit, just so long as you were doing it for the right reasons.

Jo didn't head straight for the office. She cruised around for a while. Thinking but getting nowhere. It didn't seem like there was any other option, but that didn't make it any easier.

Finally, she went to work.

Part of her was hoping Grantham wouldn't be in yet. Then she could delay this painful moment a bit longer. But the hope was moot. When Jo asked his receptionist, she said Grantham had arrived half an hour ago.

She went up to his door and knocked. She took a deep breath.

"Come in," Grantham called.

Jo entered.

"Pullinger." Grantham got up from his chair. He came around the desk and held Jo by the shoulders. "Don't take this the wrong way, but you look like crap."

"Didn't sleep much," said Jo.

"Sit down," he urged, guiding her to a chair. Once she was seated, he went back to his own seat. "I could tell when you called me last night, Jo. It was in your voice. This rattled you. I don't know why. You're usually as solid as a battleship hull. What's different?"

"He threatened my family," Jo replied. "And it was different this time because I knew he would do it. I knew he would have *fun* doing it."

Grantham nodded. "So, we're dealing with a real peach. But nothing has changed. Your family will always be a weak point that can be exploited by bad people. You just have to catch this guy, so he can't make good on any threats."

Jo shook her head. "Respectfully, sir, you don't know what I'm feeling right now."

He gave her a deep stare. "Actually, I do. But I'm not going to dig up old stories. This meeting is about you. What's on your mind? For God's sake, you're not thinking about turning in your shield, are you?"

"No, sir," Jo replied. "I just want off this case. This is one for a younger agent. Someone without so many ties."

"Someone with less to lose," Grantham said.

Jo nodded. "It's not just that I'm worried about my family. I'm also worried about my ability to perform. I had a chance to nab Raul last night, but I hesitated. It was only a few seconds, but it made the difference."

"I see." Grantham looked away. He shuffled some papers around. "Jo, you're a human being. Not a cyborg. Everyone makes mistakes. I'm confident that if you had a second chance at this guy, you would do it better. But if you want off the case, I won't try and talk you out of it."

"You kind of just did," Jo said. "But thank you, sir."

He shrugged. "No harm in trying. An agent of your caliber doesn't come along very often. Don't tell anyone I said this, but I can see you in my position. Years from now, of course. After I'm finally past my prime and have decided to retire."

Jo gave him a smile and an appreciative nod. "That won't be a for a long time, sir. I'll probably have aged out of the job by then."

He cocked a finger at her. "That kind of kissing up can get you far, Pullinger. I'll try and find some lighter work for you to do. But I'm not going to rush. Something tells me you'll be begging to be back on this case before long."

Jo left the room, letting him hold onto that illusion. Grantham was usually right about these things... but this time, Jo was anything but certain.

SEVENTY-EIGHT

Peter arrived at the meeting place early. He couldn't help it. He tried to take his time walking from the condemned house. But his nervous energy drove him on until he started moving at a fast jog.

He stood in front of the place, catching his breath. It was a small Korean restaurant. Situated halfway down a steep hill, it was easy to miss. And hard to figure out how to get into. But Peter wasn't going inside.

He'd never had Korean food before. It smelled really good. An intriguing mix of spicy and sweet aromas. The people who walked out after eating sure looked happy.

If I'm still alive after today, maybe I'll put this place on my bucket list.

When he set up the meeting with Sal, he hadn't chosen the place based on its cuisine. Nor had he picked it for the view. Though it was a lovely one, across the water. He could see all the way to West Seattle from here.

He had been a bit out of it when he chose the venue. He wanted to double-check. His phone was in his pocket. It had been turned off ever since he broke into Kari's house. Now that his uncle already knew where he'd be, Peter decided it was safe to use it again.

He turned the phone on. He opened his maps app and looked around to confirm his plan. The FBI field office was close by. All he had to do was go up the hill, turn a corner, and head over a couple of blocks.

It was his backup plan. Sal thought he was stupid. So did Raul. And maybe he was. But this time, he'd thought things through.

He kept his phone on to check the time. Then he paced in front of the restaurant for a while. Someone tried to give him money, thinking he was homeless. He thanked them and turned them away.

Finally, he saw a familiar car approaching.

It was just as he feared. This was not his uncle's car. Salvatore Russo would not be caught dead in this boxy '90s sedan.

It was Raul.

Peter tensed up. He looked around. There was no one on the sidewalk. No one to help him. And why would anyone help him anyway?

The sedan pulled up tight against the curb. The window rolled down. Raul smiled.

"Lovely to see you this morning, Peter," he said. "You should get in the car now."

"Where's my uncle?" Peter asked forcefully.

Raul's smile turned wolfish. "You are not in a position to make any kind of demand, young man. You want to make amends, yes? You have a chance. But the chance dies as soon as I drive away. You have five seconds."

Raul lifted his wrist. He flicked his watch, one strike for each second that passed. Tap. Tap. Tap. Tap...

SEVENTY-NINE

"All right!" Peter tugged the passenger door open and got inside. He buckled his seatbelt. "God, this is stupid. I shouldn't be in this car with you."

He glanced longingly at the rearview mirror. His route to the FBI office stood behind him now. As soon as Raul started driving, his backup plan would dwindle.

"Or perhaps it's the smartest choice you've ever made?" Raul offered.

"I doubt it," Peter said.

Raul laughed. He pulled into traffic and started driving. Raul drove like an old lady. Always five under the speed limit. Taking great care and hesitating before every turn. Peter appreciated that fact now. More time was never a bad thing.

"Can't you tell me where my uncle is?" he asked.

"Do you know where I found this car?" Raul asked. "At the end of someone's driveway. In Bremerton. It was right after your uncle hired me. I took the ferry from Bainbridge to Seattle. Then from Seattle to Bremerton. I brought cash with me and used it to buy a used car. And I've been driving it since then. It's a good car."

"No, it isn't," Peter said with a grunt. "It's a piece of junk that's older than I am."

Raul went on, unbothered. "That is how I move around, Peter. Leaving no trace of myself. When I am hired and have to move to a new place, I find a used car and buy it with cash. I drive carefully so as to get no tickets. When it's time to move on, I clean the car well and abandon it somewhere with the keys inside. Usually, someone steals it, and it becomes their problem."

"I guess that answers a couple of questions I had," Peter replied. "But not the big one. So, what's the deal?"

"I am trying to give you a lesson," Raul hissed. "An important lesson that would have served you well. But now, we may be reaching a point of no return. Your uncle is waiting for you at home. I will take you there. And the two of you will have a productive discussion, man to man."

Peter looked at Raul. The evil grin, the inhuman eyes. He had sensed danger the day he first met this man. Now his alarm bells were blaring so loudly he'd have to be dead not to hear them.

Peter was not going to have a productive discussion. He was going to be tied to a chair and interrogated. Whether he lived or not would be up to him. How much he wanted to give away.

Either way, the last place he wanted to be was inside this car.

He glanced at his door. He saw that Raul had not locked the doors.

It was an escape route.

Raul saw him looking. He stepped on the gas, breaking his own rules of driving. The car sped through an intersection, accelerating faster and faster.

Raul slid his hand into his jacket, reaching for his gun.

Peter unbuckled his seatbelt. He shoved the door open. The wind nearly pushed it shut again. With a final glance back at his uncle's hitman, he tossed himself out.

He seemed to hang in the air forever. His momentum caused him to keep gliding along the street. It was sloped downward, meaning he stayed in the air even longer. Watching the white painted lines flashing past.

He heard screeching brakes. Raul forcing his car to stop.

Then Peter hit the ground.

EIGHTY

Jo walked to her desk with her head hanging. She felt like a failure. But that was just the emotional side. Logically, she felt she had done the right thing.

Nothing was more important than protecting those who could not protect themselves.

She stopped by the breakroom for a caffeine fix. The pot was empty. She sighed as she poured in water for a fresh batch. Nothing was going well this morning. She kept expecting to feel a weight lifting off her shoulders. It didn't happen.

The coffee started to brew. The pot gurgled and steamed as it filled up. Jo continually resisted the urge to pour herself a cup. She waited for it to be done, yawning and wavering on her feet.

She wondered what kind of work Grantham would find for her. Knowing him, it would probably be something dreadfully boring. Data entry. Archival work. Something she'd get sick of in five minutes and go running back to him to reverse her decision.

He would be proven right. And he'd get one of his best agents back.

Thoughts of Kari entered her mind. She pushed them away. Along with feelings of guilt.

At last, the coffee was done. She filled a cup and carried it back to her desk. She was glad to see McKinley wasn't in yet. She could put off the task of telling him she had given up the case.

Jo heard a sudden commotion in the lobby. Shouting voices. Something about calling an ambulance.

Jo set her coffee down and ran toward the noise.

The glass doors were smeared with blood. A man was lying face down on the floor. His clothes were shredded, and he was bleeding from a few nasty wounds. To Jo, they looked like road rash. Multiple layers of skin scraped away.

There was also a gash on his head. It was bleeding worse than the other wounds combined. Whoever this guy was, he was in bad shape.

Agent Larkin was there. She was at the reception desk, using the phone there to call for help.

"Yes, the FBI office," she said. "Some kid just ran in here. Looks like he's hurt badly. We need an ambulance here *now*."

Jo took a step closer to the fallen man. He looked to be of an average build. He had dark hair. When he heard her approach, he turned his head. Staring at her with fearful eyes.

"Peter Russo," Jo gasped.

He got his hands under him, pushing himself off the floor. Jo crouched beside him, putting a hand on his back.

"Stay down," Jo urged. "Take it easy. There's an ambulance on the way. You'll be fine."

"Agent Pullinger," he said weakly. "You have to help me. He's coming after me. He wants to take me somewhere and hurt me. Please!"

He lost his strength. He fell back down, passing out.

Jo looked up. The lobby was filling up with spectators. Grantham arrived, parting the sea with his powerful arms.

"Make way, people," he shouted. "Get out of the way!"

He broke through, gazing down at Jo. "Agent Pullinger. Do you know this man?"

She nodded. "Sir, this is Peter Russo. Our prime suspect in the kidnapping of Kari Cross. He just asked for my help."

Grantham raised an eyebrow. "What are you going to do?"

"I'm going to give it to him," she vowed.

EIGHTY-ONE

Jo waited beside Peter until the ambulance came. She took a step back, letting the EMTs work. They performed a quick check, then brought in a stretcher. They loaded Peter onto it and wheeled him outside.

Jo followed them to the ambulance.

"Which hospital is he going to?" she asked.

"Virginia Mason," a medic told her.

"I need to be present for any paperwork," Jo said. "This is a high-priority patient. I'll be right behind you."

She found her car in the garage and drove out onto the main street. As soon as the ambulance put on its siren and took off, she fell in right behind it. She blew through every red light on the short trip to Virginia Mason.

Jo parked and jumped out of her car. She stayed six feet back, shadowing the movement of the medics. They wasted no time, running Peter inside and straight back into the emergency ward.

***

At first, it was a flurry of activity. Jo wanted to be certain that Peter was safe. She personally filled every piece of paperwork for him, using an alias on each one. For now, Peter Russo was going by the name Simon Beaumont.

Once that was done, Jo sat in the waiting room. And did exactly what the room was designed for. She did some waiting. A whole lot of it. Grantham called her once. So did McKinley. She told them what she knew, which wasn't much.

Peter was unconscious. He wouldn't be spilling any beans until he woke up. The best thing for Jo to do was stay here. That way, she'd be ready as soon as he was.

A doctor found her after more than an hour. His name was Dr. Pavel.

"Good to meet you, Agent Pullinger," he said. "You're here with Mr. Beaumont? Under what capacity?"

"The official kind," said Jo.

"Ah... I see." Dr. Pavel looked furtively around the waiting room. "Then I won't waste any time. Mr. Beaumont is going to be just fine. After some recovery time, that is. He has a rather serious concussion. We were able to stitch up his head wound and stop the bleeding there. But his other wounds... he may require skin grafts."

"Is he awake?" Jo asked.

"Somewhat," Dr. Pavel answered. "His concussion... not to mention the pain medication... he is still quite foggy."

"Then I wonder if I could go back and speak with him. I wouldn't ask if it wasn't urgent, Doctor. Innocent lives may depend on what he knows."

Dr. Pavel sighed. "Come with me."

He led her through the back halls of the hospital. Into an elevator and up two floors. They walked down more hallways and finally ended up outside a room. It was one of many on this floor. The corridor was lined with them.

"He's already out of the emergency room," Jo observed. "That's a good sign."

"He's in no immediate peril," Dr. Pavel agreed. "Go on inside, Agent Pullinger. But I can't promise he'll be of much help in his current state. If you'll excuse me..."

He wandered away, signaling to a nearby male nurse. Letting him know Peter had a visitor.

Jo opened the door and went inside, praying her suspect was lucid enough to talk.

EIGHTY-TWO

It was a large room. Full of shadows and medicinal smells. There was only one bed in it, jutting out from the wall. Peter lay on it. His mouth hung open, and his eyes looked groggy.

Jo shut the door and cleared her throat. Peter glanced toward her. He blinked twice. Then his eyes went wide.

"Agent Pullinger," he said.

"Peter," she replied. "May I come closer?"

He nodded. Jo walked up to the bed. Peter looked a lot better than he had in the FBI lobby. The blood had been cleaned off him. His road rash wounds were bandaged up. None of the damaged skin was exposed.

"How are you feeling?" Jo asked.

He grinned. "Like I'm doped up. Do I look like it?"

"You do look a little loopy," Jo agreed. "If you say no to my next question, I'll leave immediately and come back in a little while. Are you able to answer my questions?"

He nodded.

"First of all, can you tell me what happened to you?" Jo asked.

"I jumped out of a car that was going pretty fast," he replied. "Raul was driving."

"You know Raul?"

"He works for my uncle. My uncle sent him to pick me up. I never should have tried to set up that meeting." Peter tried to sit up, coughing.

"Just lay back," said Jo.

"No, he's coming after me!" Peter cried.

"He's not." Jo put a hand in the middle of his chest. Forcing him back down. "You're here under an alias. I made sure of that. You're safe."

Peter frowned. "He'll find me."

"Eventually, he might," said Jo. "But for now, you're fine. I'll stay close by."

He nodded. "Then I guess we need to start worrying about Kari."

"Where is she?" Jo demanded. "Is she all right?"

Peter winced. "Yeah, but she's in a rough part of town. She won't stay safe for long if someone doesn't go and get her."

His eyelids fluttered. His head went limp. He was drifting off into a stupor.

"Peter, stay with me for just another minute," said Jo.

His eyes snapped open again. "My uncle... I had to do it. Otherwise, she would have died. If I went to the cops, then we *both* would have died..."

"Tell me," said Jo. "What's going on? I need to know."

"I needed to get her away on the sly," Peter rambled on. "Brickwall Group..."

"What about them?"

"They had a deal worked out with my uncle. Not really a deal. More like a pact. Yeah. They signed their souls away. They helped my uncle's company smuggle things. Hiding them in the stuff they manufactured. They both got rich off it."

"Grant and Melissa Cross?" Jo asked. "Kari's parents?"

Peter nodded. "I never met them, but I knew everything. When Kari dissolved the company, the pact was broken. A debt had to be paid. My uncle's a very patient man. And he still has some kind of soul. He waited."

"Why?"

"Because Kari's grandmother... she lost her son and her daughter-in-law in the car accident. My uncle knew her. He has a soft spot for her. He didn't want to do anything to Kari. Not while her grandmother was still alive."

Jo nodded. "I see. So, when the call came in that Kari's grandmother died, you knew your uncle was going to spring into action."

"She was old," Peter whispered. "It was only a matter of time. I just had to be quicker than he was."

Jo felt goosebumps rising on her arms. "You were trying to save Kari. If I hadn't been at that rest area, everything would have been fine. But I forced you into a backup plan. And now we're all in this mess together."

EIGHTY-THREE

"That was bad luck," Peter said. "For both of us. My uncle had business connections in Mexico. *Had*. He made them angry. They would have helped me get one over on him."

"They could have made a new life for Kari," said Jo. "You would have gone back to Seattle like nothing happened. It would have been like Kari disappeared into thin air in the middle of nowhere in Oregon."

"That was the idea," Peter said with a grunt. "My hope was that my uncle would just assume she caught on that her life was in danger. And she decided to make herself scarce."

Jo pulled out her phone. She selected one of her contacts but waited to dial. "I need to know where Kari is now. An address. Or whatever you can tell me."

Peter propped himself up on one elbow. He looked delirious. His tongue darted in and out of his mouth as he tried to talk. Finally, he summoned the words. He gave her the name of a street, along with two simple words; *condemned house.*

That was all Jo needed. "I'll be back. I just need to step into the hall and get Kari some help."

She hurried out of the door, shutting it. She looked around. When she first went inside, Dr. Pavel had signaled for a nurse to keep an eye on things. There was no sign of that nurse now. The corridor was abandoned.

Jo thought that was weird. But there was too much else to worry about. She pushed it out of her mind and hit the call button on her phone.

"Ford Investigative Solutions. Dessie speaking," a bubbly voice answered.

"It's Jo Pullinger again," Jo said.

"You need to speak with Mr. Ford?" Dessie replied. "I'll transfer you to him right away."

Hold music played for a fraction of a second. Then Ford answered.

"Jo, I told that joke of yours to the wife and kid," he said. "And I got the opposite of what I was expecting. Kelly laughed her head off, and Hazel almost puked. But enough about my daughter's gag reflex. What's new with you?'

"I know where Kari Cross is," she said.

There was a brief silence. A creaking sound as Ford collapsed forward on his chair. He pulled his feet off the desk, and they thudded down on the floor.

"Where?" he asked.

Jo gave him the directions.

"I know the place exactly," he said. "I was just at a house across the street, dragging someone's son out of a drug den. That's a scary place. Is someone there with her?"

"No," said Jo. "That's why I'm calling you. I'm already busy with something. I need to stay put."

"Why not ask another agent to do it?" asked Ford. "Or the Seattle police?"

"Because I trust you," Jo replied. "I know you'll get the job done. And I thought you might like the idea of saving a young woman's life after what happened in Lapse."

He sighed. "You know me too well. All right, I'll head over there. But I'll be billing the FBI for my services."

"Thanks, Ford," she said, relieved. "I'll send McKinley over to back you up. I would send him alone, but he's still shaken up after…"

"After what happened in Lapse," Ford repeated. "I welcome the company, but I'm not going to wait for him. I'm getting Kari out of there as soon as I can."

EIGHTY-FOUR

Dessie Archer was having a rare experience. She was actually bored at work. Usually, she was fielding an unending series of phone calls. Turning clients away because Ford simply had too much work already. When she wasn't doing that, she was thinking of subtle ways to hint that he should hire another PI to help him.

Today, though, nothing was going on.

Not until Jo Pullinger called. It wasn't often a little investigative firm like this was contacted by the FBI. But Dessie didn't think of Jo that way. She was a friend of the family, so to speak. Ford had regaled Dessie with all the stories.

Jo Pullinger was a hero and a damn good agent.

After she connected Jo to Ford, Dessie sneaked over toward his office door. She listened, trying to catch a hint of the conversation.

It was something about a dangerous place. Someone that Ford needed to go and get. In other words, it wasn't much different from what he did on an ordinary day.

Dessie waited for the telltale clicking sound that meant Ford had hung up his phone. Then she knocked at the door. He called for her to come in.

She entered. As soon as she saw her boss, she knew something was different about this call. It was personal. He was moving fast, switching from his stiff office shoes to a pair of runners. He shucked his suit jacket and discarded his tie.

"Is everything all right, Bryan?" Dessie asked.

"Just have to go rescue a kidnapped girl who's locked up in a dirty basement," he replied. "Last time I had to do that, it didn't turn out very well."

"How so?" Dessie asked.

"Jo, McKinley, and I almost died," Ford replied with a grunt.

"Oh. You're talking about Lapse again. Please don't die, Bryan. I like my job a lot."

"So do I." He grinned. "Don't worry. I've been through so much crap that I'm almost starting to think I'm invincible. If anyone calls for me, tell them I'm out saving the world."

He hurried past her, leaving the building. Slamming the door shut with a bang.

"It won't be too far from the truth," Dessie said with a smile. She looked around at her boss's office. He didn't have too much clutter in here. Just a picture on his desk of his wife and daughter. Ford himself wasn't even in it.

He was a man who worried about others more than he thought about himself. He was a good person. Truly selfless. Dessie felt very proud to be working for him. When she first took this job, she thought it would just be a fun way to get some experience.

But now it was turning into a passion. Something she could keep doing for the rest of her life.

EIGHTY-FIVE

Ford had just been at the condemned house. He followed the route by heart. Hardly paying attention to the road. He spent the whole drive worrying about Kari. Wondering if she was all right. If someone else had already beaten him to her.

When he arrived outside the pitiful, decaying house, he saw there was already a car there. With a young, lanky guy standing beside it. Wearing a very nice suit that didn't fit him quite right.

It was Agent Lewis McKinley. Ford smiled. The kid still had a thing or two to learn about keeping his cool under pressure, but he was nothing if not dependable.

Ford parked his car and got out. "McKinley! I told Jo I wasn't going to wait for you."

"I know," McKinley replied. "She relayed that information to me. Which is why I got here as fast as I could."

"Good man." Ford gestured at the house. "Have you ever seen such a depressing sight in your life?"

McKinley shrugged. "You're not my therapist, so I don't feel obligated to answer that. But it seems like a good place to hide a kidnap victim. No one would ever bother looking here."

Ford stood with his hands on his hips. Giving the place a long look. "Doesn't look like we can get in through the front. Maybe the back?"

McKinley gestured onward. "I'll follow you."

"Of course," Ford said with a sigh. "Make the old guy take point. Kids these days."

The stench of the rotting house surrounded it like a cloud. There were layers to it. Getting thicker the closer they got. It was like a punch to the nasal cavity. Mold, mildew, and the ammonia of animal waste. And maybe a bit of the human kind, too.

Ford pulled his shirt up over his mouth. "Might be able to get this place for cheap, but it'd cost about a million bucks in renovations."

"Cheaper to rent a bulldozer," McKinley added.

They made their way along the weed-choked side alley, coming out behind the house. Through the collapsing fence, they could see into an alleyway. There was a car parked there. A boxy old sedan. But Ford didn't see anyone inside.

He was on high alert. But so far, he didn't sense any reason to be afraid.

There was only one obvious way of getting into the house. A broken window at the back. It led into one of the only bottom-floor rooms that wasn't currently occupied by a collapsed room from the floor above.

In the grime on the windowsill, they could see a set of smeared handprints.

"This is how Peter was getting in and out," McKinley said.

"If it's good enough for him..." Ford shrugged, jumping up and hauling himself through.

McKinley came in after. They looked around for a bit.

"Used to be a kitchen," Ford said. "Now it's a black-mold factory. Jo said Kari was in the basement. I bet that's the door there."

They slowly descended the basement steps with their weapons drawn. The room they entered was damp and smelly but in surprisingly good shape compared to the rest of the house.

They didn't see Kari.

McKinley pointed toward the back corner. There was a wall separating off a small section of the basement. "Maybe she's in there."

Ford narrowed his eyes. "This seems too easy. Why don't you hang back here? And stay out of sight. Just watch my back."

McKinley nodded. He moved off to the side, hiding in a hollow space under the steps. He hunkered down into the shadows.

Ford now felt safe to approach the back room. As he got close, he heard a soft whimpering from within. It turned into full-on shouting as soon as he came into view.

Kari was there. On a mattress, chained to a radiator. There was a thick rag tied around her mouth. Her screams were not of fear but relief. Just to make sure she knew she was safe, Ford showed her his PI credentials.

"I'm going to get you out of here," Ford said. "But it's going to take me a moment to get you free. Just hold on."

He grabbed onto the radiator. Putting one foot on the wall, he yanked back with all his might. The pipe broke free from the wall with a cracking sound. Ford grabbed the chain, snaking it around the radiator fins and finally pulling it off the broken pipe.

Kari was free. But Ford's relief died as soon as he heard footsteps in the weeds outside. He looked toward the top of the wall. At one of the narrow windows.

Someone else was here.

EIGHTY-SIX

Raul had a busy morning.

It all started to change when Peter jumped out of the car. Raul looked into the rearview mirror. Watching Peter sail through the air. He felt a surge of anger at first. A desire to kill. But logic prevailed.

He realized that Peter had some kind of plan. Maybe the best course of action was to let him follow that plan. And follow *him* in return.

So that was what Raul did.

He hit the brakes, stopping hard. Then he drove forward again. He turned the next corner. Followed the block around. He fell into the flow of traffic. In the distance, he saw Peter stumbling down the street. People glanced at him in surprise. Some tried to help. Peter shook them off.

He was on a mission. Trying to get somewhere.

Raul looked at the map on his phone. He found his location and followed Peter's trajectory. It was obvious where he was going.

The FBI building. It was only two blocks away from the Korean restaurant. Raul smiled.

Peter wasn't dumb, after all. Nor was he smart enough to avoid what was coming.

It was all quite easy after that. Raul parked down the street from the FBI building and waited. An ambulance came. He watched Agent Pullinger come outside. She got in her car and followed the ambulance.

Raul followed them both. As soon as he realized what hospital they were going to, he sped around them on side streets. He wanted to get there ahead of them.

At the hospital, he parked in a secluded spot. He opened his trunk and rummaged through a duffel bag. It was full of disguises. He found his nurse outfit and changed into it. Making sure to tuck his ponytail up inside the surgical cap.

Just in time to hear the scream of approaching sirens.

Raul hurried to the front of the hospital. He fell in with the medics who were bringing Peter inside. He walked right along beside Agent Pullinger. She never looked at him. She had no idea he was there.

But he didn't stay with her for long.

There was a set of double doors at the edge of the waiting room. They flapped in and out as people came and went. The hardest part of infiltrating a hospital was getting past those doors.

When the EMTs wheeled Peter through, Raul stayed glued to them. He got inside. No one shouted at him. No one asked to see any kind of credentials. He was through. Now he could move about the hospital at will.

And so he did. He waited until Peter was out of the emergency room. He made sure he knew what room Peter was in.

He was after the same information as Pullinger was. All he had to do now was wait. He lingered in the area, wandering around. Finally, Pullinger arrived with Dr. Pavel.

A lucky thing happened. Dr. Pavel waved at Raul. Signaling him to stay put and keep an eye on the visitor. Raul nodded and posted himself outside the door as Pullinger went in.

He listened.

When he heard where Kari was being kept, he left straight away. He knew it wouldn't be long before Pullinger headed over or sent someone else so that she could keep an eye on Peter. He was hoping for the former.

Raul got back in his car, feeling that luck was on his side. That feeling changed a bit when he got stuck in traffic on his way over. He had picked the wrong route. He made it to the condemned house several minutes later than he wanted.

He parked in the alley behind the condemned house. He stepped behind a stone wall, hiding as he changed back into more appropriate attire. After that, he headed down the alley. Trying to get a vantage point so he could watch for Pullinger.

He might as well kill two birds with one stone. He had given her a chance to walk away. She had not taken it.

Suddenly, Kari began to scream. Raul rushed back toward the condemned house. Someone else was already inside. He acted fast, getting himself into position.

EIGHTY-SEVEN

Ford held a finger to his lips. Kari held her breath, staring with wide eyes.

They listened.

The footsteps stopped for a bit. Then they came again, moving away. Fading into the distance. Toward the back of the house. The same direction Ford needed to go. Not a good sign.

He checked for other ways out. There were none. There were a half dozen windows, but they all had bars on them. Wide enough to stick an arm through, but that was all.

"Can you walk?" Ford asked.

Kari pulled her gag down. "If it means I get to leave this dump, I could probably sprout wings and fly. Are you with Agent Pullinger?"

"She sent me here," Ford confirmed.

Kari smiled. "I knew she'd find me."

"Whoa, let's not give her *all* the credit," Ford replied. "Here's what we're going to do, Kari. See those stairs?"

Kari crawled to the side so she could see beyond the dividing walls. "Yeah. Who's that guy lurking under them?"

McKinley waved.

"He's an FBI agent," Ford said. "He's with me. If anything happens, do not call out for him. Pretend like he isn't there."

"You don't want whoever's out there to know you're not alone," she said.

"You're a smart kid. Now stay behind me. Not too close, though. In case I need to make a sudden move. We're going for those stairs."

Kari nodded. Ford led the way.

They hurried across the basement toward the steps. Ford signaled McKinley to stay put.

The door at the bottom of the steps was still hanging open. Sunlight shone down through the ruined roof. To Ford, it looked more like a false promise than a beacon of hope.

But there was no other choice.

He took a step up. Beginning to climb the stairs.

There was a shadow on the wall. He didn't know it was there until it moved. He looked up the stairs. Saw someone there, darting across the doorway.

Then the shooting started.

Ford felt bullets flying past. Dust from the wall hitting his face. With one hand, he shoved Kari further back. He raised his gun and returned fire.

It all happened fast. He didn't get a good look at the person he was shooting at. He had no idea if any of his bullets hit their mark.

Suddenly, the shooting stopped.

Ford retreated, stumbling backward. The adrenaline wore off. He started to feel the pain. It felt cold and sharp at first, then became dull and hot. Throbbing.

He looked down. Blood was raining from his left hand. Speckling the floor. He looked himself up and down. He had been shot twice. Both in the left arm. One bullet grazed his shoulder. A superficial wound. The other landed in his bicep. He could still feel the bullet in there. A hot lump in his flesh.

"Crap," Ford groaned.

The first thing he thought of was Kelly. She was going to be furious. He could already hear her admonishing voice. *What's the one thing I tell you before you go to work each morning, Bryan? Don't get shot!*

Ford went to one knee. He scuttled to the side until he hit the wall. Bracing himself against it as he continued to bleed. He aimed his gun at the steps and waited.

EIGHTY-EIGHT

Raul ran out of bullets in his clip. The person down below was not Jo Pullinger, but they were still a good shot. And a difficult target. Or perhaps the angles were just bad. Either way, Raul didn't feel confident he had landed a killing shot.

He ran to the side. Diving out through the window. He hit the ground and rolled gracefully onto his feet. From there, he dashed through the broken fence. Into the alleyway.

He popped the trunk of his car open. Inside, he tossed the duffel bag of disguises to the side. Beneath it was a first aid kit. Raul brought it to the driver's seat. He left the door propped open, watching the house as he tended to his wound.

A bullet had grazed his ear. It was bleeding terribly. Raul felt ashamed of the wound. It had been a long time since one of his targets managed to hurt him.

The pain didn't bother him, however. It was a human sensation, best ignored.

He found a gauze pad in the first aid kit. He folded it around his injured ear. Squeezing tightly to stop the bleeding. He took a deep breath and turned the radio on. One of his favorite classic rock songs was playing. It calmed him.

Someone would have heard the shooting. Whether they actually called the cops was a different story. In this neighborhood, they might decide it was better not to be involved at all.

Even if they did call the cops, they would be slow to arrive. No one was in a hurry to come to this place. Not even the Seattle PD.

Raul guessed he had between fifteen and twenty minutes to seal the deal here and get away with Kari. After that, he might have to contend with the police. He didn't want to do that. Too messy. Too time-consuming.

There was now a clock hanging over his head. He felt its pressure. But he knew the person in the basement was feeling it even more. Raul knew he had landed at least one shot. Maybe two. They were down there now, bleeding. Feeling desperate.

It wouldn't be long before they acted. On the other hand, it might be better to force them into action. Raul held all the cards right now. The fate of everyone here was in his hands.

He switched out the bloody gauze pad for a fresh one. He watched the house, trying to make up his mind.

EIGHTY-NINE

Ford was happy about the presence of the wall. He felt himself sagging into it. Letting it take his weight. His strength was leaving him. Flowing out with every drop of blood.

The bleeding wasn't getting faster. But it wasn't slowing down. It was a constant drip. Like a leaky faucet. Ford tried not to think about it. He kept his eye on the stairs.

McKinley tried to come out and help him. Ford gave him a death stare until he withdrew into his hiding spot.

"Kari?" Ford called, looking around. "Where'd you go?"

He saw a hand sticking out from behind a brick pillar.

"Here," she said.

There was another pillar eight feet from the one she was using. Ford headed that way, staying low in case he collapsed. But he made it, tucking himself behind the pillar. Now he was outside the line of sight through any of the windows.

Safe for the moment.

He could see Kari now, too. And she could see him. She looked shocked.

"You're hurt," she said.

Ford nodded. "Not the first time I've been shot. It's been years, though. It's definitely *not* like riding a bike."

"I'm sorry," Kari cried.

"Don't mention it."

Ford's upper lip was wet. He licked it. Thankfully, it just tasted like sweat. No secret head wound he was unaware of. He leaned out from behind the pillar, aiming at the stairs again.

"I'm going to keep covering the steps," Ford called. "Can you make your way to me?"

Kari darted across the floor. She whimpered in fear, shrinking from the threat of flying bullets. She reached Ford's pillar safely, pressing herself against it.

"Here," she said.

"Good," Ford replied. "My phone is in my back pocket. Can you pull it out? Go to my contacts list. It's in alphabetical order. Find Jo Pullinger and call her."

Kari's hands were shaking. She dropped his phone twice. But she eventually got a good grip on it.

"What's your passcode?" she asked.

"All ones," Ford said.

"Seriously?"

Ford shrugged.

Kari unlocked the phone. She called Jo and held the phone to Ford's ear.

"Ford, did you find Kari?" Jo asked.

"She's right beside me," Ford answered. "But before you throw a parade in my honor, we're going to need some backup. Someone's here, and they seem pretty mad. Violent, too."

Jo cursed. "It must be Raul. What's your situation?"

"We're still in the basement," said Ford. "We have decent cover. The assailant retreated. Not sure where he's at now."

"I'm coming, Ford. Just hang tight. I'll be there in a few minutes."

She hung up. No goodbye. Ford knew she was already sprinting for the nearest mode of transport. She would be here as fast as humanly possible. That was the kind of friend she was. And the kind of FBI agent.

"Now we wait," Ford said. "Kari, do me a favor. Get back behind the other pillar. There's not enough room here for the both of us."

She did as he asked. Ford stretched out a bit. He lifted his left arm to try and slow the bleeding. He thought of his daughter, Hazel. All the good things he'd miss if this turned out to be his last day on Earth.

No way I'm going to let that happen, he thought. *And neither will Jo.*

NINETY

Raul made his decision. He changed the magazine in his pistol and adjusted his hair tie. He got out of the car and returned to the house. Walking along the side of the structure.

It was difficult to move stealthily here. Too many weeds. They rustled against his legs. It didn't matter. His prey already knew he was there. They were cornered and scared. The ball was in Raul's court.

Halfway along the wall, he lowered himself to the ground. Parting and crushing the weeds so he could get a good view through a basement window. He looked through.

There was blood along the floor. He studied the pattern. Following it with his eyes. The trails and circles. The footprints.

Raul had landed a shot, just as he expected. And the injured person had retreated behind a brick support pillar. One of the main structures holding up the house. Raul had a vision of shooting at the pillar over and over again. A hundred bullets. A thousand. Shooting until it crumbled away. Burying his quarry in the ensuing collapse.

It was a funny idea. But hardly practical. Besides, Sal wanted Kari alive. And Raul wanted to keep getting paid.

The glass in the window was gone. There were bars on the other side. The gap was wide enough to shoot through. Raul fed the barrel of his pistol into that gap. Aiming at the pillar.

"Hello down there," Raul called. "I see you are bleeding. I am too, but not as badly as you are. And I am outside while you are still cowering in the shadows. I have the upper hand. If you're smart, this should be obvious to you."

There was no answer. Raul smiled to himself. He was having a lot of fun.

"I believe we can settle this matter," he said. "I will offer you a very generous deal. Any man would be a fool not to accept. There are only two things you must do. Toss your gun away. And then simply leave. Climb the steps and walk away. But Kari must stay here."

Finally, he got an answer. A man's voice, sounding breathless and weak.

"What do you want with her?"

"That's not your concern," Raul said venomously. "You should worry about yourself. You must have a family. Someone who would be devastated if you died today. I have no soft feelings within me, sir. Maybe you have a child. I will not hesitate to make them an orphan. On the other hand, I do not hate you. You have my admiration, in fact. I have no strong urge to shoot you again."

Raul had to stop himself from laughing. If the man took the deal, Raul would kill him anyway. He would feel nothing other than a brief thrill, forgotten by the time he knocked Kari unconscious and threw her into the trunk of his car.

The clock was ticking. But Raul knew he would be victorious. He would bring Kari to his boss, then get himself a glass of wine. Another job well done. Another innocent life destroyed.

NINETY-ONE

Raul wasn't like other people. But he knew how they worked. The same way a hunter understood the behavior of a deer.

He knew the man behind the pillar would give in.

And so he did. After mulling Raul's offer over for a minute, he relented. He first stuck his hands out. He removed the clip from his weapon and tossed it across the floor. Then he pulled the slide back. Showing there was no round chambered.

"Just don't shoot me again," he called out.

"Of course not," Raul answered. "I'm a man of my word. And you are a man who will live on. There's only one thing left for you to do."

"Head for the stairs and get out of here," the man said.

"Not quite. First, you will approach the window. Hand your weapon to me through the bars. Then I will feel safe letting you go."

"Okay," said the man. He stepped into the open.

He looked to be in his forties. He was tall. His face was bristly with dark stubble. As he moved toward the window, he stumbled. Almost falling several times. More blood dripped onto the floor. He was fading fast. Before long, he would not have the strength to resist.

"It's good to see your face," Raul said. "I didn't get a good look at you before. What is your name?"

"You don't care who I am," said the man.

"I do not," Raul agreed. "I am prepared to let you live. But that decision depends on whether I get Kari. Where is she?"

"She's hiding," the man replied.

"Of course. As all scared little creatures do." Raul held out a hand. "Your gun, please."

Raul heard a rustling sound to his left. Something cold and metal was pressed into his skull. The barrel of a gun.

"Don't move," said a young man's voice.

Raul immediately defied that order. He flicked his head back. Twisting to the side, he grabbed his attacker's wrist and jerked it upward. He moved like lightning. A shot went out, hitting the side of the house.

Kari screamed.

Raul shot to his feet. He kicked the young man in the shin. Putting him off balance. It was enough to allow Raul to rip his gun away. He got behind the man, pulling him close. Putting his gun to his head.

Now he had a human shield. With perfect timing. The man in the basement had another magazine stashed on his person. He put it into his gun, aiming through the window bars.

"You do not have a clean shot!" Raul shouted triumphantly.

The man in the basement wheezed. He nearly fell again.

Raul slid his own gun into his waistband. He reached around the front of his human shield, pulling the man's FBI credentials out of his coat pocket.

"Agent McKinley," said Raul, putting the credentials back in McKinley's pocket. "You managed to sneak up on me. That is not an easy task. You have my respect. But you should have shot me straight away."

"I guess I should have," McKinley growled. "Next time, I won't hesitate."

"There will not be a next time," Raul said.

He heard a car pulling up outside the house. A door opening and shutting. Feet sprinting up the overgrown front walk.

"You're screwed now," McKinley said, chuckling.

"I have your gun," Raul whispered in his ear. "And now I know your name. Remember that."

He shoved McKinley toward the window. Turning around, he ran for his car before anyone could start shooting, tossing aside McKinley's gun as he did.

NINETY-TWO

Ford never saw Jo arrive. The last thing he remembered was Raul holding McKinley hostage. The blood loss and the shock caught up to him. He collapsed, falling into a semi-conscious state.

At one point, he opened his eyes and saw Kari there. She was watching him with an expression of concern on her face. Saying something. Ford couldn't make it out. His ears seemed to be full of bumblebees.

He went out again. When he came to a second time, it was Jo looming over him. She had a rag in her hand. The same one that had been tied around Kari's mouth. She was pressing it against the bullet wound on his bicep.

"Ford, can you hear me?" she asked.

She sounded like she was at the end of a tunnel. But Ford could make out her voice. He nodded.

Jo smiled, even as a tear dripped out of her eye. It streamed down her cheek. "Everything's OK, Bryan. Kari is safe. So is McKinley. We're going to get you to the hospital. Just don't do anything stupid on the way over. Like dying."

"Kelly would kill me if I did that," Ford joked.

Jo helped him sit up. She beckoned to someone. McKinley arrived, situating himself on Ford's other side. They helped him get to his feet.

"Where's the bad guy?" Ford asked.

"He got away," McKinley said quietly. "I couldn't stop him. He left my gun behind, though." He grunted. "Nice of him."

"You stopped him from killing you," Jo told him. "I'm pretty sure that's a huge win."

"You stopped him," McKinley replied. "He ran when you showed up. He didn't want to be cornered. Thanks, Jo."

"Don't thank me until this is over. Raul isn't going to hide somewhere and lick his wounds. He's going to be back with a vengeance. It's only a matter of time."

It was a painstaking process. One Ford was barely conscious for. But they made it up the stairs and out through the window. They put Ford into Jo's backseat.

"My car," Ford said wistfully.

"We'll send someone to get it for you," Jo told him. "Just try and relax."

Ford couldn't. Not until he knew the car was locked. He pulled his key fob out of his pocket with great effort. He hit the lock button until he heard a beep. Then he fell limp across the backseat.

Kari rode with McKinley. They drove ahead of Jo, leading the way.

"Where are we going?" Ford asked.

"Virginia Mason," Jo told him. "That's where Peter is already. The only way I can keep everyone safe is if we're all together."

NINETY-THREE

Ford passed out well before they reached the hospital. Jo wanted to drive faster, but Ford wasn't buckled in. She had to stop at the red lights she came to. Each time, she reached back and grabbed his wrist. Checking for a pulse.

He was alive. His heart was beating strongly.

At the third red light, Jo saw Ford's phone. It was in his back pocket. She grabbed it. The phone was locked. She held it up at an angle. Letting the sunlight shine across the screen. There was a concentrated greasy splotch on the screen. Directly over the 1 on the keycode pad.

"Seriously, Ford?" she said with a sigh.

She mashed the number 1 until the phone unlocked. It was already open to the contacts page. She scrolled down, looking for Kelly. The name wasn't there. It turned out she was in Ford's phone under the title *Lovely Wife*.

"Please pick up," Jo begged as she let the phone ring.

Kelly answered in a mock gravelly voice. "Talk to me."

"Kelly," Jo said.

There was a soft wail of anguish. "Jo, is that you? Why are you calling from his phone? Is something wrong?"

"He's alive," Jo said. "I'm taking him to Virginia Mason."

"I'll meet you there," Kelly replied. Jo didn't even hear the full last word before the call was terminated.

***

Jo and McKinley reached the hospital before Kelly. They let the doctors take Ford back. Kari, too. Then they sat in the waiting room. Feeling useless. Fidgeting restlessly.

Kelly arrived ten minutes after them. She ran in with her blonde hair flying wildly. Her purse was open, spilling its contents onto the floor. She scooped them up and sprinted to the reception desk.

"My husband," she said. "Bryan Ford."

The receptionist said something quiet and reassuring. She gestured to the waiting area. Kelly walked over slowly. Her arms folded in front of her. Hugging herself.

Jo stood up and gave her a proper hug. "Kelly, it's good to see you. Where's Hazel?"

"Still in school," Kelly replied, sighing. "But she knows. I'm having a friend pick her up and look after her for now. What happened? The receptionist didn't say anything."

"He was shot twice in the left arm," Jo said. "One was superficial. The other... I haven't heard anything yet. But he lost a lot of blood."

Kelly cried out, falling into a chair. Jo sat next to her, holding her hand.

The next hour was one of the hardest of Jo's life.

But a doctor finally came out. It was Dr. Pavel again. He walked slowly toward them, staring at a clipboard. They held their breath.

Then Dr. Pavel looked up with a smile. "Okay, so who is who here?"

Kelly raised her hand. "I'm his wife."

"It's nice to meet you," Dr. Pavel added. "And I've already met Agent Pullinger. I won't waste any more time. Mr. Ford is going to be fine."

Kelly fell back in her chair, pressing both hands to her face.

"The bullet nicked his brachial artery," Dr. Pavel explained. "A little bit further to one side, and… well, I won't go into that. But he's quite lucky. The bullet has been removed, and now we're working on the surgery. After some blood transfusions and rest, he'll be in the clear."

Jo and Kelly hugged again. This time, they cried tears of joy.

McKinley cleared his throat. "That's awesome news, doctor. And what about Kari?'

"Ah, yes." Dr. Pavel flipped a page on his clipboard. "She's dehydrated and hungry, but not dangerously so, on either account. We're keeping her in observation for now. I think any damage she has incurred will be psychological. And before I go… Mr. Beaumont is awake again, Agent Pullinger. And he's asking for you."

NINETY-FOUR

Kelly got up from her seat. She wrung her hands. Staring desperately at the doctor.

"Can I see my husband?" she asked.

Dr. Pavel sighed. "Usually, I would tell you to wait a little longer. To allow him to recover. But the man has been demanding to let you visit him since he got here. You too, Agent Pullinger."

Jo looked at Kelly. Kelly nodded. An unspoken agreement. *Yes, it's all right if you come too. It's what Bryan wants.*

"How about me?" McKinley asked. He looked haunted. Traumatized.

Jo knew how he must be feeling. He failed to apprehend Raul. It wasn't his fault that Ford was shot. But in his mind, it was his fault that the man responsible was still free.

Jo tried to think of a way to communicate this to Kelly. Luckily, she didn't have to. Kelly gave McKinley a warm smile.

"You can come as well," she said.

They all headed back to see Ford. Dr. Pavel led the way. McKinley was slow, dragging his feet. There was a gap between him and the two women. Large enough for them to whisper without him hearing.

"Who is that guy?" asked Kelly.

"That's Agent McKinley," Jo replied.

Kelly nodded. "Okay. That's kind of what I thought. Bryan has talked about him. Says he's a good kid. He specifically uses the word 'kid,' even though it looks like McKinley's only about ten years younger than him."

"Give or take," Jo agreed with a smile. "But that's Ford for you."

"Do you ever call him Bryan? Or is it always just Ford?"

Jo shrugged. "We pretty much only use last names. Think of it like a sports team. It's a unique kind of family."

"You law enforcement people are an interesting group," said Kelly. "You'd think being married to my husband for so long, I'd understand a bit better. But I appreciate you. Thanks for being such a good friend to him."

"He's a good friend to me, too," Jo replied.

They arrived at Ford's bed. He was still in ER, hooked up to beeping machines and an IV. But he looked alert.

"Look what the doc dragged in," he called out with a grin. "It's my beautiful wife and two weirdos I've never met before."

Dr. Pavel looked concerned.

"Kidding," Ford added, raising his right hand. "These are my friends. I vouch for them."

Dr. Pavel shrugged and moved away. "I'll just be in the hall."

As soon as he left, Kelly glanced around. Checking for nurses who might advise her not to do what she was about to do. Then she leaned over and gave her husband a warm embrace.

"Watch the left arm," Ford said, grunting.

"Sorry." Kelly winced, withdrawing. "How are you feeling?'

He smiled. "Pretty good. I felt like I was overdue for getting shot again anyway. I was hit in my non-dominant arm. I can't complain too much."

"Ford," McKinley said, stepping forward. "I didn't get him. Raul got away."

Ford waved his good hand. "Did you get shot too? No? Then I don't care. Jo will catch that creep sooner or later."

McKinley let out a relieved sigh. "Well, I just wanted to say sorry. I'll go back to the waiting room now."

"I think I'll go too," Jo added.

"Nonsense," Ford replied with a grunt. "I wanted you to be here."

"I was here. And I'll be back. I promise."

Ford shrugged. As Jo walked away, he was already talking to his wife in a low voice. Probably apologizing for not heeding her advice about not getting shot.

Jo left them to it. She had business with Peter Russo.

NINETY-FIVE

"You look much better already," Jo said.

She was back in Peter's room. He was sitting fully upright and fidgeting. Feeling restless and ready to move around.

"I feel better, too," he replied. "Physically, anyway. Agent Pullinger... I don't want you to think I'm a bad guy."

"I don't," she assured him. "But I *do* think you're an idiot."

He smiled. "Then you already understand me pretty well. But I feel like I should explain the full thing."

"I already know why you kidnapped Kari," Jo said. "You wanted to save her from whatever your uncle had in mind."

"He would have killed her, Agent Pullinger. To send a message and set a precedent with his other shady colleagues. He wouldn't have enjoyed it. My uncle doesn't like hurting people. He just thinks it's a necessary part of the business. He definitely wouldn't have been able to touch Kari himself. He knew her when she was just a baby."

"He would have had Raul do it?" Jo asked.

Peter nodded. "That guy loves hurting people. It's his favorite thing to do. He gets excited every time my uncle needs him to beat someone up. Or kill someone. I didn't want that to happen to Kari. But I didn't just do it out of the kindness of my heart. It was personal."

"You must have known her a long time, too," said Jo.

"That's the thing," said Peter. "I didn't. I ended up with my uncle after my parents died. He looked after me out of obligation. I was never a real part of his operation, so I never went on any trips. Never went to social functions. I never met Kari or her parents."

"Then how did you know about your uncle's plans for her?" Jo asked.

"Oh, I heard plenty about her after she shut down Brickwall Group. My uncle was pissed off. He wouldn't stop complaining and yelling about it. He couldn't believe a nineteen-year-old kid had the gall to screw him over like that. He lost one of his major smuggling partners that day. He panicked for a while. The whole thing made him swear revenge."

"Kari might not have even known about the deal her parents worked out with Sal," Jo pointed out.

"Try telling him that," Peter replied with a sigh. "My uncle's almost a good guy. *Almost.* That's why he waited for Kari's grandmother to die. But he didn't care about explaining why Kari did what she did. He just wanted her dead."

"He felt personally slighted by her," said Jo. "And in his business, respect means everything. If he let some little girl get away with doing this, he'd lose face."

"Yup. I kind of got sick of hearing about Kari. But I never forgot her name. Then, a little over a year ago, I met a guy named Martin Leone."

"The receptionist at Cornish said you were friends," Jo noted.

"We were. He was a good guy. Pretty entertaining to hang out with." Peter frowned sadly. "Professor Leone was the kind of guy who looked after his friends. Even people like me, whom he hadn't known very long. He always saw me trying to flirt with girls and getting shot down. I sometimes complained to him about being lonely.

"One day, he mentioned this girl to me. Kari Cross. He knew her personally, and he thought she and I might be a good match. I couldn't believe my ears. What a coincidence, right? I hear my uncle haranguing everyone about this girl for years, and then I hear her name from this guy I just met."

NINETY-SIX

"It seemed like fate," Peter continued. "Destiny. Do you believe in that kind of thing?"

"Some days I do," Jo replied. "Some days, I think it's a bunch of crap."

Peter grabbed a half-finished pudding cup from his bedside table. He took a small bite and put it back. "Well, I believe it. I decided I couldn't ignore whatever the universe was trying to tell me. So I asked Professor Leone about Kari. He told me all about her. How her parents died a few years back, and how she's been trying to find her way. By the end of the conversation, I knew it was the same Kari.

"Every time I talked to Professor Leone, I asked him more about her. He showed me pictures. He told me what kind of person she was. Very sweet and trusting. He worried about her. Wanted to make sure she stayed safe. He told me she had a lot of money, and it was only a matter of time before someone tried to take advantage. But I knew that was the least of her worries."

"You knew she had a guillotine blade hanging over her," said Jo. "And the trigger for it dropping was her grandmother's death."

Peter nodded. "I know it's kind of sappy since I never actually met Kari in person. As soon as I realized I wanted to save her, I knew it would be better if she never knew me. So I stayed away. But still, I fell in love. Does that sound stupid?"

Jo thought about it. "Actually, no. You made yourself stay away from her. You were willing to make her hate you for her own good. That sounds like the textbook definition of love to me."

"Then I'm not crazy." Peter grinned. "Just stupid enough to think my plan could work. I thought about going to the police. Warning them about my uncle's plan. But he has moles, you know. People on the inside."

"Who?" Jo asked.

"He never told me any names, sorry," said Peter. "But I knew if I went to the police, he would hear about it. And I'd be on the chopping block, too. I decided the best way of saving Kari was to make her disappear in some random place. Then we'd both be safe."

"You just had to wait for the right opportunity," said Jo.

"When I heard from Professor Leone that Kari was about to visit her grandmother, I thought it sounded like a good time. When he told me she was visiting because her grandmother's health was failing, I knew it might be the *only* time. I followed her down there. She made the drive to Oregon in the day, so there was no chance there. The place her grandmother lived was too busy."

Jo nodded. "So you followed her back toward Seattle. When she stopped at a dark and deserted rest area, you seized your chance. Then I came. I saw you trying to take her. I had to stop you."

"Pretty sucky timing for all concerned," Peter added. "When that failed, I came back to Seattle. Professor Leone texted me as soon as he heard Kari's grandmother was dead. I acted fast. No choice. No time to come up with a good plan.

"I broke into Kari's house and took her. Decided to lay low for a while, then find a way to get Kari out of the country. Guess my uncle figured out pretty fast that I took her. Pretty dumb idea, huh?"

"Absolutely," Jo agreed. "But you have my respect for trying to pull it off anyway. So I understand why you felt you needed to save Kari. Maybe you saw a bit of yourself in her, too. An orphan trying to find her place in the world. Like you."

Peter shrugged. "Maybe. Guess I never thought of it like that."

"There you go," Jo said with a smile. "I have two more questions right now. First, what's the deal with that plate of food we found in Kari's house?"

"Kari was still up," Peter explained. "Sort of. I guess she wanted something to eat before she went to bed. But she fell asleep at the table before taking a bite. I didn't want it going to waste. And I was nervous. When I get nervous, I eat."

Jo nodded. It was far from a reasonable explanation, but it matched what she knew of Peter. He had strange tendencies. And his behavior didn't always follow a typical pattern.

"Can you tell me more about Raul?" Jo asked.

"I don't know much about him," Peter replied. "He's from Guatemala or something. I think he used to be part of some special forces unit. Now he's a hitman for hire. He's a psychopath. Even my uncle's afraid of him."

"And so are you," Jo said.

Peter shivered. "Yeah. I'm not *that* stupid. We're both lucky to still be alive, Agent Pullinger. But Raul's going to be coming for us. Even I'm dead meat, and I'm part of the family."

NINETY-SEVEN

Olga was relieved when, yet again, she arrived at Sal's mansion for a day of ordinary cleaning tasks. When she had finished her last shift, Sal had given her a warning. She should prepare to deal with another mess in the basement's special room.

But when she got to the mansion, Sal was in a sour mood. He told her there would be no cleaning in the basement. Olga had the idea something had gone wrong. A plan had gone off the rails. Something had been meant to happen but didn't.

Of course, she didn't pry. She just nodded her head obediently. Grabbing her cleaning supplies, she went to work. It was a big house, and one shift wasn't enough to get everything. She had finished the downstairs last time. Now she headed to the second floor.

Eventually, she wound up in the guest bathroom. It hadn't been touched in a while. Dust was accumulating. Olga knew Sal would want it spotless, so she took her time.

It was dirty work, involving plenty of chemicals. She took off her family ring before starting, leaving it inside the medicine cabinet. The ring wasn't worth much money. A few hundred, maybe. But the sentimental value was high. She would never want anything to happen to it.

Once that was done, she got to work. She scrubbed out the sink and bathtub. Then she moved to the toilet. Bleaching out the bowl. Wiping every last inch of porcelain. Cleaning the seat and lid.

While she was doing that, she heard voices.

It was a quirk in the house's heating and cooling system. The vents that ran through the walls. At certain points in the house, sound traveled just right. You could hear people from several rooms away.

Or from the floor below.

It was Sal's voice that she heard first. The other voice was quiet. It sounded like it was coming through a phone.

Olga stopped scrubbing to listen.

She couldn't make out much of what they were saying. The conversation was heated. Angry. Sal was blaming the person on the phone for something. The person on the phone sounded much calmer but still annoyed.

Some of the words reached Olga's ears. Something about "retrieving the girl" and "FBI agents."

It sounded serious.

Suddenly, there were booming footsteps in the second-floor hallway. Coming toward her.

Olga went back to scrubbing just as a bodyguard arrived. He grabbed her by the arm and started pulling her away.

"Wait, I must finish!" Olga said.

"Gimme that." The guard grabbed her sponge. "I'll leave it in the bucket for you. You can finish next time. It's time for you to go."

He kept his vise-like grip on her arm all the way outside and through the gate. He gently pushed her toward her van.

"Don't come back until you hear from Mr. Russo," he said, shutting the gate. Then he remembered something. He pulled a wad of cash out of his pocket and handed it through the bars. "Here. The boss doesn't want you missing out on any wages."

Olga took the money. The guard walked away. She got back in her van and counted the cash. It was at least a week's worth of tips. But she couldn't feel happy about it. It meant Sal probably wouldn't be asking her back for a while.

Or ever, maybe.

She groaned and punched the steering wheel in frustration. There was no choice but to drive away. Head home. Sit down and start looking for other work. Just in case.

She started driving.

A half mile from the mansion, she remembered her ring and hit the brakes.

It was her great-grandmother's ring. A family heirloom. There was no way she would ever risk losing it.

She turned around and headed back to the mansion.

NINETY-EIGHT

Olga had a naïve vision in her mind. She thought she could just pull up in front of the house, buzz the gate, and explain the situation to the bodyguard. If she told him about her ring, maybe he'd escort her inside to get it. Or he would at least bring it out to her.

No. That wouldn't happen. She didn't know exactly what Sal did for a living, but she knew what he was. A crook. He didn't play by normal rules. And despite how nicely he treated her, he was not a good man.

He wouldn't understand Olga's need to get her ring back. Nor would anyone who worked for him. She'd have to find her own way to fetch it. She didn't know when she'd be called back for another cleaning session. Or if it would happen at all.

The ring might disappear forever.

Thinking fast, Olga parked a few houses down from the mansion. The road followed a curve, and there were plenty of trees. None of the guards would know she was there.

People underestimated Olga. They looked at her and saw a meek immigrant. But she was sharp. She kept her eyes open, observing everything. She knew the house inside and out by now.

She knew there was a side door that was rarely watched. Reaching it would be tricky, but she felt confident she could do it. If she was caught, she could just tell the story about her ring. She thought the worst that would happen was that she'd be kicked out again.

She ducked into the trees near the house and moved quietly through them. She came out at the right point, near the stone wall that separated Sal's property from the rest of the world. She peeked over the top. No guards in sight.

There was a camera. Watching her. She just had to hope no one was watching *it* at this crucial moment.

She climbed over the wall. It was cold and rough on her hands and legs. She scraped herself up but managed to get to the other side. After that, it was a matter of dashing to the house. She could see the side door from here.

As she expected, no one was watching it.

She ran to the door, then caught her breath for a moment. She tried to open it. It was locked.

Olga's heart sank. Then she remembered something. A month after she'd started working for him, Sal gave her a key. He said she would never need it; it was just a sign of trust. She found the key on her keyring and inserted it into the lock.

It worked. The door popped open. Olga slipped inside, carefully shutting it.

She immediately heard voices. Sal arguing with someone. They were coming from a room directly adjacent to her. Olga started moving away. Toward the stairs, so she could go up and get her ring.

Then she heard the name "Peter."

Olga stopped. She didn't like the sound of those voices. Peter must be in trouble.

The same voice as before was back on the phone with Sal. She recognized it now. Raul. She tried avoiding that creep as much as possible. But she had run into him enough times to know he was bad news.

"You keep talking about loose ends," Sal shouted. "And boy, do we got a lot of those. You did good with Leone, but now you're slipping. You need to do your job."

"The FBI is involved now," Raul hissed. He sounded like he was barely managing to swallow his pride. "The job has gotten more difficult. I will do it, but it will take more time. But now we know exactly where Peter is."

"Yes, we do," Sal said gravely. "I hate this. You know? I really hate it. But it's gotta be done. Deal with it, Raul. Get rid of the kid. Don't give me any details about the job. Just tell me when you get it done."

Olga clapped a hand over her mouth to hide her gasp. She had no idea Sal was *that* evil. To order his own nephew killed. The boy who was a great friend to Olga. Almost a son.

She forgot all about her ring. She had a completely separate mission now.

NINETY-NINE

Things at the hospital moved slowly. Hours passed between developments. Ford was finally moved from the ER around dinnertime. Jo visited him briefly. They talked while Ford and Kelly had a supper of mushy hospital food.

Ford was in good spirits, but he kept asking for Hazel. She finally arrived, along with the friend who was temporarily watching her.

"Dad?" Hazel asked reluctantly. "You're hurt."

"Not too badly," Ford said. "Get over here."

Hazel jumped up on the bed and cuddled against her father. Kelly leaned over the both of them. They shared a tender moment while Jo and the friend retreated, giving them space.

"Do you work with Bryan?" the friend asked.

"As often as I can," Jo replied. She offered her hand. "I'm Jo Pullinger. I'm with the FBI."

"Oh yeah, Kelly's told me all about you. I'm Petra." She shook Jo's hand.

"That's a beautiful name," Jo said.

"My dad was a huge explorer," said Petra. "He went all over the world. But he said the most beautiful place he ever visited was Petra, and that's why he chose the name for me."

"That's very special," Jo said. She was feeling worn out. Her emotions were all over the place. She started tearing up just thinking about Petra's dad. A man she had never met.

"Are you okay?" Petra asked.

Jo smiled. "Yeah, not too bad. Things are looking up. I guess you'll be watching Hazel for a while?"

Petra nodded. "We'll let her hang out with her dad for a while. Then Hazel and I are going for ice cream. We're having a movie night."

Jo grinned. "Nothing beats movie night."

"Nothing at all," Petra agreed. She gestured down the hall. "I was thinking about grabbing a coffee. Want anything?"

Jo shook her head. "I'm fine. Thanks."

Petra left. Jo hurried away. She didn't want anyone to see her cry. She found a bathroom and locked herself in. Then she let herself lose it for about five minutes. Afterward, she felt much better. Ready to face whatever came next. Maybe.

Her phone rang as she was dabbing her eyes. She answered.

"McKinley, what's up?" she asked. "Back at the office?"

"Yeah, but probably not for long," he said. "Something big just came in. An anonymous woman just called our office. Since you aren't in, the call was transferred to me. The woman claims to work for Salvatore Russo. She wants to help us nail him."

"Great," Jo exclaimed. "I'll take all the help I can get. Did you set anything up?"

"I'm meeting with her tonight," said McKinley. "At the ferry terminal. She's coming over from Bainbridge Island on the last boat of the night. I guess it's going to be a long one for me."

"It won't be any longer than your usual nights at work," Jo said.

"Oh. Yeah. Good point. I've asked Agent Larkin to come with me to keep an eye out. Just in case this is some kind of ambush."

"I doubt it. Much too public of a spot. But it's a good excuse to spend more time with Larkin, right?"

"I don't know what you're talking about," said McKinley. "I'll keep you informed about the meeting, though. How are things there?"

"Perfectly fine so far," said Jo. "But I'll keep you informed as well. Good luck."

ONE-HUNDRED

The evening passed slowly. It was a monotonous experience. Jo did her rounds, checking on Kari, Peter, and Ford. A lot of the rooms at the hospital were full, meaning the three people Jo cared about were spaced far apart. She did a lot of walking.

But she enjoyed it. After all, she had been through in her career, she had come to appreciate monotony. No one was currently shooting at her. Everything was fine.

It wasn't all boring and peaceful, though. There was an undercurrent of anxiety. Jo kept her head on a swivel. Her ears strained, listening for signs that Raul was there. She knew he'd be coming, for Kari at least, but probably for Peter as well.

Would he wait until they were no longer in the hospital?

Jo doubted it. It was too good an opportunity. Whatever difficulty Raul had in infiltrating the place was offset by the convenience. Both his targets were in one building.

How could he pass that up?

At least Jo wasn't alone. The Seattle PD was on the scene. They had sent three officers over. One for each room. It was all they could spare at the moment. Jo was grateful. She didn't have to worry so much when she was between rooms.

She had even gotten to know the three officers. The guy outside Kari's room was already familiar to her. He was Officer Getty. Jo had first met him outside Leone's townhouse.

It was half past midnight when Jo arrived at Kari's room for another visit. Getty was outside the door, still as a statue. He seemed tireless. Ever since Jo told him that Raul killed his friend Officer Teller, Getty's motivation was sky high.

"Heading in?" he asked. "She's probably asleep by now."

"I just want to see her with my own eyes," Jo said.

Getty opened the door for her. He left it open as Jo went in and sat beside the bed.

Jo tried to be quiet. It looked like Kari was asleep. But her eyes suddenly shot open.

"Back to check on me?" she asked.

Jo nodded. "Just making sure you're doing all right."

Kari sat up, leaning on one elbow. "I'm good. Thanks again for helping me."

"I do what I can," Jo replied. "I'm glad it was enough in your case."

Kari shrugged. "I thought I was in danger before, but I guess I wasn't. Not from Peter, anyway. He wanted to help me, right?"

"So it seems," Jo agreed.

"I hope he won't get in too much trouble." Kari winced. "I don't even want to press charges. I kind of just want to move on from all this."

Jo patted her hand. "We'll just see what happens. These cases can go a lot of different ways."

"He's going to prison, isn't he?" Kari asked.

"Probably. But you should be worrying about yourself."

"I don't need to," Kari replied. "I already have you doing that for me."

Jo smiled.

Through the open door, they heard Getty's radio come on. Through the static, a voice emerged. It was Officer Harris, the man stationed outside Ford's room.

"Hey, you guys, I just got a call from dispatch. We've got a report of a possible 11-71 on the roof of the hospital. One of us is going to have to check it out."

Jo recognized the police code. It meant *fire*. If the report was right, something was burning on the hospital's roof.

Getty looked back at Jo, raising an eyebrow. She nodded.

Getty raised the radio to his mouth. "Getty here. I'll go check that report out. Agent Pullinger's here with our VIP."

He hurried away. The door stood open. Jo watched the hall tensely.

A fire in a hospital was bad enough. But to have one at this particular moment?

She knew what it meant. Raul was coming.

ONE-HUNDRED ONE

"Is everything all right?" Kari asked.

Jo smiled and nodded. "So far, so good."

Kari stared at her. "I'm not a kid. I could just use my phone to look up whatever code that was. Can you please just tell me?"

"Someone reported a fire on the roof," Jo said. "Let's hope it was a prank call or a false report."

Kari's eyes went wide with fear. "He's coming, isn't he? The guy who shot Ford?"

Jo sighed. "That's my assumption. I thought I was being clever with the aliases, but he might have found us anyway. The fire could just be a distraction. But don't worry. While I'm here, nothing bad is going to happen."

A minute later, a breathless Officer Harris appeared in the doorway.

"Getty called me," he said. "The fire's real, but that's not all. It was arson, and he's chasing the guy who started it. He needs immediate assistance. I'm going to have to leave Ford unattended."

He didn't wait for Jo to respond before running away. She got to her feet but resisted the urge to go to Ford. He was not one of Raul's primary targets. She should stay here with Kari.

The third officer arrived soon after Harris. He looked panicked.

"Shots fired on the roof," he stammered. "I have to back my men up. Sorry, Agent Pullinger. I've called for help, and they should be here soon."

Jo nodded. "Go."

The cop sprinted out of sight.

"Raul's on the roof, then," Jo said to Kari.

"You should go help," Kari said.

Jo gave her a curious look.

"They aren't like you," Kari added. "They're just regular cops. Raul's going to eat them alive."

"You'll be alone," Jo said.

"If you can stop Raul, it won't matter."

Jo had to admit. The girl made a good point. She couldn't just sit down here and let three cops get cut down. She was obligated to help.

"You still have my number in your phone?" Jo asked. "The police already gave it back to you, right?"

Kari nodded.

"Good," Jo said. "Call me if anything happens."

She hurried out of the room, shutting the door. As she followed the signs for the stairs, Jo took a good scan around. The nearby doctors and nurses looked a little worried. Probably because they had seen three police officers running past them. But no one was panicking.

There were also no alarms blaring.

Perhaps the fire was already out. It was a small blaze, contained and controlled. Raul set it to draw the police to the roof. But why would he want them up there? Just to get into a shootout?

It didn't make sense.

Jo stopped, her shoes squeaking on the floor. She had a bad feeling that Raul was outsmarting them all.

He was already down here, moving through the hospital. Searching the rooms.

Hunting down his target.

Jo was all alone. Ford was out of commission. McKinley was probably on his way to the ferry terminal already.

It was just her to watch three rooms.

She turned in a circle as sweat poured down her face.

Where would Raul go first?

Definitely not to Ford's room. Raul probably wouldn't bother finding Ford at all.

To Kari? Probably not. He wanted Kari alive, to take her to his boss. So he would go there last.

That left Peter's room.

She was disoriented now. No idea which way she was facing. She ran up to the nearest doctor.

"Can you direct me to Simon Beaumont's room?" she asked, showing her FBI ID.

He pointed down the hall, gesturing around a corner. Jo thanked him and ran. As she got closer, she recognized where she was. She rushed into Peter's room. Shoving the door open and pulling out her sidearm.

But it was just Peter, lying in bed. He jolted upright when Jo came in.

"What's going on?" he cried.

"He's coming," Jo warned him.

She checked the room's corners. No one else was there.

Her instincts told her she was running out of time.

Thinking fast, she hid against the wall beside the door.

ONE-HUNDRED TWO

Raul whistled to himself as he wandered the empty halls of the hospital. The idiotic police on the roof must have found a fire extinguisher. If not, alarms would have been going off by now. Raul would have liked the extra confusion. But it was no matter. He didn't even bother finding an alarm and triggering it himself.

He had faith in himself to get the job done either way.

He wondered if the police had also discovered his little trick, the box of 9mm bullets he had left at the bottom of the bonfire. Maybe one of them had been hit by an exploding shell. That would be lovely.

Raul made sure to keep his hands in his pockets as he walked. He found an operating room and slipped inside. He used the sink to wash his hands. The water ran black with soot. Getting the fire going had been harder than anticipated.

He had many skills, but Raul wasn't very good at arson.

Once the evidence was scrubbed from his hands, he felt fully confident to stroll the rest of the way to his target.

So far, it had been an unpleasant day. First, he failed to apprehend Kari at the condemned house. Then, when he called Sal, he got yelled at for a while. Then he had to come to this hospital and walk around for hours. He knew what room Peter was in already, but he didn't know where Kari was.

He would have to check almost every room to find her. A painstaking process. The hospital staff would have been suspicious if Raul had simply gone down the halls, opening every door, one after the other. Sticking his head in and taking a peek.

Thus, he had been forced to search gradually.

His fingers itched as he made his way toward Peter's room. He was restless. He needed to hurt someone. He needed to take a life.

In just a moment, he would fulfill his desire.

Raul opened the door to Peter's room.

Peter was already awake. Staring toward the door. His face was sweaty, and he was breathing heavily. He already looked terrified.

Maybe he had a bad dream, or maybe he knew Raul was coming. Someone must have tipped him off.

Raul reached into his nurse scrubs. He unholstered his silenced pistol and drew it out.

Peter started screaming when he saw the gun. Covering his face with his hands.

"Don't do it!" he begged.

"Shut up," Raul snapped.

Killing Peter could wait for a moment because Raul had a sense there was a third person in the room. Besides, he wanted to relish watching the life go out of the brat's eyes.

He looked all around but didn't see anyone. The sheets on the bed weren't very long, so he could tell there was no one under there either.

That left only one place.

ONE-HUNDRED THREE

Jo held her breath. In her mind, she went back to her childhood. Playing hide and seek with her friends. A low-stakes game. But back then, staying hidden felt like the most important thing in the universe.

She could stay in one spot for hours. Not moving. Hardly breathing. If that's what it took, she would do it.

Jo channeled that now. She stayed perfectly still.

The door opened. It swung toward her, inching toward her nose. If it hit her, the person opening it would know she was there. Jo tried to make herself even flatter, shoving the back of her head into the wall.

The door stopped.

Peter screamed and begged for his life.

"Shut up," an accented voice said.

Jo waited a moment. She prayed Raul would step further into the room. Getting close to his target. That way, he'd become a target as well. Jo would have a clean shot.

But Raul hesitated. Nothing happened for a moment. Jo's heart raced. Somehow, he knew it was a trap.

"I said *shut up*," Raul barked. "Before you bring attention. You think I am just here to kill you? I only want to know which room Kari is in. Tell me that, and I won't hurt you."

"No way," Peter shouted. "I'm not telling you anything."

"There is no car to jump out of this time, Peter. But there is a window. And we are on the fourth floor. Perhaps not a fatal drop, but very painful. I could help you get through the glass, if you'd like."

"I'm not giving you Kari," Peter said sternly.

Raul said nothing, but Jo could hear him breathing heavily. He sounded angry. Ready to hurt someone.

She had to stop him now before he started shooting.

Jo took a step to the side, trying to get out from behind the door. But suddenly, the door swung away from her. Raul was pulling it shut.

She didn't know what he was doing, but she took advantage of it. She stepped forward.

The door suddenly slammed open. It hit Jo in the face with a cracking sound. She flew back, smashing against the wall. Blood erupted from her nose. Her head was spinning. Stars burst in front of her eyes.

When the door swung away again, she fell to her knees. She nearly lost consciousness. Her vision shrank to a tiny pinpoint, but then it came back.

ONE-HUNDRED FOUR

Jo still couldn't see much. Her vision was cloudy. But she heard Raul enter the room. His shoes slid noisily on the rubber floor.

She said a quick prayer in her head. Then she sprang forward, reaching with both arms. She collided with someone who felt skinny. She hoped it was Raul.

Blood dripped into her mouth. She spat out the coppery taste as she twisted around, trying to wrench Raul off balance. A shot sounded. Then a second one. The silencer could only do much. In this small room, the noise was still thunderous.

"Agent Pullinger!" Peter cried. "Someone, help! We need help in here!"

No one came.

They would be here soon, Jo knew. A hospital staff member would arrive. See what was going on. They would run to find one of the police officers or at least a security guard. It might take a couple of minutes before Jo had any real backup.

She had to stay alive until then. And keep Peter breathing as well.

Adrenaline kicked through her body like a drug. It woke her back up. Her vision cleared, and the pain faded. She found herself face to face with Raul.

At one point, he probably had a good tan. But the Pacific Northwest's climate had done him no favors. He was pale and thin. His cheeks were sunken, like a vampire's. His eyes were dark but shallow, like a mirror.

There was no soul behind them, but they saw everything.

Raul grabbed her wrists, pulling them away from him. "Good to see you again, Agent Pullinger. I didn't want to kill you, but now I must. What is that I see in your face? Hope?"

She stomped on his feet. Then she kicked backward, pulling her wrists free. Her gun had fallen from her hands at some point. No time to look around for it.

Raul aimed. Swinging his pistol around to shoot at her. Jo ducked to the side and lunged forward. She aimed a punch at one of his kidneys, not expecting it to land.

But it did. A crushing blow that would have disabled most people, at least for a moment. But Raul absorbed it. He grunted but remained stationary.

Jo followed through with another punch, sending an uppercut toward his jaw. With his free hand, he caught her fist and twisted it painfully. He was a wiry man, but he had tremendous power. Jo was forced to move along with the twisting motion. It was the only way to save her shoulder from being dislocated.

Raul knocked her in the chin with the butt of his pistol. Jo landed on her back. Swallowing more blood.

He smiled down at her. "There is no hope. I will kill Peter and then find Kari. I want you to know these things before you die."

"Why?" Jo asked.

"Because it entertains me," he replied.

He pointed his gun at her forehead.

ONE-HUNDRED FIVE

Jo stared into the barrel of the silencer. Any second, a bullet would fly out of it. Into her head. She would die quickly. Most likely, she would never even hear the shot. So, if there was any time for her life to flash before her eyes, it was now.

The first thing she thought of was her niece, Chrissy.

Then she thought about McKinley. He was coming into his own, but he still had things to learn. He was still firmly in the camp of protégé. But he was already a great agent. He would only get better. Jo was sad that she'd never get to see it.

She braced herself.

Something long and metal came flying into view. It clunked against Raul's head, knocking him forward. He stumbled, reaching out to catch himself on the door. He succeeded, but the door swung under his weight. Pulling him further away.

The long, metal thing fell to the floor. It was the stand that held Peter's IV bags. Peter was sitting up in bed with his arm outstretched. He had thrown it like a spear, nailing his target. He was smiling, proud of his accuracy.

Jo sat up. She saw her gun on the floor nearby. She flipped onto her side and quickly crawled for it.

Raul foresaw her move. He kicked at her. She dodged. Instead of hitting her in the face, his foot landed on her shoulder. It bruised her flesh and sent her sliding across the floor. Away from her gun.

Raul stood up, shoving the doorway. His anger got the best of him. It would have been wise to shoot Jo first, but Peter was the one who had thrown the IV stand at his head.

He aimed his weapon toward the bed.

This gave Jo enough time to dive for the gun.

Not hers. His.

She grabbed the silencer, tugging it down. Raul squeezed the trigger reflexively. Trying to hit her. The bullet struck right between her knees, sending bits of rubber flying upward.

Jo wrenched sideways. Trying to twist the gun out of his hands. His grip was strong, though it was starting to slip. His fingers were peeling away, but not fast enough.

Raul still had a free hand. He would punch her in the face soon. Or just grab his gun with both hands, preventing her from taking it. He was stronger than she was.

These were both viable options. But Raul didn't get the chance to use them.

Peter leaped off of his bed, grabbing Raul from behind. Wrapping his arms around the hitman's windpipe. Peter pulled back with all his weight, trying to choke the man.

Now Raul had to use his free hand to pull at the arm that was cutting off his air. He did so, digging his nails into Peter's flesh. Peter hissed in pain but held strong.

Raul didn't look panicked. Not quite. But he seemed to experience a realization.

He used his thumb to hit the magazine release on his pistol. The clip fell out. Then he let the gun go.

The magazine hit the floor. But it was still closer to Jo than her own gun. She grabbed for it.

At the same time, Raul used both of his hands to yank Peter's arm away. He twisted around, slamming an elbow into Peter's face. Blood burst out of his nose.

Peter fell backward. He was out of the fight.

But Jo wasn't. She slammed the magazine back into Raul's gun.

By the time she had the weapon ready, its owner was gone. Raul had taken off into the hallway.

Jo gave chase. She stepped through the door, bringing the gunsights around. She found Raul, but she didn't have a clean shot. A few nurses were in the corridor. On their way to see what the commotion was about.

"Out of the way!" Jo shouted.

The nurses flattened themselves against the wall. But it was too late. Raul disappeared around a corner.

Jo ran after him, using her forearm to wipe the blood off her face. When she got to the corner, there was no sign of Raul. He was too fast. But he had to be somewhere.

Jo kept going. Trying to follow his trail.

ONE-HUNDRED SIX

McKinley sat in his car longer than he should have. He was parked under the ferry terminal, in the place where people left their cars if they were taking a day trip across the water on foot. But he wasn't getting on the boat. Agent Larkin was parked a few rows behind him, watching his back.

In truth, he felt awkward. He looked at the flowers sitting on the seat next to him. They weren't that beautiful. They looked sad and a little wilted. He bought them from a random convenience store. The best he could do on short notice.

It almost felt like a real date. He thought about Agent Larkin. How she might look in an evening gown.

The vision of her resplendent in a formal dress made his hands start sweating.

Get it together, Lewis, he thought.

He looked in his side mirror. He could see people flowing down the terminal steps. Just a few stragglers. These late-night ferries were fairly unpatronized.

It was time.

McKinley got out of the car. He looked around. The lot was dark. There were only a few other cars. He didn't see anyone. As far as he could tell, he wasn't being shadowed. He couldn't be so sure about the woman he was here to meet.

He heard a car door shut. He looked back, saw Larkin was standing beside her car.

She waved. McKinely waved back and began walking.

He still knew nothing about the lady he was meeting. All he knew was she would be wearing a blue sun hat with flowers on it. Her "gardening hat," as she called it over the phone. It was something they had agreed on, so he would recognize her.

McKinley grabbed the flowers from the passenger seat. He checked his hair in the mirror. Slicking it back, making himself look presentable.

He walked across the parking lot. He took one quick glance, saw Larkin was following at a discrete distance.

I wonder what kind of flowers she likes? he thought as he looked ahead again. *Not that I'd ever ask, but still... Oh, get it together, Lewis.*

A few ferry passengers were waiting for buses or taxis at the curb. Only one of them was standing off to the side, leaning on the railing and looking out over the water.

She was wearing a blue hat with flowers on it.

McKinley approached, clearing his throat. "These are for you."

She looked back. He handed her the flowers. She took them. Gave them a cautious sniff.

"Who are you?" she asked reluctantly.

McKinley sized her up. She was a tall, skinny woman. Pale and blonde. She had the cheekbones and jaw of a supermodel. If he had to guess her age, he would have said she was in her late thirties.

"I'm McKinley," he said.

"Can I see your credentials?" she asked.

He shook his head. "You'll just have to trust me."

She shrugged. "What are the flowers for?"

"Appearances," McKinley replied. "In case Sal has anyone following you, they'll just think you came to Seattle on a date."

"A very late one," she pointed out. "But it works well as a cover. Thank you."

"They're crappy flowers," said McKinley. "You can just throw them away later. So, who are you?"

"My name is Olga Aleksandrov."

"Russian?"

She nodded. "I came to America ten years ago. It was not as easy as I had hoped, but there's still more opportunity than in my home country."

"You found a job with the Russo family."

"Yes. As a cleaning lady. I learned that American people love stereotypes. When they meet a foreign lady like me, there are only a few jobs they think I will have. Cleaning lady is one of them. I decided I might as well take advantage of this. It would give me a better chance of being hired."

McKinley smiled. "Did it work?"

"Too well," Olga replied with a sigh. "When I responded to Sal's job posting, I thought it was too good to be true. I get to clean a lovely mansion and get paid twice as much as my usual work. And I was right. It was too good to be true."

"How much do you know?" McKinley asked.

"Not a lot," she admitted. "He is careful not to discuss business around me. But I am often tasked with cleaning blood from the floors, and I wouldn't like to speak much more about that. The point is, Agent McKinley, I have access to the house."

"Great," said McKinley. "That's all we need. If you really want to help, it's going to be a simple job. I'll give you a listening device. Don't worry. It's not like an old spy movie. These new devices are tiny. No one would ever notice."

"I just have to put it somewhere in the house?" Olga asked.

"Somewhere Sal likes to use for business discussions."

"I know just the place," said Olga. "But there is a slight problem. I had to leave my shift early today. Something bad is happening, and I was kicked out. I don't know when Sal will ask me to come back."

"Don't worry," McKinley assured her. "You can plant the device any time."

Olga bit her lip. "I do know a way I can sneak in. I can do it tomorrow, maybe."

McKinley's eyebrows went up. "I won't tell you not to, but you have to be careful."

"Don't worry, I have a plan for what to say if I am caught," she replied with a laugh. "I left something important in the bathroom. I'm just trying to get it back before it's lost."

ONE-HUNDRED SEVEN

Jo had already cheated death twice tonight. She was feeling lucky, so she went with her gut.

She continued down the hall. When she saw people looking out of their rooms, she waved them back.

"FBI," she said. "The situation is under control."

It was a lie, but they didn't need to know that. They glanced at the two pistols she was holding and retreated without question.

She reached the end of the hall. There were two choices now. She could turn back and search elsewhere. Or she could take the stairs.

This was the way Raul had gone, and she hadn't seen him, so he was either on a different floor by now or else hiding in one of the rooms.

It was another gamble, but Jo decided on the stairs. Once she entered the stairwell, she had to make another decision.

Up or down?

As she was looking around, trying to make up her mind, she saw something. A hint of blood smeared on a railing. The kind that would be deposited by someone rushing by with blood on their clothes.

My blood or Peter's? she wondered.

She ran down the steps.

She was on the fourth floor. She went down all the way to the first, then opened the door and stuck her head out. She was back in the lobby now. No one down here seemed to have any idea that a madman was running around. The receptionist sat calmly at her station. The people in the waiting room hung their heads morosely.

Jo cursed. Had she missed Raul? Maybe he had exited onto the second or third level.

She turned to head back up. Then she saw that she wasn't at the bottom of the stairwell. There was another flight, going down. The parking garage. She looked down into the shadows and knew it was where Raul had gone.

Moving slowly, she descended beneath the lobby. She opened the heavy door at the bottom and darted through. The door tried slamming shut behind her. She grabbed the handle to stop it.

She needed to be quiet.

Jo carefully shut the door. Then she scanned the garage. It was full of columns and darkness. Dozens of bright lights glowed from the ceiling, but it wasn't enough to dispel every shadow.

Raul could be in any of them.

She ran over to a parked van and stood behind it. She made sure her legs were in line with one of the tires. That way, he wouldn't be able to see her beneath the vehicle.

"Raul?" she called. "Are you down here?"

There was no verbal answer. But she heard a scuffling sound. He was somewhere nearby. Moving to a new hiding place.

"The hunter becomes the hunted," Jo shouted. "I have your gun now."

There was a shot. The side mirror on the van exploded. Jo sprinted around the back of the van. She scooted to one side, taking a quick look out.

She didn't see anything.

"And I have a backup weapon," Raul cackled.

There was a thick cement pillar nearby. It would make better cover than the van. Jo ran for it. She managed to duck behind it just in time. Another shot came, causing a cloud of dust to spray out from the pillar.

"You are very skilled," Raul said. "Perhaps you are one of the best I've ever come up against. But I am better."

"How do you know that?" Jo asked. "The way I see it, me and my friends have already kicked your butt twice. First at the condemned house, now here."

"I survived despite being outnumbered on both occasions. Now it's only the two of us. Now I think I'll kill you more slowly so that you have time to fully regret the choices you've made."

ONE-HUNDRED EIGHT

A heavy clicking sound echoed across the parking garage. Someone was opening the door to the stairwell.

Jo thought Raul must be trying to escape. She didn't have an angle on the door. She ran back to the van to see what was going on.

The door was wide open, but it wasn't Raul standing in it. It was Officer Getty. His face was streaked with soot. His forehead was beaded with sweat.

"Agent Pullinger?" he asked.

She gave him a wide-eyed stare, gesturing for him to go back.

Raul took the shot. Luckily for Getty, he was still holding the door open. The bullet hit the door instead of his head. Getty screamed and threw his hands up. The door started swinging shut, but he ran out of its way.

Coming toward Jo.

"*Hurry!*" Jo hissed.

Getty tripped over his own feet while trying to get to her, stumbling and falling. Like Leone dropping his keys, this sudden failure worked out for him. Raul's next shot missed.

Jo ran into the open. She used Raul's gun, firing in his general direction. She had no idea where Raul was. She just knew he was to her left.

"Come on!" she said. Grabbing the back of Getty's shirt, she pulled at him.

He shot to his feet. They both ran for cover as Jo laid down more suppressing fire. Some of her bullets hit parked cars. Alarms went off, filling the garage with noise. Collateral damage. She'd feel bad about it later.

Once they were safely behind the concrete pillar, Jo turned to Getty.

"Why are you down here?" she asked.

"To help," he said with a grunt. "We put that fire out. There was never a shooter on the roof. He just put a box of bullets in the fire to trick us. I went back to Kari's room to find you. She told me you left. Then I found Peter, and he gave me the full story."

"Where are the other officers?" Jo asked.

Getty poked a thumb toward the ceiling. "Watching Peter and Kari. To be honest, I regret coming down here."

"Me too," Jo replied. She leaned close, whispering. "Here's the play, if you're ready for it."

"I played football in high school," said Getty, "but something tells me this isn't going to be like that."

"Nope, but we can call it a Hail Mary if it'll make you feel better. I'll go out first. Draw his attention. Once he starts shooting at me, you go the other way. Stay in cover as much as possible. If you get a shot, take it."

Getty licked his lips and nodded. "After you."

Jo moved. To give Getty a better chance at success, she took the more dangerous route. Back toward the doors. The only shelter that way was the van and a line of two smart cars connected to charging ports.

As Jo predicted, Raul didn't hesitate to shoot.

Jo crouched behind one of the tiny smart cars. The rear window and windshield both shattered as a bullet passed through. Jo winced.

That'll be expensive.

She bowed her head toward the floor. Glancing beneath the van. She caught sight of Getty. He was making a run for it. Trying to flank Raul. He didn't make it far before he threw himself back into cover.

But Raul didn't shoot at him.

As soon as Getty stopped moving, Jo started. She advanced to the next smart car. The windows on this one remained intact.

What's going on?

Jo raised her head into the open, looking around.

She saw lights glowing on the far wall. Then she heard a dinging sound.

It was an elevator, and the doors were sliding shut.

ONE-HUNDRED NINE

Jo watched the elevator doors shut. She waited as the light above them changed. Counting the floors. It went all the way to the fourth, then stopped.

The same floor Kari and Peter were on.

Jo ran for the elevator. She knew full well it could be another trick. Raul might not be on the elevator at all. He might be hiding off to the side. Ready to shoot whoever was stupid enough to fall for the ruse.

Jo wasn't feeling particularly stupid, but she was feeling desperate in spades.

"Getty!" she called. "Stay back until I give the all clear."

She sidled between two parked trucks and emerged on the other side. The elevator doors were ten feet away. She was standing in an alcove that was free of any obstructions. No parked cars. No pillars. Just open space.

Raul wasn't here.

But a security guard was.

The man was lying on the floor in a puddle of blood. Motionless. Jo squatted beside him, checking his pulse. She pressed her fingers to his neck and then his wrist. She got nothing from both spots.

Scanning his body, she saw the empty gun holster. Now she knew where Raul's backup weapon came from. If he'd already had one, he would have shot her back in Peter's room instead of running away.

"It's safe," she said.

Getty arrived. He made a mournful sound when he saw the guard.

"This man was just trying to do his job," he groaned. "Just like Teller. And now he's dead. Agent Pullinger, you need to take this guy out."

Jo looked at the floor lights. The elevator was still on the fourth level. She could call it down here, but chances were it would make a couple of stops on its way. Letting other people on. It might stop again on the way up.

It would take too long.

Jo returned to the stairs instead. She put all her running fitness to the test, jumping up them like a mountain goat. She reached the fourth level and flew down the corridor.

When she reached Peter's room, she didn't know whether to laugh or cry.

He was safe. Officer Harris was outside the door, keeping watch. A nurse and a doctor were in the room, checking Peter over.

That was good.

But Raul was gone. He had tricked Jo once more. When he reached the fourth floor, he probably ran directly for the stairwell on the other side of the building.

By now, he was long gone, out in the streets, and ready to try killing her again.

ONE-HUNDRED TEN

"Look at us," said Peter. He pointed to his bloody face. "Broken nose brothers."

Jo chuckled. "I'm a woman."

"Oh. Broken nose *siblings*," Peter replied.

They were both sitting in Peter's room. Two nurses were there, tending to them. Wiping the blood away.

Next came the painful part. Peter's nose wasn't actually broken, but Jo's was. A doctor came in and felt around. Moving the cartilage.

"It's not too bad," he said. "But I'll have to move some stuff back into place. It's going to hurt."

"Good thing I love pain," Jo said. "And I'm also a good liar. I'm scared, doc."

He used his thumbs to crunch her nose back into place. Somehow, it felt even worse than open heart surgery. Tears poured out of Jo's eyes. Fresh blood seeped from her nostrils. But the nurse was there quickly to mop it up.

"All set," said the doctor. "You'll want to use an ice pack on that. And make sure to keep your head elevated when you sleep. I'd like to see you back in a couple of days to see how it's going. It was a simple fracture, so it shouldn't need any surgery."

He smiled and nodded, slowly leaving the room. As soon as he was in the hall, Jo heard him running. Busy shift. Too many people to see.

A moment later, Officer Getty poked his head into the room. "Hey, Agent Pullinger. Can you do me a favor?"

She wiped her tears away and stood up. "Yeah. Need some help in the parking garage?"

"Nah, we're all set down there," said Getty. "We even found the owners of the cars that got shot up. They all have good insurance, thankfully. But Ford's been bugging us every chance he gets. He wants to see you."

Jo followed Getty into the hall. They parted ways. Jo made her way to Ford's room. He was sitting up, looking exhausted.

"Where's Kelly?" Jo asked.

Ford smiled. "The babysitter called. She did her best, but Hazel needed her mom."

Jo nodded. "It's been a stressful day."

"More for you than me," Ford replied with a grunt.

"Do I need to remind you that you got shot?"

"In the arm," Ford said indignantly. "If this was an action movie, I'd be fine. Besides, you almost got shot too. You could have used me. You should have called for backup."

She laid a comforting hand on his uninjured arm. "You've done enough today, my friend. Besides, there was no time. I had to move."

"He got away again," Ford said with a sigh.

"But his luck's going to run out," Jo told him. "Raul's alive, true. But he failed his assignment. Again. Kari and Peter are still alive."

Ford pushed his head back into his pillow, nestling in. "That's some comfort."

There was a knock at the door. McKinley came in, smiling.

"Back from your meeting?" asked Jo. "You missed some excitement here."

"So I heard," McKinley replied. "I wish I could have been here. But I'm glad everyone's all right. Jo, I've got something."

Jo ushered him toward Ford's bed. Then she pulled the curtains shut around them.

"The anonymous woman is Olga Aleksandrov," McKinley said in a quiet voice. "A Russian immigrant. She's Salvatore Russo's cleaning lady. I gave her a listening device. She's agreed to plant it at Sal's place. As soon as we get evidence that Raul's working for him..."

"We come down like a hammer," said Jo. "Did she say when she was going to plant the device?"

"In the morning," said McKinley. "She's really serious about taking this guy down. I get the feeling she badly wants out of this particular criminal enterprise."

Jo nodded. "Then I guess we're heading to Bainbridge Island."

ONE-HUNDRED ELEVEN

After she met with McKinley, Olga knew she was in for a rough night. She was able to catch the final ferry from Seattle to Bainbridge Island at 1:35 AM. It was a foggy night on Puget Sound. Cold and clammy. But she stood out on the deck anyway, breathing in the briny air.

Now and then, she saw a splash out in the water. Too far out to be caused by the ferry's wake. A dolphin, perhaps. She had seen them out here before.

She imagined herself as one of them. With the whole open ocean to explore, she could go anywhere. No mobsters and hitmen to deal with. No wayward nephews to worry over. She watched the dolphin splashing in the water and felt envious.

At least someone's having a relaxing evening, she thought.

Olga kept putting her hand in her pocket. Making sure the listening device was there. McKinley had given it to her in a sturdy paper sachet. He had explained it all to her. The adhesive was already applied. It was already programmed to broadcast at a certain frequency. All she had to do was stick it under a table or something.

Easy.

But not quite. She had no idea if she'd be able to get into the house at all. She might have to wait longer. Days. Weeks, maybe. It wouldn't be too late to catch Sal and Raul.

But it might be too late for Peter.

She had no choice. She had to get into the house. The thought of it made her stomach stir. She ran back inside the passenger cabin. She found a bathroom and squatted in front of the toilet.

Nothing came up. She washed her hands and left the bathroom just as the ferry approached the Bainbridge dock.

Suddenly, an idea occurred to her.

It was slightly risky. It might make Sal angry. But safer than trying to sneak into the mansion again.

She took out her phone. Sal had given her a contact number to use in case of emergency. She called it now.

A man answered. Not Sal. One of his guards.

"Hello?" he grumbled. "Who is this?"

"Olga Aleksandrov."

"The cleaning lady? You know it's the middle of the night, right?"

"Yes, and I thought this was the emergency line," she replied. "For use any time."

He sighed. "Fine. What do you want?"

"I left something at the house, very important to me," said Olga. "I understand Mr. Russo won't need my services for a little while, but I would like to retrieve this item in person."

"I would need to ask the boss."

"Okay, I will wait."

"What? You want me to wake Sal up right now?" the guard stammered.

"Is my accent too strong? Yes, that is what I am implying."

"Come on, lady. Is this thing you left really that important?'

"To me, it is."

After a bit more hemming and hawing, the guard did as she asked. He brought to phone to Sal.

"Olga?" Sal's sleepy voice answered. "Is everything all right?"

"Mr. Russo, I left my family ring in your house."

She heard a shuffling sound as Sal sat up in bed. "Is it important to you?'

"Yes, very important."

"Okay, Olga. Do you remember where you left it?"

"Yes. I know just where it is."

"Then you can come get it. No worries. Sometime between six and seven AM would be good. I don't have any important business happening then. I won't let any of my guards hassle you."

"Thank you, Mr. Russo," she said.

It wasn't hard to make herself sound grateful because she actually was. She felt somewhat bad for betraying Sal.

But it has to be done, she quietly reminded herself.

ONE-HUNDRED TWELVE

At 5:15 AM, a white van arrived at the Seattle ferry terminal. It waited in line with the others. Ready to drive onto the lower deck of the ship.

To the outside observer, it seemed to be the van for a plumbing company. And it was. Or at least it had been. The FBI had purchased it from the original users. They changed a few minor things on the logo stencil. And they had outfitted the back with a full surveillance setup.

Jo and McKinley were in the front seat. Jo was driving. Both of them wore coveralls. On the floor between McKinley's feet was a tote holding a small set of tools in case they needed props to help them fit in. Pipe wrenches. A soldering torch. Various fittings and valves.

"Remind me again," said Jo. "What did Olga say to you?"

"She called me at two o'clock," McKinley reiterated. "Using the burner phone, I lent her. She told me she would be planting the device by seven at the latest. By the time we get into position, we should be ready to start eavesdropping."

"She really came through for us," Jo said. "Did she ask for any favors?"

McKinley shook his head. "I think she's just trapped and wants to be free."

"We can help her with that."

The ferry arrived. Jo drove the van onto the lower deck. Since she was one of the first cars in line, she got to park at the opposite end of the boat. That way, she'd also be first in line to get off at Bainbridge.

It was tempting for Jo and McKinley to get out and stretch their legs, explore the boat, but they stayed in the van for the duration of the trip. When it was time to drive off, they were ready.

McKinley routed them to where they needed to go. Rockaway Beach was directly south but across Eagle Harbor, a large inlet of water that nearly cut the island in half. They had to drive west to get around. The detour would give Olga plenty of time to get her end of the job done.

They were still a mile out when McKinley's phone rang

"It's Olga," he said. He answered. "McKinley here. Yes. That's great. We'll be there very soon. In the meantime, make sure you shut off the water main. No, ma'am, I'm just a plumber. Thank you."

He hung up and smiled at Jo.

"She wanted to know if shutting off the water main was code for something," he said. "I forgot to tell her we would be posing as plumbers."

"You're a great method actor, McKinley," Jo replied.

"Hey, I'm just trying to stay in character. Give me your best plumber lingo, Jo. Go on. I want to make sure you're with me."

Jo shrugged. "Boy, I sure can't wait to cut in this new water line. Soldering copper is my biggest passion in life."

McKinley shook his head. "Too enthusiastic, I think. I'm sure you'll have time to work on it. Olga said she was able to plant the device in the living room. She's already out of the house and safe."

They reached Rockaway Beach. Jo slowed down, keeping an eye out for Sal's mansion. It wasn't hard to spot.

"What's the range on the listening device?" she asked.

"About five hundred feet, maybe," said McKinley.

"Then we can park a couple of houses down. Here we go." She pulled into a neighbor's driveway and put the van in park. "Do you want to talk to them?"

"Sure," said McKinley.

He got out and ran up the house. Rang the doorbell. An old woman answered with a polite smile. As McKinley spoke, she nodded enthusiastically.

McKinley got back in the van. "All set. I told her we were conducting free inspections in the neighborhood today and we needed a place to park. She told me we could use her driveway until dinner time."

"Should be long enough," said Jo.

"Hopefully," McKinley said with a sigh. "Should we head back?"

They stepped outside and opened the van's rear doors. They climbed inside, shutting the doors behind them. There were screens lining both walls, but none of them were active. All Jo and McKinley needed were their headphones.

They put them on and started listening.

ONE-HUNDRED THIRTEEN

The last thing Raul wanted was to speak to Sal. The man was a cretin. A slimeball who would be better off as a bloodstain on his own basement floor. But he paid well. And Raul wasn't used to failure.

He needed to salvage this job. Peter needed to die. Kari needed to be delivered to Sal. And Jo Pullinger had to be dealt with.

Raul pulled up in front of Sal's mansion. He got out and punched his gate code in, leaving his car on the side of the road. He walked inside, in no rush to be yelled at and berated by the old man.

A guard was waiting just inside. He gestured toward the living room. "Mr. Russo would like to see you now."

"That is not the word choice I would have gone with," Raul replied.

He went into the living room. Sal was lounging on the couch, pretending to be relaxed. But he had a glass of whiskey in his hand. Sal never drank this early in the day.

"Nice of you to grace us with your presence," Sal sneered. "Sit down, Raul."

Raul looked at the whiskey decanter. It was on the table next to Sal. Heavy, thick glass. It was a third of the way empty.

"Are you drunk?" Raul asked.

"It's my house," Sal replied with a grunt. "I can be whatever I want to be."

"I will not speak with you while you're in this state, Sal. It's pathetic and unprofessional."

"*No!*" Sal jumped to his feet. Wobbling a bit. "The only unprofessional thing in this room is you, Raul. You've failed me too many times. You came highly recommended, but you're a *joke*. You can't even wipe out one punk kid and grab a college girl for me? What am I even paying you for?"

"This FBI agent has proven highly tenacious," Raul said calmly. "And resilient."

"I don't care!" Sal roared. "I brought you into my home, Raul. I've paid you more money than most people can dream of. Why do you think I did that? Because I think you're pleasant to be around?"

Raul said nothing. He breathed slowly through his nose, eying the whiskey decanter again.

"Aren't you going to answer me?" Sal demanded.

"Sometimes operations like this take time," Raul replied.

"Yeah, and how much time? Enough time for the FBI to finally get their way and put me in prison? Does that sound like enough time to you, Raul? You're worthless. If I go down because of your incompetence, the last thing I'll do is let all of my colleagues know to stay away from you."

Sal stepped forward, stabbing a finger into Raul's chest.

"You'll never get the big bucks again," Sal went on. "You'll be stuck making ten dollars an hour for some back-alley pill-pusher. You hear me? You're finished!"

Raul smiled. "Then I suppose I will try and rectify my mistakes, Sal. Can I start by getting you a refill?"

Sal hiccupped. He looked down at his glass. "Yes. It's the least you could do, Raul."

Raul nodded. Bowing his head respectfully. He stepped around Sal, picking up the decanter.

He turned around and smashed the decanter over Sal's head.

It took a lot of force to break that material. Roughly the same amount of force it took to crush a man's skull.

Raul felt the pain. He ignored it. Watching his boss crumple to the floor was just too satisfying. It made everything worth it.

He laughed. "Don't worry, Sal. I'll still finish the job for you. But only because these people have angered me as well."

ONE-HUNDRED FOURTEEN

"Slow morning," McKinley said. At least, that's what Jo thought he said. The words were distorted by a loud yawn.

Jo was on her phone, checking the map of the area. "Hmm. Don't see anything walkable. If we want coffee and donuts, we'll have to call some help in."

"Coffee and donuts are required for an assignment like this," said McKinley. "I wonder who might be available to help? I can check and see if the FBI has any people in the area..."

He reached for his laptop.

"Or we can call the office," Jo suggested. "See if Agent Larkin is available to drop off some critical assets. She might be glad for the chance to get away from her desk. And see you."

McKinley shoved his laptop away. "That's all right. I'll just walk. How far away is the closest bakery?"

"About three miles," Jo replied with a smirk.

"About two hours round trip?" said McKinley. "No problem."

"You just don't want me calling Larkin."

"Huh? Who said that? No idea what you're talking about."

McKinley waved as he popped the rear doors open and stepped out. Jo laughed. She knew he was just making a big show of it. He'd walk about as far as the street before coming back. Then he'd return to his seat and admit he didn't want coffee and donuts *that* bad.

But his expression changed suddenly. It went from embarrassed and goofy to completely sober. He glanced to his right, following something with his eyes. He then slowly climbed back into the van. He shut the door.

"I assume that was Raul's car that just showed up at Sal's gates," he said. "It matches Peter's description."

Jo had been sitting with one ear of her headphones pushed back so she could hear McKinley. She pulled it forward now. "Then it might be showtime."

They went silent.

Through the listening device, they heard a door open. Clumsy footfalls crossing a floor. Then a *clunk* as something heavy was set down. A soft *woosh* as someone fell onto a couch cushion.

"Sir," a distant voice said. "He's here. Should I send him to you?"

"Yes, Devon. Straight away. Let's see what this moron has to say for himself."

The second voice belonged to Salvatore Russo.

A minute later, Raul arrived.

Jo and McKinley listened with increasing glee as the conversation happened. They were getting everything they needed. Direct verbal confirmation Raul was working for Sal. Sal had hired him to take care of his dirty work. He had ordered Raul to kidnap Kari and murder Peter, his own nephew.

"Sal is going down for good," Jo whispered to herself. She knew it was true. She just didn't know how quickly it would happen.

Raul sounded so calm. Professional. Jo assumed he would leave soon. Go about the business Sal had asked him to do. He wouldn't succeed. By the time he came back, his boss would be in cuffs.

Instead, they heard a loud cracking sound. The splinter of shattering glass. A thud of a body hitting the floor.

And then, nothing.

Jo pulled one of her ear pads back again. "What just happened?"

"I think..." McKinley licked his lips. "I think Raul just murdered Sal."

"Someone got put down," Jo agreed.

"Should we go in?" McKinley asked.

Jo shook her head. "Sal has armed guards. And Raul's still in there. We'll wait out here and see what happens. Might be time to call for backup."

An ear-splitting noise suddenly came through the headphones. She winced. She had heard everything she needed to hear.

"Gunshots," she said.

"Are we still calling for backup?" McKinley asked.

Jo didn't answer. She climbed up into the driver's seat. She kept her headphones on.

ONE-HUNDRED FIFTEEN

Raul couldn't stop staring at his fallen boss.

Sal's eyes were frozen open. Those strange blue eyes. They were still sharp enough to cut through diamonds. Even in death.

But was Sal really gone? Maybe he was just braindead. On the threshold between life and whatever came after.

Raul crouched down. Jammed his fingers into Sal's meaty neck. There was no pulse. He held his hand in front of Sal's mouth and nose. No breath, either.

"I hope the whiskey was good," Raul whispered. "Because I've heard the hangover is a killer. It might give you a splitting headache."

He laughed as he stood up. He went to a cabinet on the wall. Pulled it open. There were guns inside. Raul grabbed two pistols and loaded them. He slid one into his belt. When he ran out of ammo, grabbing the extra gun would be quicker than reloading.

He turned to the door just as the guard came in.

"Sir, is everything all right?" Devon asked. "I heard a... hey!"

Devon drew his sidearm. Raul shot him in the face.

Another guard arrived. Dumbfounded. In shock. He stood right in the doorway and took way too long to react.

He was far too easy to kill. It wasn't even fun.

Raul stepped over the two men's corpses. He looked both ways down the hall, listening to the approaching footsteps.

He knew Sal had twenty house guards on the payroll. They worked in shifts. Sometimes there were only eight in the house at once. Sometimes as many as twelve. Raul didn't know how many were here today.

He only knew that he would kill as many as he had to.

"Stop right there!" a voice roared.

Raul looked to his right. There was a man halfway through a doorway, using it as cover. His gun arm was sticking through. Flat against the wall.

Raul shot him through the hand, making him drop his gun. The guard fell back through the doorway, yelping in pain.

"Show your ugly face to me again," Raul shouted, "and I will put a new hole through it."

He turned his back to the guard and walked away.

There was a shuffling sound behind him. The guard, trying to go for his fallen gun.

Raul turned quickly. He made good on his vow, and the guard was dead.

He made his way out into the foyer. Just ten feet from the front door and freedom. He was almost reluctant to go for it. It would be a shame to leave while there were still men left to kill.

But Raul hadn't gotten this far by being a fool. He could ignore his impulses when he needed to. And use them when they were advantageous. Such as when he killed Sal. The man was going to ruin Raul's career.

Two more guards arrived. One from each side. Raul dove forward. He shot one in midair. He landed, rolling to the other side. Shooting the other guard before the man could pull his trigger.

Raul got to his feet.

He had already killed the dumbest guards. The ones who charged in, making plenty of noise. But there were others still in the house. Three more, at least. He hadn't heard any sign of them. Maybe they were smart enough to run away or hide.

Or maybe they were just dumb enough to try and sneak up on him.

Raul ran to his left. He twisted around as he moved, firing several shots down the hallway. He never saw anything. But when the sound of the last gunshot faded, he heard someone slump to the floor.

He strolled back into the foyer. There was a dead guard halfway down the hallway. He had taken two bullets to the chest. The others had missed, but no matter.

Six guards down.

Was it good enough? Raul decided so. He had already taken seven lives today. And now that he didn't need to worry about protecting Sal, he could finish the job in his own way. Without mercy or caution.

By sunset, three more lives would be ended. Kari Cross. Peter Russo. Jo Pullinger.

And perhaps he would pay a visit to Pullinger's family after all.

He left the house and stepped through the front gate. He was heading for his car when he heard a screaming engine to his right.

He looked over. A huge white van was racing toward him.

ONE-HUNDRED SIXTEEN

The listening device planted in the living room was weak. But gunshots were loud. Jo was able to hear each one, echoing through the house. She multitasked, driving down the road and listening to gunfire.

"Jo?" McKinley asked. "What's the plan?"

"There isn't one," she said. "But we do have an objective. Stop Raul. I need you to do something for me, McKinley. Find out what kind of guns Sal keeps in his living room. Maybe Olga knows."

"The living room?" he said. "She already told me, when we were talking at the ferry terminal about safe places to plant the device. They're just 9mm pistols. That's where Raul got his silenced weapon from."

That's what she wanted to hear. She just had to hope Raul hadn't brought something different with him.

As soon as she got the van on the road, Jo saw Raul's car. An old boxy sedan. Then she saw the man himself, coming through the front gate. His head whipped around, his ponytail flapping. He stared toward the van. Through the windshield. Directly into Jo's eyes.

He smiled.

Jo pushed the accelerator down. Driving faster.

"You're going to hit him?" McKinley asked with a gasp.

"He won't let me," Jo replied, grunting. "But I'm going to try."

Raul saw the van barreling toward him. Then he stepped gracefully aside. He went back through the open gate. There were thick stone columns on either side of it. He hid behind one of them.

The van surged past the gate. Jo slammed on the brakes. Tires squealed. Smoke puffed into the air. McKinley fell off his chair in the back and slid across the floor.

"Sorry!" Jo told him. "Stay there. Call for backup."

She opened the driver's door and jumped out. She hit the ground running. Headed for Raul's car.

She aimed at the column he was hiding behind. She put three shots into it in quick succession. Keeping him pinned down. She ducked by the rear of the car and waited.

"Interesting tactics, Agent Pullinger," Raul called to her. "When I first saw the van, I thought the cleaning lady was back. Then I saw who was driving it. You do not give up, even when you should. I was beginning to admire you, but now I begin to wonder if you're just stupid."

"I heard what you said," Jo replied. "In the house. After you killed Sal. You said you were going to finish the job. That means coming after me. And my family."

"That was never what Sal asked me to do."

"No, but you're a psychopath."

"Hmm. Perhaps you have a good point there. I suppose you are not stupid, Agent Pullinger. You simply think too highly of your skills. This shootout only ends one way."

"With you tucking your tail between your legs and running like a coward?" Jo asked. "That seems to be a trend with you."

"I run to survive, and I kill to live," said Raul.

"Well, that's good for you, Raul. But it's not going to end like that. Not this time. You're done. This is where it ends."

He laughed. "You sound so sure of yourself. It will be a pleasure to kill you, Agent Pullinger."

"Let's see about that," she whispered to herself.

She jumped out of cover. Charged toward the gate. She fired at the column several more times. Chipping away at it. She kept going until her gun clicked. Her magazine was empty.

Jo stopped in the middle of the road. She cursed loudly. Then she dropped the empty mag out of her gun. She reached to her belt for a fresh one.

Raul heard this. He seized the opportunity. Running out from behind his column, he aimed at Jo.

ONE-HUNDRED
SEVENTEEN

Raul pulled the trigger. Nothing happened.

He glanced at his gun curiously. Then his eyes flicked toward Jo. For the first time, she saw fear in them.

Raul dropped the empty gun. He reached for the second one tucked into his belt.

Jo slapped the full magazine into her pistol. She shot Raul in the right knee.

He made no sound as he fell. No grunt or scream of pain. The veins on his neck and forehead bulged out. His eyes went wide, glowing with hatred.

"Show me your hands," Jo demanded. "If you reach for that gun again, you're dead."

Raul's face went red with rage. He slowly lifted both hands above his head.

"McKinley?" Jo shouted.

The rear van doors sprang open. McKinley came out, peeking around. Checking if it was safe. He came out to meet her.

"Cuff him," said Jo.

McKinley did so, pushing Raul's hands together behind his back. Slapping the manacles around his wrists. Then McKinley jumped away, as if Raul were a deadly snake.

Jo stepped closer. Towering over Raul.

"You were right, Raul," she said. "I *am* sure of my abilities. And so were you. Not anymore, huh?"

"You will die," he seethed. Spittle flew out of his mouth. "Along with everyone you love."

Jo shook her head. "You don't even know what love is. That's a nice pistol you have there. Did you get it from Sal's living room? It looks just like the one you had on you at the hospital. We learn a lot about weapons in FBI training."

Raul gave her a devilish smile. "You counted my shots. I suppose I shouldn't have fired so many down the hallway."

Jo shrugged. "What you really shouldn't have done was underestimate me and my team. When you assume you're better than everyone else, you tend to make stupid mistakes. Like forgetting to keep track of how many bullets you use."

"I should have done whatever it took to kill you at the hospital," Raul replied.

"On that, we disagree," Jo said. "I kind of like being alive."

***

Backup arrived soon after. Raul was taken away under heavy guard. CSI teams swept into the house, making it pretty much inaccessible. Jo and McKinley stood outside, sipping coffee and munching on donuts.

"I guess that's another case wrapped up," said McKinley. "I wonder how long of a break we'll get before something crazy happens again."

"Probably not very long," Jo answered. "But for now, we can bask in the glory of the moment. It feels good, doesn't it? Knowing we brought down someone who thought they were invincible?"

"It does," McKinley agreed. "In fact, it feels so good that we ought to spread the word. What do you think?"

Jo nodded. "There's nothing more we can do here."

They got back in their van and drove away.

ONE-HUNDRED EIGHTEEN

Peter Russo looked rough. He had two black eyes from Raul hitting him. There were cotton balls jammed up his nostrils. But he smiled when he saw Jo enter his room.

"Agent Pullinger!"

"I'm back," she said. She pulled up a chair and sat next to his bed. "And I have some news. Some of it's good. Some of it's bad. What do you want to hear first?" Peter cringed. "The bad, I guess. Is someone dead?"

Jo nodded. "Your uncle. Raul killed him."

Peter sighed, covering his eyes with his hands. "I knew this would happen. No way we could get through all this without something terrible happening. It's my fault."

Jo touched his arm. "It's Raul's fault, actually. And Sal's. Your uncle might have had some good qualities, but he more than made up for them with his bad ones. He wanted to kill Kari. He wanted to kill *you*, Peter."

Peter nodded. "Yeah. If I didn't do what I did, Kari would be dead. She's the only innocent person in all this, yeah? So I did the right thing."

"You did," Jo assured him. "You did the only thing you could do. Maybe you didn't go about it in the smartest way, but..."

Peter burst out laughing. He hid his face in shame. "Oh, man. I'm an idiot. But at least I tried to be good." His expression turned serious. "But it's not going to be enough, is it? I can't just tell the judge my heart was in the right place. I'm still a kidnapper."

"Technically," said Jo. "But your case is going to be different. There are extenuating factors here. You won't avoid jail time, but I'd be shocked if you didn't get a light sentence."

Peter's eyes welled up with tears. "I don't want to go to prison. I'm going to die in there."

"No," Jo whispered. "You won't. You're strong. I know you are. It takes a lot of guts to do what you did, Peter. You'll be fine."

He wiped his eyes, nodding to himself. "What about Raul? Where is he?"

"He's in custody," Jo said. "FBI custody, to be specific."

Peter sat up, his eyes going wide. "He's still alive? He's gonna come after me again. Nothing's going to stop him."

Jo waved a hand at him. "Don't worry. He's not going anywhere. Trust me. We know how dangerous he is. The right precautions will be taken."

Peter took a deep breath, trying to relax. "Thanks. I guess I'll be okay. At least tell me you hurt him, though."

Jo grinned. "I shot him in the knee."

"Nice!" Peter put up his hand.

They high-fived.

***

Jo's next stop was Kari's room. Officer Getty was still there, keeping his vigil. He let her inside.

Kari was out of bed. She was on a yoga mat in the middle of the room, stretching and holding poses. When she saw Jo enter, she broke out of her routine and stood up.

"Doing some rehab?" Jo asked.

Kari nodded. "Just trying to get back in the swing of things. Officer Getty told me you would probably be coming. And you had good news."

"You're free, Kari," Jo said. "You can start living your life again. The men who were after you have been dealt with."

"Can I ask how?" said Kari.

"You can. Salvatore Russo is dead. And Raul will spend the rest of his life in the highest security prison available."

Kari took a deep breath and let it out through her nose. "How's Peter dealing with this?"

"His uncle has been killed and he's going to jail," Jo said. "But he's taking it well enough."

"If it were up to me," said Kari, "he wouldn't go at all."

"I'm right there with you," Jo said. "I'll be at his trial, Kari. I'll do what I can. But I'm not a lawyer or a judge. They'll make the final decision."

"Is there nothing else you can do?" Kari asked.

"Sorry. Peter's just the nephew of a dead mobster. If he was related to a president or he possessed vital information, I could probably pull a string. But..."

Kari nodded. "I understand. Thanks for everything, Jo. You saved my life."

"So did Peter," Jo said quietly.

ONE-HUNDRED NINETEEN

Peter was sick of the book he was reading. It was pretty good. Lots of action. But he couldn't keep his mind engaged. He was too worried about everything that was happening in real life.

He had thought a great sense of relief would come over him when his uncle and Raul were gone. Instead, he found himself staring down the barrel of a different gun. One scary word that started with a P.

Prison.

And not just that. Months of trials. Scary courtroom appointments where he'd be judged and scrutinized. The media circus that would surround him.

He didn't know if he could survive all of that. It was too just big.

Maybe if Jo was there, he'd find a way to make it through, but he'd forgot to ask her about that.

Peter looked at the clock. It was already eight PM. Hours since Jo had been in his room. But maybe she was still around.

"Hey, Harris," Peter called.

The cop sitting by the door perked up. He looked at Peter questioningly.

"Are you as bored as I am?" Peter asked.

Harris shrugged. "I'm getting paid to sit here. You're not. I'll manage."

"Can't you just... leave?" Peter asked.

"If I want to lose my job," Harris replied with a grunt. "You're a criminal awaiting trial. I'm here to make sure you don't try and run away. Or did you just think I like the way this chair puts my legs to sleep?"

"All right, fine," Peter said with a sigh. "But I have another question. Is Agent Pullinger still around?"

"Haven't seen her. I think she left a long time ago. But maybe I could get her back here."

"No," said Peter. "That's fine. She's probably with her family. I'm not going to bother her. How's Kari doing?"

"She checked herself out of the hospital this afternoon," Harris told him. "She's doing well, I guess. And I'm not supposed to be telling you this, so you didn't hear it. Got it?"

"Got it," said Peter.

They went back to being bored in silence.

There was a knock at the door. Harris got up to open it. A man in a suit stepped in. He looked official. Like someone important.

He also looked familiar.

Peter narrowed his eyes, studying the man's face. It only took a second to realize who it was.

His name was Philip Bennett. He used to work for Sal as a guard, but he had quit a couple of years back. From what Peter had heard, Bennett had a moral crisis that forced him to leave the position.

What's he doing here? Peter thought.

"Can I help you?" Harris asked.

Bennett pulled out a set of credentials. "Agent Griffith, FBI. Are you the man in charge of watching Peter Russo?"

An alias. A badge that was most likely fake. What was going on here?

Harris nodded. "That's me."

"Just one cop?" Bennett asked with a sigh. "Not good enough. This hospital's security has already been compromised to a high degree. There was even a shootout in the parking garage."

"Hey, that was Pullinger," Harris said defensively. "She's one of yours."

"That doesn't matter," said Bennett. "I'm here to transfer Peter to a place with higher security. You're dismissed, officer."

Harris stepped aside, blushing. Bennett approached the bed, grabbing Peter by the arm.

"Come with me," Bennett said.

Peter followed him into the hall.

"Don't worry," said Bennett. "There's a change of clothes in the car. You can get out of that hospital gown."

"What's happening right now?" Peter asked. "Why are you pretending to be—"

"*Shh!*" Bennet hissed. "Just walk with me."

They exited the hospital after Bennett showed his credentials to a few more people. There was a car with tinted windows parked at the curb. Bennett opened the back door and pushed Peter in. As soon as Peter's legs were clear, he slammed the door shut.

There was a woman driving the car. She looked back.

"Olga!" Peter said.

She smiled. "Peter. It's wonderful to see you."

Bennett got into the passenger seat. "We should drive."

Olga nodded. She took them out of the parking lot.

"What's going on?" Peter asked.

"Olga tracked me down," Bennett explained. "She knew I could pull this job off. Smuggling you out of the hospital like that. You're a good kid, Peter. Olga and I both know it. I told her I'd do the job for free."

"Does this mean I'm not going to prison?" Peter asked.

"That's exactly what it means," Olga replied.

Peter laughed. He found a stack of clothes on the seat next to him and started pulling them on.

EPILOGUE

It was half past seven. Jo had spent the past forty-five minutes in front of her bedroom mirror. Trying on clothes. Posing and checking herself out from every angle.

Finally, she settled on the perfect outfit. A little black dress and a set of heels. It was more than she ever dressed up. She had these clothes in her closet, but this was the first time she'd put them on.

She felt good.

Next, she thought she ought to accessorize. She opened the jewelry box on her dresser and laughed at the tiny collection inside.

"Guess it'll be easy to pick what to wear," she said.

As she put the seashell necklace on, she thought back to recent events.

It had been three days since Sal was killed, and Raul was taken into custody. Three nights since she'd gotten the call from the hospital. The one that told her Peter was gone.

She wondered where he was. She had a pretty good idea. If she wanted to hunt him down, she was confident she could find him.

She didn't want to. There were plenty of actual bad guys out there. Her time was better spent on them.

She had figured out Raul had killed Leone because he had seen her talking to him at Kari's place. He had feared Leone might spill something to Jo and so had eliminated him.

Jo finished adjusting the necklace and smiled.

Tonight wasn't about work. It was about her.

It had been a whirlwind of a week. The afternoon after Peter went missing, Jo had gotten a call. She had forgotten all about Ted, the truck driver in the mess of the Russo case. But when she heard his voice, all the feelings came back.

He was going to be in Seattle. He wanted to meet up. Jo didn't hesitate to say yes. He wanted to know if she had any good spots in mind. She suggested a nice bar near the water.

It was a date.

Jo finally managed to shut the tiny clasp on the necklace. She looked at the time.

"Gotta go!" she said. "I'm coming, Ted."

She giggled to herself as she rushed out of her apartment.

BIO

THOMAS FINCHAM holds a graduate degree in Economics. His travels throughout the world have given him an appreciation for other cultures and beliefs. He has lived in Africa, Asia, and North America. An avid reader of mysteries and thrillers, he decided to give writing a try. Several novels later, he can honestly say he has found his calling. He is married with two kids, and he lives in a hundred-year-old house. He is the author of **LEE CALLAWAY** series, the **HYDER ALI** series, the **MARTIN RHODES** series, and the **ECHO ROSE** series.

Made in the USA
Middletown, DE
15 September 2024

60976851R10212